SIMON'S MANSION

Reviews for author William Poe

Simple Simon's message of reconciliation and hope is truly for anyone who has struggled to resolve the truth they know about themselves with the way others see them. The power of forgiveness and acceptance can resonate with all readers.

—Melissa Wuske, Foreword Reviews, on Simple Simon

Poe's narrative moves quickly and smoothly and fills in the blanks left in Simon Says. These first novels by Poe will leave his readership wondering—and waiting for— what he comes up with next.

—Publishers Weekly on Simple Simon

Stark and gritty, Poe's story about the search for self-discovery is a sobering testament to the author's own personal journey which makes the story resonate that much more.

—Publishers Weekly on Simon Says

SIMON'S MANSION

William Poe

Paperback Edition

ISBN-13: 9781729078433

Independently Published: Kindle Direct Publishing

You'll get back to where you came from.

—*William Golding, Lord of the Flies*

CHAPTER ONE

G rowing up in the small town of Sibley, Arkansas, living in the timber mansion his family built prior to the Civil War, Simon Powell felt out of place and out of time. It is said that culture takes root early in a child's life, but that didn't apply to Simon; he claimed allegiance to a home planet orbiting a distant star, an idea that occurred to him after watching *Forbidden Planet* on a Friday night when his mother allowed him to stay up late. So impressed was Simon with the movie that he said to himself, Always remember, you were eight years old when you saw this. That was the age when Simon realized that he felt different from other boys, an awareness that scared him. *Forbidden Planet* taught Simon that what dwells inside us can destroy us.

Secluded in his bedroom, Simon wondered about life on his home planet of Zenon, recognizing Zenon culture in the paintings of Jackson Pollock and Emile Nolde, which he first saw on the pages of a Funk & Wagnalls yearbook. Pollock and Nolde spoke to Simon's alienation, and he began emulating their style, working with finger paints to explore Pollock's sense of ordered chaos, drawing family members in a child's version of Nolde, applying vibrant colors from the box of Crayola crayons that his mother, always attentive to Simon's loneliness, gave him as a present on his birthday, never commenting on his strange images and always defending Simon against his father, a man quick to ridicule his peculiar son.

"Why paint his face red? And why's that tree purple?" Lenny had once asked about a rendering of Simon's uncle Jared, identified by the title *Jared of Magnolia* scrawled at the bottom of the page. "That's something a crazy person would do."

"Leave the boy be." Vivian glared at Lenny. Then she turned to Simon and offered, "You enjoy yourself, son." She pointed at a wobbly planet orbiting in a hazy solar system drawn above the red-hued cousin and visible through the leaves of the purple tree. "That's your world, isn't it, Simon?"

Simon nodded.

In the evenings, Simon occupied himself by sketching scenes of flying saucers piloted by bug-eyed monsters and attacking neighborhoods on Earth as he sat on a TV pillow shaped like a cocker spaniel. Lenny would be watching his favorite television programs, half-asleep from a long day of work as a plumber, fighting to stay awake in order to catch the ending of *Gunsmoke* if it were a Wednesday. Vivian, who didn't share Lenny's affection for television, spent her evenings reading Harlequin Romances, dutifully seated on a sofa next to Lenny's La-Z-Boy recliner. When not engaged in drawing monsters, Simon rested on the cocker spaniel pillow, hugging its neck. Vivian periodically lowered her reading glasses and gazed upon Simon; then, believing him content with his pillow friend and drawings, she would return to her fiction.

Upstairs in the timber-hewn mansion, outside the door of Simon's bedroom, hung a gallery of charcoal images, portraits of gloomy ancestors rendered in their Sunday best, framed in oak that had aged dark as ebony through years of being treated with Old

English furniture oil. Placing his art alongside those stern faces would have affronted the ancient gods, which was how Simon's young mind perceived the characters in those portraits, none allowing Simon to walk by without telegraphing their displeasure. Simon's art only made sense in his bedroom, where his drawings crowded the spaces between his paintings like fanciful wallpaper.

Lenny's mother, whom everyone called Mandy, had been a woman well into her seventies when Simon was born. She had cared for him as a baby and sat with him at the mansion during his preschool days since both Lenny and Vivian worked full-time. It was she who had instilled in Simon an appreciation for family heritage, bringing the gallery of ancestors to life through tales as vivid as if she had witnessed them herself. Mandy had conveyed stories of actual people, not the ephemeral beings with the voyeuristic eyes that peered from the portraits, nor the apparitions known from carvings on the grave markers across the road in the family cemetery—a plot of land within sight of Simon's bedroom window and denoted by an elaborately molded wrought-iron archway as rusted as the gate it supported.

Simon's favorite among Mandy's tales was the story of his ancestor James Thomas Powell, "JT" as he was known, the family patriarch, the man who had lived in the mansion during the Civil War and who had met his end when marauders strung him up because he dared to harbor a wounded Union soldier after the nearby battle of Jenkins' Ferry.

"Hanged him from that limb right there," Mandy would say. "That old tree stands as proud as the day JT's body swung in the wind."

Mandy would point an arthritic finger at the red oak dominating the front yard, the limb that once secured the hangman's rope now supporting a tire swing, and under the swing, a sandbox, favorite playground of Simon's oldest niece, Cheryl, and her younger sister, Victoria. They would play there when Simon's only

3

sister, Connie, ten years his senior, and her husband, Derek, came for visits from the town of Tulip, where they'd moved to be closer to Derek's parents.

According to JT's will, the oldest child in each generation inherited responsibility for the property—the *mansion,* as everyone called it, qualifying for such a grand name due to its size, not for any hint of elegance. Responsibility fell to Lenny upon the death of Aunt Opal, sister to Lenny's father, a woman who'd spent her final years as caretaker and lone resident and who now guarded the property from a prominent position in the family cemetery, her grave marked by a delicately carved angel, its marble head bowed with graceful hands placed over a sorrowful face, the less-than-life-sized statue sitting on a granite platform, now marred by vandals who sometime in recent years had spray-painted block letters on its edge that read, if one were to look closely enough, *witch.*

Sibley residents had long accused Simon's great-aunt of ungodly behavior, commenting on the fact that she hung talismans from trees around the property, even though many of the area's residents performed a similar act of superstition, placing colored bottles on the ends of dead branches in the belief they captured evil spirits and prevented misfortune. On Halloween, Aunt Opal strung an effigy of JT on the red oak to ward off trick-or-treaters. Aunt Opal knew the good people of Sibley were more likely to leave her alone if they feared being cursed for walking across the property, and Opal valued privacy, finding solace in her life as a recluse.

Lenny had once confided to Simon that if he had been JT, the Union soldier would have become garden fertilizer. In later years, Lenny claimed he had moved the family from Little Rock to Sibley following Opal's death because his older brother didn't want to move into the mansion. Lenny portrayed the move as a noble act of family duty when in fact a darker truth underpinned the decision.

Following the integration of Little Rock High School in 1957, Lenny couldn't tolerate the idea of Simon and Connie attending mixed-race schools. Moving to Sibley all but guaranteed the continuation of segregation, given the makeup of the population at the time. If descendants of the men and women enslaved by Sibley's founders had stayed behind after the Civil War, they were long gone, chased away by Jim Crow and the Ku Klux Klan, prevented from reentry by the imposing statue of General Marmaduke that stood in front of the county courthouse, a monument to the battle fought for preservation of the South at Jenkins' Ferry on the Saline River, a conflict symbolizing the dangers of slave rebellion in the eyes of Sibley's residents, since it was well known that former slaves had fought and died alongside Northern soldiers.

When Simon came home from school during the second grade and announced that he had made a new friend, a boy with brown skin and eyes different from his, Lenny flew into a rage and stormed off to speak to the principal, who told Lenny that Simon's newfound friend had recently moved with his family from Hawaii to work in a local company analyzing defunct bauxite strip mines that threatened Sibley's groundwater. Flummoxed, Lenny informed Simon that if a classmate wasn't white, he wasn't to play with them. Simon refused to take the order to heart and never shunned a girl or boy for not looking the same as him. Simon knew what it was like to be different, and a boy from Zenon must always be on guard.

Racism wasn't the only source of Lenny's rage. He especially disliked people who failed to behave the way they should. That Lenny despised homosexuals became evident whenever Liberace appeared on television. "Damn faggot's queer as a three-dollar bill," Lenny would rail, wagging a finger at the sequined performer, outbursts that instilled fear in Simon's young heart, for Simon identified with the showmanship of the pianist. Those were the earliest stirrings of what later became apparent: if Simon wasn't from Zenon, then he was a stranger to his friends, because his desires were different from theirs. Words from *Forbidden Planet* echoed in his thoughts: "My evil self is at that door, and I have no power to stop it!"

Just as Vivian had supported Simon's art, she recognized Simon's love of music, allowing him to take piano lessons from a woman who lived farther down the unpaved road that led from Sibley's town center to the mansion. The teacher's home was within sight of Simon's front porch, where Vivian would stand as she watched him leave for his lessons, her confidence that Simon would find his way heightened by the prominence of the neighbor's white gravel driveway, causing it to stand out against the orange dust of the road.

After a few lessons, the woman told Vivian that if Simon kept practicing, he might become a professional, so quick was the boy to associate the notes on the page with the piano's black and white keys.

Lenny heard about the neighbor's praise at dinner one night and said, "No son of mine's going to be a goddamn sissy pianist."

And so ended Simon's potential career as a future Liberace.

CHAPTER TWO

God is a judgmental being, always ready to punish his children. Such was the viewpoint Simon internalized as a boy, beliefs reinforced each Sunday by the pastor of the Southern Baptist church his family attended, roots going back to its very founding. The pastor, an admirer of the colonial theologian Jonathan Edwards, who articulated the belief that all people are sinners in the hands of an angry God, claimed that God demonstrated his concern for humanity through judgment, which he described as an act of love toward disobedient children.

Lifting his head from the scribbles of flying saucers and space aliens he'd drawn in pencil on the margins of the church bulletin, Simon began to understand from the pastor's sermons how Lenny justified his prejudices. On a succession of Sundays, the pastor made it clear that some people were better than others, quoting Ephesians: "Slaves, obey your earthly masters with respect and fear, and with sincerity of heart, just as you would obey Christ," and, adding his own touch, explained that slaves were in bondage because their skin color indicated a curse from Genesis: the mark of Cain.

Lenny declaimed against all sorts of people of whom he disapproved, using the words *queer* and *faggot* to identify any male who wasn't masculine enough or any woman who wore pants, at least until the invention of culottes, which confounded his arguments and led to Lenny's use of new terms for women who wore them. Vivian, in a rare moment of defiance, stood up to Lenny and said that culottes were not pants and that she planned to wear them whether Lenny approved or not.

In young Simon's mind, God and Lenny merged—one in heaven, all aware, observing every action, listening to every thought; the other on earth, limited, unaware, avoidable. If God knew what Simon did with his friend Ernie during sleepovers, he would make an exception (Simon was from Zenon, after all), but Lenny must never find out.

Though the word *homosexual* had not entered Simon's vocabulary, he understood what the pastor meant when preaching about Sodom and Gomorrah. Nothing put fire in the man's eyes like rage against sex between men. The sermons began to sink in, and Simon soon began to doubt that God would continue to excuse his behavior. After all, Ernie was a human from Earth, even if Simon was from Zenon. Simon began paying closer attention to the pastor's infrequent sermons about God's compassion, explaining that sin is forgiven through the blood of Christ. Simon learned the words to the congregation's favorite hymns, "Are You Washed in the Blood?" and "White as Snow." Simon began to feel the need for salvation, moved by the choir's singing and the pastor's weekly call to confession:

Come home, come home
Ye who are weary, come home
Earnestly, tenderly, Jesus is calling
Calling, "O sinner, come home."

Simon needed to confess the sin taught as a secret game by Ernie's older brother and conveyed to Simon when Ernie explored his body in a secluded spot deep in the woods. Simon knew that what he and Ernie did was wrong, and he hoped that being washed in the blood would provide forgiveness; but even more urgently, he hoped to wash away the desire that increased each time they played their games. Simon enjoyed the intimate acts with his friend, acts that created a profound sense of guilt.

Hoping that he might be wrong about God's expectations, Simon questioned his Sunday School teacher when she explained that God is love. "If God is love," Simon asked, "how can some love be wrong?" Simon had recently learned that the two men who lived next door to Ernie were together because they loved each other. At least, that was the answer one of them had given when Ernie asked why they didn't have wives. Ernie mentioned the neighbor's response to his mother, who made sure he understood that men were not allowed to love in that way, that the neighbors were committing sin, and that God would judge them in his own time. The Sunday School teacher answered Simon's question by explaining that the devil corrupts God's love by giving people lustful thoughts.

Simon remembered the message of *Forbidden Planet*—that what is within us can destroy us—and decided that what really mattered was what people found out about us. If only Dr. Morbius had not learned of his daughter's attraction to the commander, all might have been well on the planet of the Krell. Simon would never mention his desires to Lenny or Vivian. But what about the all-knowing God? Simon could no longer sustain the fantasy that he was a boy from Zenon. The rules applied to him, just as they did to others.

On a Sunday morning, as the choir sang, "Earnestly, tenderly, Jesus is calling, calling, 'O sinner, come home,'" the pressure became too great. All of Simon's Sunday School friends had made the journey down the aisle to salvation, and now it was his turn.

Breaking free of Vivian's hand, Simon left the pew and walked toward the pulpit, toward the pastor, who met him with a reassuring embrace, whispering into his ear, "Do you accept the Lord Jesus Christ as your personal lord and savior?" Simon burst into tears, sure that the devil would leave his heart as Jesus entered. God knew what Simon had done, but he would forgive. Upon his salvation, Simon would be free from unholy desires, as innocent as they were at his young age—he had not yet celebrated his tenth birthday.

Congregants came from all over central Arkansas to attend the church Simon's family attended, not least because of its famous sanctuary, illuminated by brilliant hues filtering through twenty-foot stained glass windows imported from Germany, each panel depicting stories from the Bible. The windows proceeded chronologically, starting with Eve taking fruit from a serpent, then moving to Noah adrift in a sea of darkness, releasing a raven to test for land; Joseph parading his multicolored coat before jealous brothers; Daniel praying heavenward, surrounded by lions as tame as lambs; Ezekiel riding to heaven on a vehicle not unlike a flying saucer; and a pregnant Mary aglow in the presence of Gabriel. From there the windows progressed to an angry Jesus overturning moneylenders' tables, smiting a fig tree, and telling his chosen that one of them would betray him, then ending in the largest panel, filling an entire window: Jesus nailed to a cross. According to what Simon understood, the church believed in the cleansing ablution of Christ's blood, though resurrection seldom factored into Sunday sermons, other than to mention, in passing, that Jesus had conquered death, and those who believed in him would be carried to heaven after his return to judge humanity.

A choir loft, spacious enough to seat fifty choristers, rose behind an alabaster pulpit framed by green velvet curtains, which remained closed, except during baptisms, when they opened to reveal a four-foot wall of glass holding back sacred waters depicted on a painted diorama of the river Jordan, the image complete with desert sands and waving palm trees, as if the minister in his hip boots and white baptismal gown, weighted at the bottom edge to keep the material from floating, stood in the midst of a blossoming oasis.

Twelve boys awaited redemption the Sunday evening Simon's name appeared on the schedule—the church's tradition required boys and girls to participate on alternate Sundays. A middle-aged man, handsome and fit, dressed in dark slacks with a crisp seam and a white shirt with French cuffs (Simon noticed the brilliant opal settings of the cufflinks) escorted Simon into a changing room, similar to the fitting rooms at the J. C. Penney where Vivian bought his school clothes. The man shut the door for privacy as Simon began to undress.

"You won't be naked under the gown," the man assured, as Simon stood before him in his underpants. The man took a pair of boy-sized jockey shorts from his back pocket. "Let's slip you into these so yours will be dry when you return."

Before Simon had a chance to comply, the man hooked his thumbs through the elastic waistband of his shorts and tugged them to the floor. Simon ground his teeth to resist the feel of the man's hairy arm raking across his body as he reached around his waist to insert each foot through the shorts. Simon feared for his salvation as his body reacted, and the man pinched the front of his shorts through the white gown. He had just slipped the gauzy material over Simon's head and made sure the hem fell evenly around the ankles. "This will go away as soon as you step into the cold water," the man said with a nervous laugh. "Anyway, the gown will keep it hidden."

Boys had begun to queue near an antechamber outside the baptismal font. As each boy received the go-ahead, indicated by a hand signal from the attendant, the next boy in line passed through a door, having been instructed beforehand to carefully descend the font's three steps into the water—steps representing acceptance of the Trinity. As Simon left the dressing room to take his place in line, frightened the other boys would see evidence of his sinful heart, the man bent down and whispered, "Come back after you're baptized, and I'll dry you off." Simon nodded weakly and joined the procession. Contrary to what the man had said about the gown, Simon clearly saw that each boy wore shorts similar to his and wondered if their attendants had also helped them change out of their clothes.

The moment of his salvation approaching, Simon found himself tainted by the thoughts he hoped to escape, desires he knew were wrong, inflamed by the touch of the man in the dressing room. Simon struggled with his feelings until he concluded that the man was Satan; the devil had made a last attempt to sway him from salvation.

The boy in front of Simon in the procession climbed from the waters on the other side of the baptismal font with the help of an attendant. Simon began his descent down the treacherous steps, finding himself in water almost as deep as he was tall; his gown, puffed with air, caused him to float toward the pastor, anchored by his hip boots and weighted garment. Simon fought to keep the fabric of his gown from rising around him, frantically chopping the cold water. In a quick motion, the minister pulled Simon forward, placed a rough hand over his nose and mouth, and dipped him backward, invoking the names of Father, Son, and Holy Ghost. The minister raised Simon's head from the water and set him in the direction of the exit. The attendant grabbed Simon's arm and pulled him from the water, the gown quickly deflating into a second skin.

"Is it done?" Simon asked, to a slight chuckle from the attendant. Simon had forgotten to repent during the minister's appeal to the triune God. Remembering instructions given by his Sunday School teacher that salvation depended upon repentance at that moment of submersion, Simon wondered if salvation had taken effect. He barely recalled the sequence of events that had just occurred, his focus remaining on the gown that adhered so tightly to his flesh.

The attendant provided an arm for balance, placing sandals at Simon's feet and pointing toward the dressing room, down a corridor of linoleum tiles with rubber footprints to provide traction and lead the way. Simon spotted the man from the dressing room assisting another boy and scurried as fast as he could to reach his clothes, finding them folded on a bench, except for the promised dry shorts. Simon scrambled from his wet garments, dried off with the flimsy towel provided, and slipped into his suit pants—rough against his body—tucked in his shirt, slipped on his socks, and stepped into his black loafers, his heart racing as he joined the other boys in the room where the parents had been told to wait.

"It's a blessing your boy found Jesus at such a young age," the man from the dressing room said to Vivian. The man parted his lips slightly as he looked down at Simon, patting his coat pocket where the underpants made a slight bulge.

Vivian smiled, taking Simon by the hand and leading him into the sanctuary, too briskly for Simon to keep up easily due to the roughness of the chafing suit. If Jesus had entered Simon's heart during submersion, he'd left just as quickly, recognizing an unrepentant soul—or so Simon surmised. An overwhelming sense of disappointment clouded Simon's mind.

Vivian never understood why Simon threw tantrums at the mere suggestion that he attend church services following his baptism, flying into fits of rage that no threat of punishment would quieten. But Simon could not bear the thought of sitting in the sanctuary, pondering the miracle of salvation through the blood of Jesus Christ as he scanned every face for the man from the dressing room, damnably hoping that if they met again, the man would wrap his muscular arms around his waist, and Simon again would know the touch of a caressing hand.

CHAPTER THREE

Vivian never used the word *boyfriend* when referring to the relationship between Simon and Thad after they arrived (Simon used the word *escaped*) from Hollywood, Simon having lost to addiction everything except the contents of his house, belongings that Thad, Simon's tall and spritely boyfriend, transported to Sibley in a rental truck, volunteering to help in the hope that Simon would take him back after a period of estrangement that saw Thad go into rehab for dependence on cocaine, followed by Simon. Vivian preferred to think of Thad as Simon's companion. A relationship as close as *companion* allowed Vivian, when she saw a certain look in their eyes and knew they were about to sneak a kiss, to divert her gaze and pretend it was merely a *companionable* gesture.

Connie and Derek never visited the mansion without asking Thad when he planned to go back to Hollywood. Only gradually did Simon's sister and brother-in-law realize the nature of their relationship. Connie's first thought was one of gratitude that Lenny had not lived to see it. Lenny and Vivian had suffered enough during Simon's involvement with a fringe religious group—the Moonies, people called them—listening as relatives condemned Simon, enduring the pity of friends horrified that an Antichrist, and an Asian one at that, had stolen Simon's young adult life. Connie blamed Simon's rejection of his Christian heritage for his later descent into cocaine use and, now, homosexuality. Lenny's heart surely would have given out sooner if he had known the truth about Simon.

Derek avoided thinking about the relationship between Simon and Thad because it contradicted his belief that his work with Connie, opposing Sun Myung Moon's Unification Church by traveling a lecture circuit to conservative church groups, would result in Simon's rescue and his return to Christ, never acknowledging that Simon seemed to have left the church long before his teenage years. Further confounding Derek, Simon had been married to a Japanese woman while a member of the Unification Church. Simon and Masako had visited after their marriage, and they seemed happy. Masako played dolls with Cheryl and Victoria, instantly winning them over and leading to Simon's nieces calling her Aunt Masako. She similarly charmed everyone else in the family, even disarming Lenny, who had responded with a racial slur from World War II when Simon announced his betrothal. Masako, who had been a nurse before joining the church, gave Lenny advice about changing to a healthier diet, suggesting foods Lenny actually liked and that Vivian could prepare, followed by what Lenny described as the best shoulder rub he had ever received—shiatsu, which Masako had studied as an apprentice in Japan. Masako won over Vivian by helping her prepare dinner the night Simon and Masako stayed at the mansion.

Derek concluded that Simon's drug use, and then his decision to divorce Masako after leaving the apostate church, were steps along Simon's path to godlessness. Derek would never give up hope that Simon might again return to Christ. Until then, he would refrain from further condemnation and accept Thad as Simon's friend, but no more than that.

Since leaving rehab, Simon had begun to think about the lucrative business he had established in Los Angeles after working for an Italian entrepreneur introduced to him by his friends from a law firm he had hired while still in the church. What opportunities he had let slip, and what a disaster at the end when he'd entrusted daily affairs to his secretary, Charlotte, who, while Simon was en route from Hollywood to Sibley, had stolen over $200,000 when it arrived from a deal Simon had concluded with a company in Spain. Charlotte could have had no idea she was taking money the Spaniards wanted Simon to use for procurement of new films to release on the Spanish video market. Though Simon had hoped to keep his own involvement legal, he knew the Spaniards intended to use the movies to launder profits from drug smuggling and distribution of pornography into countries where such films were banned. Simon didn't know where Charlotte had gone after the theft, but he knew that Rudy, the mutual friend who'd introduced them, had helped her.

During rehab, Simon's counselor had advised him to reflect on his life and learn to accept the many experiences that had led him to depend on cocaine. Worry about Charlotte's theft and the dread of being pursued once the Spaniards realized he had disappeared threatened to derail Simon's path of recovery, but as much as possible, Simon tried to follow his counselor's advice and continue to examine his life, as he had done during rehab. He realized how the prospect of living a celibate life as a follower of Sun Myung Moon had given him permission to set aside his personal struggles, celibacy being the sacrifice required of members until Moon chose a spouse for them. Because the group emphasized the importance of marriage, Simon came to believe that anything interfering with the union of a husband and wife, especially homosexuality, was Satanic by definition, and he wholeheartedly believed that on the

17

day Sun Myung Moon joined him to his betrothed in holy marriage, the oppression of his feelings for other men would be lifted, and the salvation promised in youth through baptism would find realization through the rituals of the new messiah. When nothing changed following the church's ceremonies—communion wine spiked with a drop of Sun Myung Moon's blood, caning in an act reminiscent of Jacob wrestling God's angel at the Ford of Jabbok, the mass wedding ceremony itself, when the messiah and his wife sprinkled holy water on the participants—Simon never lost hope for the realization of his long-awaited miracle. But after he went back to his work helping lawyers prepare an appeal to Sun Myung Moon's conviction on charges of income tax evasion and conspiracy to defraud the IRA, affections for his own sex grew even stronger. Simon descended into despair and, within months, left the church, choosing to party with his newfound friends from the law firm—Scott Mansfield, a young gay lawyer, and Sandra Banks, the firm's ribald secretary, introduced him to the dangerous comfort of cocaine—and male hustlers.

Vivian knew nothing of Simon's struggles—with faith, drugs, or sexuality—but she recognized the deep loneliness Simon experienced when the thousands of church members he had called brothers and sisters turned their backs on him after he left the group. She was happy that Simon and Thad were together, though she could never have comprehended their ordeal with cocaine or the near-murderous fights in which they engaged along the way. Vivian wished Lenny were alive now that Simon had come home, unaffiliated with the strange religion that had torn the family apart; she thought Lenny would have understood Simon's struggle with addiction, and she would have helped Lenny find a way to accept Thad.

Vivian understood how desperately Lenny's death had affected Simon, happening so soon after he'd abandoned his faith. Reconciliation might not have been possible, but Simon mourned the fact he would never have the chance to try.

CHAPTER FOUR

Some months after Thad arrived from Los Angeles and Simon completed his time in rehab, Vivian's sister reminded her of a long-planned family reunion in their hometown of Magnolia. Vivian asked Simon to take her, with trepidation, knowing that Simon resented her family because of the way they'd spoken about him in the past but hoping the reunion might offer a chance at reconciling. Simon agreed, though he knew Vivian wouldn't want Thad to join them. Then Vivian asked Simon, "See if Thad wants to go."

Simon wasn't worried about having to tell Vivian that Thad had agreed to go, aware that the idea of visiting another hole-in-the-wall town was more than Thad would be able to think about. Sibley, with a population of less than two thousand at the last census, served well enough to invoke memories of a childhood in Idaho that Thad preferred to forget. Besides, if Thad went, Simon would be put upon to lie about their relationship—or worse, tell the truth to his small-town relatives and be chased out of town with pitchforks. Neither option, lie or speak the truth, seemed like a good idea. Better to avoid the situation entirely.

"I'll stay put and catch up on the backlog of daytime dramas that Vivian recorded," Thad responded when Simon asked; then, going into the parlor, he made sure Vivian knew he appreciated the invitation.

Vivian's 1979 canary-yellow Pontiac Grand Prix needed new spark plugs, service on the transmission, and at least to get the tires retreaded, but Simon trusted the durable car would make it to Magnolia and back. The morning he and Vivian set out, mist still crept along the grass from the swamp making up the lower part of the property and feeding a pond that had served to water the horses and other animals Lenny had kept as long as he was able, trailing past the corral and around the house all the way to the base of JT's red oak, mist that was soon to burn off as the sun's rays crept down the trunks of the tall pines that dominated the woods on both sides of the mansion. Simon could not recall a time since childhood that he had been alone with his mother for any length of time. The opportunity allowed him to broach questions he'd frequently mulled over since Lenny died. Generally, Simon couched his words in euphemism when speaking to Vivian, but this time he decided on a direct approach, asking straightforwardly, "Why did Lenny hate me so much? Did he know I was gay?"

Vivian didn't seem surprised, but after addressing the first part with a simple statement, she chose to answer the second using anecdote. Speaking in a halting voice as she struggled through the effects of a recent stroke that had affected her motor skills but left her mind intact, Vivian offered, "Honey, your father didn't hate you. Lenny used to see Dr. Stanley when he got sick. You know he went to the funeral when her friend died."

Dr. Stanley, an unmarried woman in her sixties when Simon was a boy, had lived with a *companion* of thirty years in a house on the edge of the county, set back from the main road down a wooded lane of poplar trees and known for multicolored azaleas that bloomed profusely in the spring. The community referred to her as a spinster, even though they knew the truth. Simon too had always understood what was going on with Pat Stanley, who lived as a couple with her *friend*. No Sibley resident suggested inappropriateness in their relationship—after all, Dr. Stanley had delivered many of their children.

Vivian reasoned that if Lenny had found out about Simon, he would not have hated his son, but even so, some things were better left unspoken. Simon had understood that. He never told Lenny, or Vivian, that the men who came with him on the long drive from Los Angeles to Sibley each Christmas were more than traveling companions. Simon had no doubt what Lenny would have said about his sleeping in the same bed with Thad—the memory of Lenny's reaction to Liberace remained a guidepost. Still, Vivian provided a comforting image, one of Lenny sitting in the pew at the funeral of his lesbian doctor's companion. That was enough to settle the issue for Vivian, and, through her story, to let Simon know she understood his relationship with Thad. Simon could never be sure what Lenny's reaction to Thad might have been, but more importantly, taking a cue from his counseling in rehab—did it matter?

Sunlight filtered through the old-growth forest along the highway, left intact to hide the less comely forest of pine trees behind them, planted and quickly harvested by a northern company since the days of Reconstruction to provide lumber and fencing, and mulch for paper mill in Pine Bluff, and shone directly overhead as Simon and his mother arrived at Vivian's hometown, driving through a square picturesque with ancient magnolias, tall and wide, as if guarding the courthouse they surrounded. Simon lowered his window to savor the delicate aroma of the cream-colored blossoms and to admire the dark beauty of the waxy leaves in which they nestled. Vivian's sister lived on a thirty-acre tomato farm two miles beyond the city limits, the house standing on the same plot of land as the dogtrot cabin built during pioneer days.

Vivian was the middle child of nine, and all her siblings were still living, with the exception of Wesley, who had died as a teenager and whom Vivian saw reflected in Simon's every mannerism. Wesley's portrait greeted Simon each morning as he left his bedroom, the most recent addition to the gallery of ancestors. A few cousins still lived within a few hours' traveling distance of Magnolia, but the majority had departed long ago to seek work in areas less economically depressed, and with more for the men to do during leisure time than chew the fat with neighbors, or to fish, or to hunt—or to get into trouble with a neighbor's wife or daughter.

A crowd of about thirty people stood around picnic tables and makeshift serving platforms in the field beside the house of Simon's aunt. One platform was constructed of planks supported by cinder blocks, another fashioned from a discarded door, with broken hinges dangling from one side, set across corroded oil barrels. Steam rose from casseroles kept warm atop Sterno burners, a fryer sizzled with chicken wings, and aromatic smoke billowed from the grease dripping off a locally raised hog onto a bed of hot coals. Pies, made from scratch, vied for symmetrical perfection, none able to compete with the rhubarb prepared by Vivian's oldest sister, Cassie, the entry easily identified by the burgundy filling that oozed from its lattice crust.

Vivian held Simon's arm for support as she made her way to a row of folding chairs, easing into a seat beside Cassie and their youngest surviving brother, Jared. First and second cousins that Simon had not seen since his teenage years updated each other on recent events in their lives and, in one overheard conversation, railed about liberals destroying the country—"won't even let kids pray together before a game any longer...Judgment Day is coming, that's for sure." None of the relatives acknowledged Simon when they greeted Vivian, though Simon caught the furtive glances cast his direction, darting away if their eyes met. Vivian asked Simon to fetch her a glass of punch from a bowl sitting precariously on a wobbly TV stand. As soon as Simon stood up, Jared (pronounced as if his named rhymed with scared) leaned close to whisper something into Vivian's ear. Vivian's lips pursed as her eyes fixed in the way Simon had always dreaded as a little boy.

When Simon returned with a paper cup brimming with sweet red punch, Jared voiced what was on his mind. "Why did you come here? Don't you know how much embarrassment you've caused this family?"

Simon wondered what troubled Uncle Jared, unless Vivian had told them about Simon's drug problems, which Simon was sure she hadn't; they couldn't know about his relationship with Thad, and Simon's past association with Sun Myung Moon's religion was a long time ago—at least from Simon's perspective.

"Uncle Jared," Simon began, "the truth is, I hardly know you or anyone else at this reunion—not since I was a child. How could I possibly be an embarrassment to you?"

Alerted to the confrontation, several cousins approached. Aunt Cassie gave up trying to conceal her disdain, looking Simon square in the eye; but it was Simon's aunt Josephine, who had not greeted Vivian or Simon when they arrived, who marched over to say, "You turned your back on Jesus to follow that blaspheming Korean."

Simon wondered if her disdain originated with his presumed rejection of Jesus or the fact that he had believed in the divinity of an Asian.

"Have you repented and asked the Lord's forgiveness?" Jared demanded.

Simon began to understand. Just as it had been for Connie and Derek, Simon's leaving the fold of Sun Myung Moon's religion wasn't enough. They expected him to profess faith in their beliefs.

Vivian leaned forward, covering her face, signaling her shame at the way family was treating Simon.

"See what you've done to your mother," Jared accused.

Vivian straightened her back and through reddened eyes said with force and clarity that defied the symptoms of her stroke, "If you want to treat my son like he's not family, I don't know why *I* came." She stood, appearing deceptively stable, and took a step forward as Simon extended his arm to assist.

As Simon and Vivian slowly walked toward the car, Simon noticed the adults' attitude reflected in the eyes of his youngest cousins, taking the lesson to heart: those not like us should be driven away.

Simon remembered why he had adopted the persona of an alien from Zenon, a being who could observe the prejudices of his relatives without being affected by them. Now, considering his many transgressions since leaving Sun Myung Moon's religion, Simon mused, If they only knew!

Vivian and Simon drove away from the reunion in silence. Vivian's tears had dried, the look on her face hardened into one of firm resolve.

"What brought that on?" Simon asked.

"It must be Connie's doing. She and Derek filled everyone with stories about how you were following the Antichrist. But Lordy mercy, I would have thought that wouldn't matter anymore. Hon, I'm sorry about today. I sure never expected anything like that, or I wouldn't have asked for you to take me."

"If I had known how they felt, I would have dropped you off and come back when the reunion ended."

"I would never let you do something like that. I'm not ashamed of you, and I'll be damned if anyone is going to condemn you, family or no family."

Simon marveled at Vivian's use of a curse word, unable to recall any other example of Vivian using such language. Passing Uncle Jared's house on the north side of town, Vivian turned toward Simon. "Simon, what you believe is your own business."

It had not occurred to Simon that Vivian thought he still believed in Sun Myung Moon, but in her mind, he knew, a person must believe in something, and Simon had not responded to Jared's question about repentance, nor had he attended church when invited by Connie and Derek.

Vivian's beliefs were constant and straightforward: she believed that Christ died for her sins and that though she might fall short of God's expectations, Christ forgave her. Vivian had learned long ago not to insist that the family attend church. Though she never knew why, Simon's tantrums after being molested by the baptism attendant ensured that he'd never go, and Lenny had rarely attended services after the pastor of the church during World War II refused to let husbands and wives meet together for prayer, strictly enforcing a church prohibition against mixing the sexes outside Sunday sermon. In Lenny's mind, this was an idea that violated the spirit of worship and led him to settle on his one article of faith: once saved, always saved.

If Simon had proclaimed himself agnostic, Vivian would never have accepted it. Belief in God was natural, like breathing. Doctrines might err, but everyone knew that God existed. They needed only to open their hearts to Christ in order to experience him fully.

"I wish your grandmother was alive," Vivian said as they entered a stretch of highway shaded by oak and walnut trees. They had to slow down as they approached trucks transporting logs to the lumber mill in Warren.

"Why's that?" Simon asked, though he too missed his grandmother.

"Mother would never have let your uncle Jared get away with challenging you about your faith. She followed the example of Jesus and let people be. When did the Lord ever condemn anyone?"

"I'm afraid Christians don't try very hard to act like Jesus," Simon cautiously noted, realizing that his words might give Vivian more reason to assume he still held his prior beliefs.

"Judge not lest you be judged," Vivian insisted. "That's the plain truth." She nervously tugged the hem of her dress as she considered her words. "I sure wish you and your father had learned to talk to each other. You are so much alike."

Without meaning to, Simon laughed. "Lenny and me? Alike?"

"More than you know. At least it's not too late for you." Vivian reached for a Kleenex, carefully balancing her purse on a knee, and, with the elbow of her bad arm as leverage, unclasped the lock. She dabbed beads of sweat from her hairline, where perspiration always formed when Vivian felt nervous. "You enjoyed drawing so much when you were little. Remember how I used to bring home construction paper and boxes of Crayolas? You loved the red one best. You'd spend hours sitting in front of the TV on that dog pillow drawing the craziest pictures I ever saw." Vivian smiled, thinking about them.

Simon remembered the drawings, attempts to visualize his home planet of Zenon, the imaginary world where he felt welcome, where no ancestors followed his every move, and where Lenny never criticized his attempts to find friends or engage in his favorite pastimes, whether it was learning to play piano or drawing pictures of spacemen.

"And those paintings in your room," Vivian recollected. "You had such an imagination. I don't know where you got it from."

"Remember those books that arrived every year as part of our Funk & Wagnalls encyclopedia? I never told you, but one year I cut out images of modern art with a razor blade and taped them to my headboard."

"I wondered where those came from." Vivian sighed, an old mystery having finally been solved. "You never told me what you did with the paintings you had in your room when you joined those people."

Vivian had always characterized Unification Church members as *those people*, asking, on visits home, when he planned on returning to *those people*; or, when challenging Simon about things he said during attempts to explain his beliefs, saying that *those people* had put crazy ideas in his head.

Simon dreaded Vivian asking what he had done with the paintings. She knew how important they were to Simon, even if she didn't understand why he'd painted them. From Vivian's point of view, the paintings had vanished into thin air—and, in fact, they had.

"Do you remember the Bible story about Abraham sacrificing his son Isaac?" Simon began.

"But the angel of God stopped him," Vivian said, anticipating his story.

"In the church that I belonged to, we believed that new members should dedicate themselves to God by sacrificing the thing they loved the most."

"Oh, son, all those paintings?"

A pain shot through Simon's chest as he considered what he had done those many years ago. While Vivian and Lenny were at work, Simon had collected his canvases and taken them into the woods, built a bonfire, and watched them go up in flames on a bier of dry leaves, dead branches, and wadded-up drawings.

"An angel might have stayed Abraham's hand, but no one stopped the fire I set in the woods. Everything burned to ashes."

Vivian started to say something but hesitated, having no words to express the sympathy she felt for provoking such a painful memory.

"We ought to buy some dahlia bulbs on the way home," Vivian suggested as if the prior conversation never happened. "Snider's Feed has the best ones. The pictures on the boxes looked so pretty when Connie and I were up there the other day."

"Planting for next spring sounds like a good idea," Simon agreed, recognizing Vivian's desire for a happier future.

"You really are a lot like your father," Vivian again insisted. "When he was a boy, all he cared about was animals."

Simon had seen pictures of Lenny as a teenager in his backyard holding a baby raccoon, surrounded by geese and chickens.

"Lenny would go into the woods to look for animals that needed care," Vivian continued. "He rescued foxes and rabbits that got caught in those awful traps that broke their legs. He'd nurse them back to health and then let them go. Lenny wanted to be a veterinarian. That was all he talked about when we first met."

Vivian and Lenny were young when they began dating. Vivian's mother had departed Magnolia with Vivian and the younger siblings and moved to Little Rock, an event that forever shaped Vivian's emotions. Vivian met Lenny two years later, and they married as soon as they turned eighteen. The answer to why Vivian's parents had separated depended on whom Simon asked. Vivian claimed that her father had gone into a rage and beaten her brother, Wesley, whose memory, if not his ghost, haunted Simon's childhood. Simon had been born on the same day as Wesley, and, as Vivian pointed out when she noticed Simon separating the vegetables on his plate, ate his food like him. Wesley was left-handed like Simon, and Wesley loved art. One of Vivian's dearest possessions was a leather notebook etched with images of 1930s cartoon characters surrounding a World War I biplane. Simon often wondered if Vivian thought he was her brother's reincarnation—one of those doctrinal errors she might think God would forgive.

"Couldn't Lenny have gotten a GI loan and gone to veterinary school after he came home from the war?"

"He sure wanted to do that," Vivian confirmed, and then said in a tone of deep melancholy, "but I caused trouble by getting pregnant. We met when he was on leave. I drove to where he was stationed in Alabama." Vivian sighed deeply, thinking of Connie. "I wanted a child so much." A tear formed in Vivian's eye, and she reached for another Kleenex. "We didn't have much money. You know we lived with Mandy and Bart in Little Rock. Mandy never worked a day in her life, and of course, Bart lost the mercantile store when the Depression hit."

Lenny's father, Bartholomew "Bart" Powell, had lost his store in downtown Little Rock because he'd allowed the store's debtors to default on their bills, never suing any of them to recover his money on the feed he was providing through credit. As a child, whenever Simon questioned Bart's wisdom, he was told to respect his deceased grandfather because Bart had demonstrated his nature as a good Christian. The family motto became deeply entrenched through repeated telling: Better that one family suffer than for others to go without. As a follower of Sun Myung Moon, Simon had believed in the motto as a message from his ancestors as a way of preparing him to receive the new messiah and to agree to the sacrifices that discipleship required. Now Simon wondered if Bart's attitude had been a wise one. The farms failed anyway, and if he had taken even a few cents on the dollar, he might have secured a future for his business and a livelihood that Lenny might have inherited, allowing him to attend veterinary school after the war.

"Your father took responsibility for the care of his parents," Vivian explained. "We both worked, but it was hard to make ends meet. If Lenny had gone to school, we couldn't have managed."

"Then I came along. He must have loved that."

"That might have added to his bitterness—one of the reasons you and your father didn't get along. I know he loved you, but he didn't want more children. Your sister was enough for him. I was the one who wanted a large family."

"And I can see from the reaction at the reunion what a blessing family can be." Simon immediately regretted his sarcasm.

"Don't think badly of them," Vivian consoled. "If only Momma was alive. She didn't judge people because of what they thought. She cared about how people behaved themselves. She knew you were a good person."

The last time Simon had gone to a reunion of Vivian's family was during his time as a leader of the church's fundraising activities in Texas. His secretary at the Dallas headquarters had driven with him to Magnolia. Vivian knew it might be the last opportunity for Simon to see his grandmother and had insisted that he come. Many of the same relatives had attended that reunion, but they had mostly held their tongues. Only one person, a cousin by marriage, couldn't hold back. "Are you as brainwashed as that son of Vivian's?" he rudely asked the secretary. "What kind of person follows a man who thinks he's Jesus? That Moon fellow should be sent back to wherever he came from."

For her part, the secretary, a woman in her fifties who had never endured abuse from anyone, who had bravely raised her children on a commune in Northern California, turning her back on the whole of American society, replied calmly and eruditely, "If you took some time to study our philosophy, you might come to understand that Sun Myung Moon does not think he is Jesus."

The cousin by marriage had no interest in debating theology. "Ain't readin' none of your crap," he said, steadfast in his conviction that people did not have a right to their own beliefs.

Simon stood near his grandmother, who, overhearing the exchange, took his hand and pulled him close, overcoming the debility of a recent stroke, a malady suffered by all the elderly members of Vivian's family. "Don't you listen to them," she had said. "You are family. If we start chasing away people because of what they believe, what kind of people will we be?"

As Vivian had feared, that was the last time Simon saw his grandmother. Driving home from the recent reunion, Simon wished her children had inherited his grandmother's personal convictions instead of the ones taught at their church.

"Your mother was a decent person," Simon assured. "It's not easy to accept people's differences the way she did."

"I miss her," Vivian said. "It's not the same anymore when the family gets together. That was the last picnic I'm attending. If they want to see me, they can come to Sibley."

"I wouldn't count on that, not while I'm there with Thad."

"Well, I'm sorry for them, then," Vivian said resolutely. "Thad is welcome to stay as long as he wants. I hope you know that."

"I know," Simon responded.

He really did know.

CHAPTER FIVE

"What are we going to do?" Thad asked, lying awake with his head on Simon's chest, enjoying the comfort of luxuriating in a lover's arms.

"Breakfast," Simon responded.

"You know what I mean." Thad reached under the covers, turned Simon on his side, and playfully slapped him on the butt.

"Okay, I do know what you mean," Simon admitted. "It isn't like I haven't thought about it. Vivian has said we can stay at the mansion as long as we like. I could take over the place after Vivian's gone, though I hope that's not anytime soon."

"She's a sweet person," Thad confessed.

"What? Hard-ass Thad, sentimental?"

Instead of a slap, Simon earned a grab. "You're the one who's hard," Thad joked.

"I don't want to go downstairs just yet," Simon whispered.

Thad placed a hand gently on Simon's face and pulled him close. The pair kissed, losing themselves in lovemaking, savoring each other like two people starved of love.

Afterward Thad turned onto his back and laughed.

"That was some serious sex. Why are you laughing?" Simon asked, but he found himself laughing as well. "It's like being high on drugs, isn't it? Better, though."

"I was laughing because right at the crucial moment, I heard your mother calling. I almost lost it."

"Glad you didn't!"

"Bubby," came Vivian's barely audible voice. Simon would never outgrow his childhood nickname.

Vivian slept in a room on the ground floor once occupied by Aunt Opal, where Lenny had stayed when his heart condition made it impossible to navigate a flight of stairs, especially toward the end, when he needed to pull an oxygen tank on rollers everywhere he went.

"We'll be there shortly," Simon called out.

"All right, hon," Vivian acknowledged, straining to project her voice.

Simon and Thad found Vivian was sitting at the dinette table looking out at the pond and biting into a slice of toast, her plate a messy affair, evidence of trying to manage a butter knife to spread jelly with one hand. Cicero, Simon's Boston terrier, who had accompanied him on his dash from Los Angeles, the beloved dog that Thad had once kidnapped to punish Simon for a perceived flirtation at the Spotlight Bar, sat attentively beside Vivian's chair. Cicero had become her dog, a surprising turn since, throughout Vivian's life, she had professed a dislike for animals (secretly pleased that Lenny never became a veterinarian). Cicero now slept on her bed and always earned a food reward, no matter how many times Vivian scolded him for begging at the table. It was a kind of heaven for Cicero after enduring ill treatment during Simon's drug abuse, often going unfed for days and, when Simon met Thad, becoming a pawn in their tumultuous relationship.

Cicero had spent his first six months as a puppy in the window of a pet shop at the Beverly Center in Los Angeles, awkwardly standing on the wire floor of his cage, which over time had caused the outer toe on each paw to retract. Simon had bought Cicero during a period of sobriety at the height of his business success, a time when Simon often made purchases on a whim. Before Cicero reached two years old, Simon relapsed into his addiction, the beginning of the rough period for Simon but also for Cicero, culminating in harsh mistreatment when Simon left Hollywood on his final road trip to Sibley, when Cicero would find himself locked in motel bathrooms, unfed because Simon, stoned to near unconsciousness, forgot he was inside. Cicero had managed to survive his trials and forgave Simon; even so, when Simon came into the room, Cicero nudged close to Vivian's leg.

"It's such a beautiful morning," Vivian remarked. "Let's walk out to the pond. I want to check on the barn."

Thad didn't like to think about barns and ponds, and so he offered to stay behind to make a proper breakfast. Vivian had gotten very little nourishment from her toast-making effort.

"I suppose goat herding is country enough for you?" Simon teased, a question Thad ignored with a curled lip. He was willing to help but unhappy that, when Vivian had received a goat from the people who'd moved into the Corley house beyond the creek—Ernie's old house—she had asked him to position the animal around the property in order to keep the grass short. Thad would have preferred to take out Vivian's riding lawn mower, but Vivian thought that would be too much to ask. Connie's oldest daughter, Cheryl, mischievously named the goat Ferdinand, partly because her younger sister, Victoria, had trouble pronouncing it, but also because Cheryl once had proudly recited back the name Ferdinand Fitz-Fossillus Feltspar when Simon finished reading to her the Edgar Allan Poe story "Lionizing." Cheryl had not understood the story, but she delighted in the odd names of the characters.

Vivian held onto Simon's arm as they made their way through the morning air, walking the dewy acre that separated the mansion from the swamp's watershed, which the Powell family had always called the pond. The clay forming the bank in that part being too hard for cypress to sprout, the terminus had become an algae-filled nursery for mosquitos, with flat-top granite outcroppings beloved by snapping turtles as a place to warm themselves.

Simon couldn't stop thinking about Ernie, how they'd met as preschoolers soon after the family had moved into the mansion, how they'd become instant friends, concocting imaginative games whenever they were together, a picnic table serving as a whaling ship, with stripped mimosa limbs their harpoons, each woodland hill the site of a long-lost fort—Simon and Ernie, the Inseparables. When Ernie's older brother Jay began molesting him, and Ernie taught Simon the *games* they played, the innocent adventures soured, and the two companions, though still spending time together, felt separated by secret emotions they couldn't understand, emotions that became barely recognized as guilt and self-loathing once they approached puberty, when finally, with sexuality ruling their bodies, jealousy tore them apart.

Ernie and Simon might have become lifelong companions, but Ernie never came to terms with his feelings for Simon; instead, he tried to be like other boys and date girls. Loneliness caused Simon to experiment with hallucinogens, excused as a way to seek mystical enlightenment—anything to avoid the question of his sexual identity. Ernie, driven by his own denials, began sniffing glue, progressing to heroin by the time he reached high school. The religion of Sun Myung Moon, despite its falsehoods and deceits, rescued Simon from imminent destruction, but no savior redeemed Ernie. He died at the age of twenty-two, victim to heroin, dying alone in a liquor store parking lot slumped in the front seat of his truck, needle hanging from his arm, a pint of whiskey spilling onto the seat beside him.

"It's so sad what happened to Ernie," Vivian remarked, noticing Simon's gaze in the direction of the Corley house. "You were the cutest little boys. I remember watching you and Ernie play out here by the barn. It didn't take much to keep you entertained."

"We were close for a long time," Simon said. "Closer than you might know. I truly loved Ernie."

Vivian squeezed Simon's arm. "I wish I had understood what you were going through."

"At least you and Dad didn't get divorced like Ernie's parents. That was one trauma I didn't have to face."

"Stay away from those awful drugs," Vivian said, nearly in tears. "You weren't yourself when you came home."

"The drugs tempt me," Simon admitted. "But these days, I want more from life."

"That's why I wanted you to come out here to the barn with me," Vivian said as they made their way through the wooden double doors. "Derek replaced the hinges. See how freely the doors open? It's awful stuffy, but at least the water doesn't get in. The roof's still good, and Lenny had the floor concreted before he died. You know how he spent all our money during those last few months. He even had that heater over there installed." Vivian pointed to a stove that looked like the one in the mansion's upstairs bathroom, but this one stood alone rather than being recessed into the wall. "I think he wanted to turn this into a workshop, but I can't imagine what he thought he was going to build. He couldn't even walk out here with his oxygen tank."

Simon realized then what Vivian was planning to suggest.

"You and Thad could live at the mansion, and you could paint here in the barn. It's sure big enough."

When Simon had driven away from Hollywood, his idea was to make it to New York City and establish himself as an artist—a cocaine fantasy, but one with a germ of truth. Simon had dreamed of becoming a professional artist since childhood.

"I'll give it some thought," Simon promised, forming a mental image of himself slinging paint onto a twenty-foot canvas as the Jackson Pollock of Arkansas. "I hope the bats would leave me alone." For years, the rafters above the planked ceiling had been home to a colony of fruit bats.

"I haven't seen them fly out of here in a while," Vivian said. "Maybe they found a better home. There's a raccoon living around here somewhere for sure. He goes down to the creek to wash the food he steals from the garbage can—no matter how tight I push down the lid, he gets into it."

Thad called from the back porch, "Breakfast!"

The three residents of the mansion sat down to a banquet of vegetable omelets, hash browns, link sausages, and fresh biscuits with giblet gravy.

Cicero sat by Vivian's chair with an irresistible expression of longing. He would soon get all the table scraps he could eat.

CHAPTER SIX

Vivian's proposal warranted careful consideration, but before broaching the idea with Thad, Simon decided to explore possibilities. If he stayed in Sibley, money would be a challenge. Simon had left rehab penniless, and the money Charlotte had stolen from his Spanish client—Hollywood Pictures, SA, run by Emilio, who produced hardcore pornography, and husband-and-wife team David and Irene, who managed general business affairs—never strayed far from Simon's thoughts. It was foolhardy to think that Sibley's remoteness would protect him, but Simon needed to believe it.

Simon had known the deal with the Spanish company held great risks when he went into it, having learned while in Spain, negotiating, that the company engaged in nefarious activities. Still, the warnings had come from one of Emilio's porn stars, and Simon chose to doubt it. Simon's small enterprise licensing video rights for low-budget American films to foreign countries made a good profit, but at the rate he was going, Simon would never get rich—and that was what Simon wanted, because at that point, he fantasized, he would embark on a new career as an artist.

Rudy Gutierrez had introduced Simon to Charlotte. Rudy was an acquaintance from the Spotlight, a gay haunt at Selma and Cahuenga in Hollywood, advertised by its owner as the crummiest bar in Hollywood, an assessment with which an uninitiated customer, encountering the male hustlers and drug dealers who frequented the establishment, clandestinely plying their trade, might agree. Charlotte was a former exotic dancer and manager of a dance club in Miami before relocating to Hollywood, fleeing her own unsavory dealings with Miami's underworld, representatives of which demanded monthly payments from strip clubs such as the one Charlotte managed, and whom Charlotte tried to cheat—something that should have alarmed Simon when he learned about it but that instead, in a twisted turn of reasoning, had caused him to trust her more.

Unfazed by Simon's carousing and drug use, Charlotte ran his business affairs for several months before moving into Simon's house in the Los Angeles neighborhood of Silverlake, expertly making excuses when Simon failed to return phone calls and/or to show up for meetings. Charlotte knew Simon could ruin her plum situation and often warned him about the extent of his drug use, varying the theme "you're going to lose everything if you don't slow down."

Simon's business associates had reached their limits when he failed to show up at an all-important film market in Milan, Italy, called MIFED—an acronym derived from the name of the industrial convention center that hosted the event—because he was too high on cocaine to make it. The failure served as one of the triggers that sent Simon fleeing Hollywood hoping to outrun his addiction, a ploy that led to worse effects on his mental health and that strained his family's tolerance to its limits when he showed up on the doorstep of the mansion, nearly dead. Simon's flight

set Charlotte on her determined path to salvage what she could before he ended up in jail, or worse.

Simon ventured to contact the one film supplier who might work with him, Wally Freeze, creator of sexy but relatively unobjectionable videos, who, along with a silent partner named Martin Fast, owned a company called Fast-Freeze Productions. Simon hoped for an exclusive deal to market Wally's newest videos, but when he reached him from Sibley, Wally insisted that Simon could only market videos listed on their original contract.

"Even that feels like a risk," Wally said sharply. "I heard through the grapevine that you had left town and cleaned up your act, but I've seen too many people, you know, relapse. Anyway, the new company I'm working with should have luck in overseas markets, but..." Wally's voice trailed off as if he had not meant to bring up the arrangement with a different company. When Simon asked who it was, Wally replied, "Just someone I've spoken to. We can discuss the future when our contract expires...a little over a year, right?"

"Something like that," Simon demurred.

"There's a call coming in. I have to take it. Let me know when you've made sales. Your lab letters are still in effect; I just need to give them the go-ahead to copy the master tape and let the customs broker know."

Before Simon could say good-bye, Wally hung up the phone.

At least Simon had some hope of making money, but few markets remained for Wally's videos. Simon had given up trying to make sales before he left Los Angeles, waiting instead to benefit from Fast-Freeze's strategy of churning out a new title every month, drawing upon a stable of athletes, cheerleaders, and struggling university students from the Southern California area to produce an hour-long video of the twenty-something men and women taking off most of their clothes. *Bel Air Babes* and *Co-ed Jell-O Wrestling* were among the titles that had launched Simon's business when he'd left his job as a salesman with Nicolò, the Italian entrepreneur introduced to Simon by Scott Mansfield.

Simon found Thad upstairs, sprawled on the bed reading a Harlequin Romance, one of dozens stacked in a crawlspace under the stairs—Vivian's stockpile, books she had devoured each time a new one showed up on the rack of the grocery store where she had been a bookkeeper and sales clerk until her stroke made working impossible. Those novels had transported Vivian to exotic locales and stimulated vicarious emotions she'd never experienced with Lenny. Thad read the romances as comic relief, often remarking with amazement that anyone could find the stories believable and yet admitting with a laugh that recent events seemed just as preposterous as the contrived dramas, even suggesting that he might submit his own story for publication: the saga of Thad and Simon's epic romance.

The image in front of Simon was a pulp fiction dust jacket: Thad's lithe body stretched supine from headboard to base, smooth skin beckoning, nylon gym shorts betraying any semblance of modesty. Fortune had blessed Simon with a handsome boyfriend, one whose time-tested commitment promised a love that would endure. Looking up from his book, Thad's eyes appeared bluer than ever, his sandy blond hair, grown long since arriving in Sibley, forming a frame around his boyishly cute face.

"Are you comfortable at the mansion?" Simon asked.

Hoping Simon's next statement would be "Let's go back to Hollywood," Thad cautiously responded, "Bored, but comfortable enough."

"What if I decided to remain in Sibley for a few years?"

Thad set the paperback facedown on the bedspread. "I've been wondering what you decided to do."

"Part of me wants to go back to Hollywood and try to rebuild my reputation."

Thad knew what a difficult task that could prove to be; he put on a stony expression as Simon went on.

"I spoke to Wally. He didn't sound happy about it but agreed that I could still market his films. I'd have to start small and negotiate to pay back the money I owe to the other producers; after all, I'm not the only person who has crashed and burned because of cocaine. I hate to think about it, but I need to consider paying back the Spaniards, if I could work out something with them. But I'm scared to contact them."

"Could you make enough sales to repay them? I mean, that was the biggest contract you'd ever made."

"I'd have to avoid going to Europe for MIFED this year, and it would be risky to attend the American Film Market in Hollywood until I worked something out."

Thad's expression grew pensive. "If only I had gotten into rehab sooner. I should have taken over what Charlotte was doing for you. I'd never have ripped you off."

"That's sobriety talking." Simon smiled. "You're forgetting. You did rip me off once."

"The jewelry I charged on your credit card. You're right, but I was mad at you, and I was using heavily. I'd like to think that if I'd sobered up sooner, I could have helped you."

"You know how addiction works, Thad. Nothing anyone could have said or done would have gotten me to stop until I decided it on my own."

"Yeah, but still," Thad sighed.

"The biggest stumbling block right now is the lack of films in my portfolio. I'm afraid to reach out to anyone other than Wally."

Thad could see Simon becoming increasingly melancholy and tried to comfort him. "We've been through a lot, haven't we? My life was going nowhere when we met, and then you showed me all the great things a person can do if they believe in themselves. I hated witnessing what happened to you, even if I was part of it." Thad stood up and wrapped his arms around Simon, kissing him on the neck. "I've seen you out there in the barn, and I knew you were imagining what it would be like to start painting again. The one time I saw you working on an oil painting at the Silverlake house, it was like you were in a trance."

"I never thought about cocaine when I was painting. I should have kept at it, but I felt guilty for being creative—that is how screwed up I've been. I'm still shaking off the feeling that I betrayed everything I believed in."

"You did betray everything you believed in! They were ridiculous beliefs and needed to be betrayed. I mean, come on, they taught you that being gay is evil." Thad hugged Simon closer. "Go ahead and set up the barn. I'll find some way to get by here in Sibley."

Simon wasn't sure Thad would be satisfied, but he was grateful for the support.

CHAPTER SEVEN

To operate his business, Simon needed the equipment he'd originally brought with him to the mansion but that he'd left with a friend whom he'd met after Lenny died, a time when Simon went out to bars in Little Rock and drank heavily. Dean Pickett was a former Jesuit priest who understood Simon's struggles better than most, having been a counselor who dealt with the drug addictions among college students. Before entering rehab, Simon had asked Dean to take the computer, which held his business files, and video equipment used to copy preview tapes, all of which Simon had thrown into the trunk of his car before driving away from Hollywood. Dean had thought the request signaled that Simon might be preparing for suicide and explained his concern to Vivian, whom Dean had met on visits to the mansion. "Simon is showing classic signs," he told her. Dean's fears might have materialized if Thad had not intervened and escorted Simon through the doors of a rehab center.

Simon had only spoken to Dean once in recent days, to express his gratitude for never giving up on him and for consoling Vivian while he was in rehab, as well as being a friend to Thad.

"You think you can make a go of it from Sibley?" Dean asked when Simon called and told him of the new plans.

"I have to try," Simon said. "Time will tell. If things don't work out, I'll sell the equipment and figure out something else."

"It's good to have you back. Everyone missed you."

"You mean at the bars?" Simon sounded surprised.

"No, my friend, I mean your family—Vivian, Connie and Derek, and your nieces. It's not what I do anymore, but at their request, I came to the mansion to pray with them while you were in rehab. They needed to hear from someone who understood what was happening, especially after you nearly jumped off that bridge right after you got there."

Simon preferred to forget how crazy he had become when a fellow rehabber challenged him about being gay. Something had snapped in Simon's mind, and he wanted his pain to be gone for good. Vivian, Connie, and Thad, along with sympathetic words from Harris, Simon's counselor, had enticed him to take another chance on life.

The news about Dean holding the prayer meeting gave Simon a chill. He'd always thought of Dean as a secular friend, despite Dean's history in the clergy, and didn't want to picture him praying. "I'm sure they appreciated it," Simon allowed, then, "Was Thad part of it?" Simon couldn't imagine such a scenario—Thad had long proclaimed his atheism.

Dean smiled. "Thad handled it well. He took my advice and said that his own beliefs didn't allow prayer in groups and that he would be upstairs. Connie really wanted to dig into it, but Vivian gave her such a look. Thad stayed upstairs until later and joined us for dinner. Derek cooked steaks on the grill, and Connie prepared boiled potatoes and wonderfully seasoned corn. I visited Vivian a few times, but the family came over just that once. I'm not sure if Thad mentioned that he stayed at my house quite a bit while you were away, but mostly he tended to Vivian."

"I'm glad he had you as a friend."

Simon set up an office upstairs in a bedroom that had not been used in many years and contacted an agent with whom he had worked in the past, a businessman who had relationships with buyers in the smaller foreign markets. The agent negotiated a deal for a market that included Pacific island nations and wired a portion of the proceeds to an account that Simon had established at Sibley Commerce Bank. As a precaution to hide his whereabouts, Simon asked the agent to send Wally's portion directly to him. The deal was the speediest Simon had ever managed, placing sorely needed cash in his pocket and allowing him to proceed with plans to fix up the barn.

Simon installed halogen lights in the ceiling and dusted off the tarpaulin that had once shielded Lenny's bush hog tractor, an item that Vivian had sold after Lenny's death to help pay hospital expenses not covered by Medicaid, which Lenny was forced to seek despite protesting that government assistance offended his sense of pride. The tarpaulin, cut into several pieces, covered Simon's paintings to prevent dust from the corral sticking to the wet paint.

Within a few months, five large paintings covered the walls, and ten assemblage sculptures filled the former horse stalls. Arranging objects from his childhood into three-dimensional constructions, Simon reexamined his life. Roller skates, stuffed animals, marbles, and other items grew from a workbench made of broken furniture, the painter in Simon decking out the array in a sequence of nostalgically somber tones. Another piece, incorporating items discarded during efforts to remodel the mansion's interior, took shape in the form of a 1950s sunburst ceiling lamp, painted gold and attached to a metal stand with an antique telephone. Simon called the piece *Time Communicator* and the workbench *Alien Builder.*

In the best of all possible worlds, Simon's art would sell, and he could withdraw from the business affairs that put him at risk of being discovered by the Spanish company to whom he owed such a large sum of money; but with no credentials, he saw limited prospects. A bona fide novice might create a stir with unschooled art, but Simon's paintings spoke of familiarity with Modernism; as a former university art student, he could never pretend naiveté, despite those studies being cut short by his participation in Sun Myung Moon's errant crusade.

Simon thought about going back to school and earning his credentials. He wondered if the university still had his records. Could he pick up where he'd left off?

Thad and Simon lounged downstairs in the parlor when Vivian took a nap. "I've watched you paint out there in the barn, and I've never seen you happier," Thad said. "But it's so private. I don't think you realize how many hours you work. Your mother is kind— I can even get along with your sister—but I'm going a bit stir-crazy."

"What are you thinking about doing?"

"Going back to LA."

"I don't want to lose you," Simon gasped. "Thad, I love you."

Thad pulled away from Simon and walked to the bedroom window. The wisteria, almost as old as the mansion itself, had overwhelmed the trellis and attached itself to the timbers, curlicue runners crisscrossing the screen. Simon's heart filled with ancient dread as he watched Thad at the window. Was this to be the end of Thad and Simon?

"When I was in rehab," Thad began, "you were all I could think about. The counselor cautioned me to focus on myself, but I remembered how good you had been to me and what an asshole I had been toward you."

"I have to admit that during my bout of hepatitis B, when you disappeared in my car to see that Marvin guy in San Diego, and the time you ran off with Cicero to spite me, I wanted to knock your brains out."

Thad's look of despair made Simon regret bringing up the hurts of the past. The truth about his illness was that he had contracted it when cheating on Thad at MIFED after they'd first met, and he would always bear responsibility for having introduced Thad to cocaine. The craziness of their addiction had caused Thad to lash out, at the expense of poor Cicero.

"Don't go right away," Simon pleaded.

"I'm not in a hurry. I don't know what's best." Thad came away from the window and kissed Simon. "I didn't mean that I want us to break up. You started talking about starting up your business again. I don't know. I have the crazy idea that I could go out there and make enough money to support the two of us."

Simon pictured in his mind an old map with the words *There be monsters*—a sailor's fear that demons lay in wait for those venturing beyond safe harbor. Simon knew that cocaine waited for them like a stalking beast. Working on his art in Sibley filled Simon with life as surely as cocaine threatened his destruction. Vivian needed Simon—more reason for him to stay—and despite unpleasant memories from his childhood, the mansion was home. Thad, however, was unmoored outside their love.

"I'm bored out of my mind," Thad confessed. "Sibley is a ghost town."

"What if we both go to college?"

The question made Thad smile. "Do you have any idea how bad my grades were in high school? I barely managed to get my diploma."

"But you're smart," Simon insisted.

"School bored me to death, and so did Idaho. Do you know the name of the city where I grew up?"

"I forget."

"It was called Mile Run. The saying in town was that a person had to run a mile to find a neighbor."

"Sibley isn't that bad," Simon argued.

"Not as bad as Mile Run, but if I walk to the grocery store where Vivian used to work, guess what, it's a mile! I'm lucky to see three shoppers, and if they know who I am, they start gossiping about the queer boy who came home with Simon from California."

"They do not."

"Yes, they do. I overheard a conversation just like that."

"Okay, maybe. But people around here gossip about the Powell family no matter what we do. It goes all the way back to the beginning, when JT was killed. You know, we used to hang an effigy on Halloween—dangled it from the tree out front to dare anyone to step foot on the property."

"And that's another thing! All these stories! Who gives a fuck? It's ancient history, Simon. You tell me these things like they happened yesterday, and like they matter. No one cares! I'll admit it. I can't stand this place."

"Are you saying you don't want to go back to school?"

Thad laughed again. "You do that to me every time."

"I don't know what to say, Thad. This creaky old mansion, the stories, the portraits hanging in the hallway, the family graveyard across the street—they're in my DNA. This place *is* me."

"I'm just bored. I need something to do."

"What kind of job would make you happy?"

"Working in porn."

Now it was Simon's turn to laugh. "That came out of the blue. Are you serious?"

Thad didn't smile back.

"Sibley isn't exactly the porn capital of North America."

"I'm serious," Thad insisted.

Simon started for the bedroom door.

"Don't freak out on me," Thad called after him. "Listen for a minute."

"How can I not freak out? Was I fooling myself to think we could be lovers? If you can have sex with just anyone, you aren't in love with me."

"Simon, it's as if the modern world passed you by."

"It did."

"You mean all those years you were in that religious cult, or whatever it's called?"

"We believed that having sex was a sacred act, that it should only happen after a man and woman are married. It's hard to shake that kind of conditioning. I came close to killing myself because I knew, deep down, I'd never stop desiring sex with a man, and giving into that would mean Satan had won my soul. Now I accept the fact that I'm gay, but I can't forget the idea that fidelity to your partner means something."

"So am I the devil?" Thad fashioned his index fingers into a set of horns and placed them on either side of his forehead.

"You joke, Thad, but those beliefs still affect me. You find it easy not to believe in God, but I don't know what I believe. At least when I'm in the studio, I'm able to stare down my demons."

Thad put a hand on Simon's shoulder. "I didn't mean to upset you, Simon. I know you struggle with your past. I was lucky to be brought up by unbelievers—probably the only thing I appreciate about my upbringing. I was never any good at science, but at least I understood the point of it."

"Going back to what you suggested, Thad, even if you wanted to do it, I doubt there are pornographers in Arkansas."

Thad squinted. "They'd be shooting scenes with farm animals if there were."

"I hope you're not willing to go that far."

Thad rolled his eyes. "Joking, for God's sake. When you were sick with hepatitis B, and I was in San Diego, I met someone in the porn business."

"Let's be clear, Thad. You weren't simply *in San Diego*. You took my car and disappeared when I needed you most."

"Your illness scared me, Simon. Our relationship scared me."

"And being with the HIV-positive marine didn't?"

"Simon, I've told you the story. The marine's name was Marvin. I'd known him since before I met you, since the times I went to San Diego on weekends—I liked the nude beach. That's where I met Marvin. I was planning to leave you once you recovered. I thought I was in love with Marvin. When he tested positive, I couldn't handle it. That's why I took pills to kill myself. When I felt myself fading, you were the person on my mind, not Marvin. I called you to say good-bye, but after we hung up, Marvin found me and dialed 911. After I got better, I went to the Spotlight and found you sitting right where we had our first drink. You forgave me, and here we are."

"I heard a different story about your suicide attempt."

"Who told you a different story?"

"Patricia. According to her, you thought I'd forget about you if I believed you were dead, and then the marine and you could go on with your lives. I believed her until you showed up at the bar... without Marvin."

"That queen would have said anything to turn you against me. She's always been in love with you."

Patricia was among the craziest of Simon's friends from the Spotlight Bar, but she had cared for him after Thad disappeared, when hepatitis had made Simon so weak, he couldn't even make it to the toilet. Patricia had proved to be a good friend, though even then, Simon knew she wished it to be more.

"As soon as you kissed me that night at the bar when it seemed you had risen from the dead, I was yours," Simon confessed.

"I don't know how to explain it," Thad said, struggling. "Except that love can be overwhelming."

"My anger can be worse. I will never let you make me as mad as when you took Cicero."

"I was drunk when I did that, Simon. I'd never hurt little Cicero. I wanted to bring him back as soon as I sobered up, but you were crazy with rage."

"How did we get into this conversation?" Simon interjected. "What has all this got to do with pornography?"

"That's what I was trying to explain. Marvin had a friend who made gay videos—mostly guys pretending to be straight and sucking dick for the first time, stuff like that. I did the sound effects.

The job paid good money. When I said I wanted to work in porn, I didn't mean performing. I'd just add sound effects after the filming ends. You know, postproduction stuff."

"And you're still in touch with this pornographer?"

"If the guy's phone number hasn't changed. It's been a long time since I spoke to him."

"We'd need quarter-inch machines and a mixing board if you worked from here, and that equipment's expensive. We'd have to set up a recording studio in the barn. Can you imagine if Vivian or, God forbid, Connie or Derek heard you slurping and moaning!"

"It is a noisy business." Thad chuckled. "Let me talk to the guy. I'm sure he'll remember me. Let me find out if I can work from here. Maybe he'd supply the equipment. Who knows?"

Thad was right that Simon tended to be old-fashioned, but to Simon, this felt like flirting with the devil.

CHAPTER EIGHT

Howard Price, the pornographer Thad had worked for in the past, now lived in Chatsworth, a suburb north of Hollywood. Thad had to get a new number from Marvin, admitting to Simon that he and Marvin had kept in touch and arguing that Simon would have been upset if he had known. Simon bristled at Thad's statement but realized that, even as he was managing to get in touch with himself along the quest for self-discovery, Thad still felt the need to protect his feelings.

"It's good that Marvin is responding to AZT," Simon told Thad. "Please don't be afraid to tell me things."

Simon could tell that Thad wanted to say more.

"I haven't called Howie yet," Thad said. "I wanted to talk to you first."

"Howie? Cute nickname."

"See, already you're making something of it."

"You're right, the idea of you staring at naked hunks all day bothers me."

"You can watch with me if I work from here."

"Sounds exhausting," Simon quipped.

"You get used to the images—after a while, there's nothing sexy about them. It's only work and not easy to do. I used a lot of lip balm when I was working before; it takes hours."

"It's important you never mention my name. You realize that, right? I don't know what the Spaniards are thinking. If they want to find me, they'll ask around Hollywood. Howard Price wouldn't know me, but I bet he knows Wally Freeze. Wally made hardcore videos before he got out of the business to make his wrestling tapes and the like."

"I won't say anything," Thad assured, picking up the phone to place the call, fingers crossed for good luck.

Howard remembered Thad, commenting that he had been the best, making the most believable sounds of anyone on his staff. But he couldn't think of a way for Thad to work remotely. Instead he offered to fly Thad to Hollywood whenever a video entered postproduction and to let him stay at the Antelope Valley ranch, where Howard ran Chatsworth Price Productions. To keep Howard from knowing his whereabouts, Thad claimed not to have his own phone, saying that he would check in from time to time. Howard agreed to leave a message with his secretary when a film entered postproduction.

When the first opportunity arose, Simon panicked.

"Thad, are you sure this is a good idea? The pornographers I knew about in Hollywood were into some pretty heavy drugs. I'm worried sick about you going out there, especially staying at Howard's ranch. I visited William Higgins's house once. His 'stars' hung out there before filming. Higgins thought that if they paired up on their own, they'd produce steamier sex on screen. You'll be tempted by sex and drugs. I know you're determined to remain clean—but still."

"That porn star, Jerry, living with Scott, told me about Higgins when I was staying there during that long breakup of ours." Thad had brought up another contentious situation from their past.

"Then you know what I'm talking about. And don't go falling in love with someone like Jerry. I know how you crushed on him."

"I wasn't born yesterday," Thad said, embracing Simon. "When will you settle down and realize how much I love you? I don't want anyone else. You are my old-fashioned guy."

The touch of Thad's hair on Simon's cheek, the feel of his lips as they kissed, the warmth of their bodies pressing together— Simon believed he had nothing to worry about.

Thad knew he shouldn't have mentioned Jerry. Scott Mansfield had met Jerry through an organization of gay-film producers that he represented, a group that filed frequent lawsuits against distributors for copyright infringement, all unknown to his boss, Maury Fender, partner in one of the law firms that represented Sun Myung Moon in his appeal of federal charges, a man who frowned on his attorneys moonlighting. Jerry had received an award at an annual ceremony that Scott attended, and Scott had pursued him. Showing up at Scott's house while Thad was there, Simon had accused him of being in love with Jerry. Thad had denied it, and Jerry feigned ignorance about why Simon would care. Thad eventually moved to San Diego to get away from Simon's fits of jealousy and relentless pursuit.

Reversing months of personal neglect, Thad ironed his sleek designer jeans and wardrobe of stylish shirts, attire that made him look like a model from the pages of *Gentlemen's Quarterly* as he modeled for Simon in a pair of freshly pressed slacks and a soft yellow shirt. The color drained from Simon's face as the reality hit him—Thad really was going back to California.

"Don't be afraid, Simon," Thad consoled, seeing a familiar look of terror on Simon's face. "I'm excited about the opportunity, that's all. Ironing these clothes and all, I realized how down in the dumps I've been." Thad rubbed his chin. "It's been a week since I shaved, and you never said anything."

"I kind of liked the soft stubble." Simon smiled. "You may be in your twenties, but I swear, your beard is peach fuzz."

Thad blushed. "It's the blond hair." He pulled a little square of tissue from his neck. "Every time I use a razor, my neck bleeds."

"I'm scared," Simon admitted as Thad draped his freshly pressed shirts over the backs of the chairs.

"Me too, a little, but trust me, Simon, I won't go back to using, and even though it's not the big deal to me it is to you, I won't have sex with anyone. I'm yours."

"I believe you," Simon said, lacking conviction.

Simon's worst day since leaving rehab began the morning he awoke without Thad beside him. Despite his commitment to sobriety, loneliness nearly overwhelmed him. Simon thought he had developed mechanisms to cope, but old patterns felt as strong as ever. When the idea crossed Simon's mind to get in Vivian's Pontiac and drive to the Little Rock housing projects where he was sure to make contact with Snake, BT, or one of the other drug dealers he knew from the first months after arriving back in Arkansas, he considered handcuffing himself to the bedposts. Instead, Simon escaped to his studio, where he could stare down his fears in swirling colors as they morphed into images, his brushes and palette knives serving as the weapons of war as surely as crayons had been swords against the bug-eyed monsters from the planet Zenon.

CHAPTER NINE

B efore Thad left for Hollywood, he and Simon relaxed in the parlor, reminiscing, wondering what was going on in Hollywood with Scott and Sandra and the crew at the Spotlight. Vivian paid no attention as she watched one of her favorite television programs. Simon picked up a magazine from the table beside his chair and remarked to Thad about an article he had just read in it about a human ancestor recently discovered in the Afar region of Ethiopia.

"We didn't come from no monkey," Vivian said, her attention turning abruptly from *Murder, She Wrote*. She addressed Simon but stared at Thad. "We came from God's children, Adam and Eve. You don't think we came from a monkey, do you, Simon?"

"I don't think humans came from a monkey," Simon replied.

Satisfied with the response, afraid to pursue the question further, Vivian turned up the volume on the television.

Simon had not lied to Vivian, reminding himself that all primates, including humans and monkeys, descended from a common ancestor, facts he'd learned when taking classes in anthropology, a field that remained one of Simon's interests, sparked during his first attempt at college shortly after high school. That education had ended when he joined the Unification Church, but he'd continued to nourish his fascination with anthropology during his ten years in the church, when he would stop by libraries to read scholarly journals—no matter that the reading conflicted with beliefs more aligned with Vivian's idea about Adam and Eve than speciation through the process of natural selection. Simon remembered a day at school when he'd held the plaster cast of a *Homo habilis* skull and pondered how anyone could doubt Darwin's explanation of human origins.

Thad cared little for religion or science and tried to change the subject whenever Simon strayed into scholarly musings. Growing up, Thad had never heard his parents mention God except to deride people's beliefs as utter nonsense. Thad readily accepted that humans were a species of brainy ape and didn't see any need to look into it further.

With time on his hands and a little money in the bank from the sales of Wally's videos, Simon investigated the possibility of returning to college, taking a trip one afternoon into Little Rock to visit the registration office. Simon always told people he'd left college with a four-point average, but that wasn't the case; he had forgotten about the final exam in physical anthropology, taken shortly after accepting the Divine Principle and becoming a follower of Sun Myung Moon. Simon had not answered the essay questions with arguments based on science, producing a rambling justification of spontaneous generation instead.

Simon's incoherent paper earned him a failing grade with a note of extreme disappointment from Professor Hardeman, who became so concerned about the abrupt change in Simon's personality that she attended Divine Principle lectures to discover for herself what had enthralled him so. Professor Hardeman had hoped to debate the ideas, to bring Simon to his senses, not understanding that Simon's reasons for joining had little to do with the teachings and far more to do with his sense of being doomed to a life of loneliness as a gay man, strengthened by his sadness at being estranged from Lenny and emphasized by bitter heartache after rejection by his first love.

Professor Hardeman eventually recognized that Simon would have to reach his own conclusions but still insisted that he call her anytime he wanted to talk. Simon had never taken advantage of her offer, but he always remembered their final conversation.

"If nothing else," Professor Hardeman had advised, "look at the next few years as fieldwork. You're a natural scholar, Simon. You'll collect a dissertation's worth of information."

Simon found his anthropology exam in the dusty admissions folder handed to him by the university's registrar, and he cringed as he perused it. Also enclosed was an essay written for his psychology class. Simon barely remembered the cold-blooded professor who'd espoused the behaviorist teachings of B. F. Skinner—that humans are little more than programmable automatons. Horrified by the lectures, Simon had taken it upon himself to explore alternative theories, and in his essay, which referenced the importance of self-actualization, apex of human motivation in Abraham Maslow's hierarchy of needs, he wove a justification of humanity's significance that became nearly religious in its assertions.

"You'll need to replace your high school transcript and ACT scores," the registrar explained after reviewing the materials in Simon's folder. "After that, you can re-enroll. Our administration prides itself on encouraging nontraditional students."

Simon smiled at the thought of being *nontraditional.*

The day after visiting the university admissions office, Simon went to Sibley High School to retrieve his records. The teachers that Simon remembered had moved to other districts, except in the case of his gay art teacher, Darsey Faber, who'd switched professions to become a florist before getting caught having sex with students. Simon had not reported Darsey after Simon's first love broke his heart and Darsey seduced him.

"I'm here to get a copy of my transcripts and my ACT scores," Simon said to the woman who greeted him at the counter in the principal's office.

"And your last name?"

When Simon responded, "Powell, Simon Powell," the woman looked puzzled for a moment, and then her face brightened. "Oh my word, that's yours over there, isn't it?"

The woman pointed toward a sixteen-by-twenty-inch canvas in a simple black frame hanging by the door of the principal's office. Simon had always mourned having burned his early works, forgetting about the ones that remained with friends or their parents, gifts the church deemed exempt from his Isaac sacrifice. The portrait, rendered in the Mannerist style of Modigliani but without his somber tones, this work glistening with bright reds and blue-green hues, took on a ghostly presence as Simon recalled the circumstance of its painting.

"Remarkable it still exists," Simon marveled. "It's a portrait of Mrs. Jenkins. Her son, Jake, and I attended school here."

"I'm Melissa Jenkins-Woodley," the woman explained. "Jake was my nephew. I'm his father's sister."

Her use of past tense gave Simon a chill. "Is Jake all right?"

"I'm so sorry," Mrs. Woodley replied. "I would have thought you'd heard."

"My life took me far from Sibley."

"I hate to bear sad news, but Jake and his family were driving on Stagecoach Road when a drunk driver collided with them, head on, about ten at night. It gets very dark along that section of the road, you know."

Simon grasped the counter to steady himself. Throughout junior high and much of high school, Jake had been Simon's close friend, a friendship that had deepened after graduation when Simon renewed his friendship with Jake and his girlfriend, Jewell, along with a crew of hippies who lived communally and with whom Simon resided briefly when he lost hope after being scorned by his first boyfriend and betrayed by his art teacher. For a time, before joining Sun Myung Moon's group, Jake's mother, Dorothy, a free-spirited, one-time beatnik, had encouraged Simon to pursue his art as a career. She'd hung several of his paintings in her house, including the one by the principal's office, Dorothy Jenkins's portrait, titled *Dot with Dotted Eye,* referencing Dorothy's nickname as well as the fact that, instead of the typical crosshatch over one eye favored by Modigliani, Simon had applied dots similar to the ben-day pattern used by printers.

"How long ago was the accident?"

Mrs. Woodley by that time had come around the counter to stand beside Simon. "Nearly eight years ago," she said, touching Simon's arm in a consoling gesture. "I'm so sorry you didn't know."

"The whole family?"

"Dot was driving. Jake and his father were visiting from Alaska. The other boys were in the back seat. Death came instantly. Jake's cousins inherited most of Dot's books and all those record albums she collected from the 1940s and 1950s."

"I remember that. Dot introduced me to Edith Piaf and Josephine Baker."

"No one claimed the paintings, so I took them. I have three others at home. My children have a few of your sketches. You signed them with a dedication to Dorothy."

"I remember each one."

"Do you want them back?"

It took a moment for Simon to realize what Mrs. Woodley was offering. "I could never do that. I gave them to her because she was such a great and positive influence. Please keep them in your family."

"We get a lot of comments on that painting," Mrs. Woodley said, pointing to *Dot with Dotted Eye*. "People recognize Dorothy."

"I can think of no better tribute to Jake and his parents, or to my time here at Sibley High, than having it displayed so prominently."

Mrs. Woodley led Simon behind the counter for a closer look at the painting. The work sparked other memories. Jake and Jewell and the rest of the communal gang had infiltrated a speech by Sun Myung Moon when he came to Little Rock while Simon still lived at the local church center. The band of friends waited until Sun Myung Moon took the stage, then stood on their chairs, threw their arms forward in a Nazi salute, and shouted, "Heil, Moon." Guards swiftly escorted the cadre from the building. Simon's friends recognized what Simon refused to admit: that the man to whom he had dedicated his life was little more than a self-deluded charismatic craving adulation from a horde of worshippers and, in the case of his public speaking, the general population.

"What are those boxes?" Simon asked, breaking out of his reverie and noticing a stack of cardboard crates marked with the year of his graduation.

"It's an amazing coincidence you showed up today," Mrs. Woodley remarked. "These boxes are headed for county storage. This pile is scheduled for shipment tomorrow." Mrs. Woodley ran her finger over the labels. "Here it is, N through P," she said as she shuffled the boxes to get to N–P. Lifting the dusty cover, she retrieved a manila envelope, unwound its clasp, and checked inside. "Yes, this is it: Powell, Simon."

The envelope contained everything the university needed: the transcripts, including many classes in art and journalism, and the ACT scores, sufficient at the time to qualify for scholarships. If only Lenny had not convinced Simon to remain near home by attending the university in Little Rock, telling Simon Vivian might need him if Lenny's upcoming heart surgery did not go well. It was a request Simon had honored—the last nail in the coffin of his dreams.

Mrs. Woodley made copies of the file and again consoled Simon about Jake and his family, asking, "Did you know my brother, Jake's father?"

"I only met him once," Simon recalled, "but Jake often spoke of him. I knew that Jake went to Alaska to visit his father, but I didn't know he stayed there. I'm sorry we lost touch."

Simon departed from his old school before other ghosts could appear. If his demons were allowed to surface, Simon would blame himself for what had happened to Jake and his family, the consequence of his abandoning discipleship to Christ's second coming. In Moon's theology, sin demanded a price—the greater the sin, the heavier the burden. If Jesus's death atoned for the sin of Adam and Eve, Simon's transgression, denying the blessing of marriage bestowed on him by the third Adam, Sun Myung Moon, was a crime that reached out to everyone who knew him, even damning his ancestors. Were Simon to allow those old ideas to resurface, he would view the deaths of Jake and his family as Satan claiming those he loved as payment, as if an individual's actions influenced the workings of the universe. Still, the self-important religious mind-set held a grip on Simon's fears.

"How can you harbor such thoughts!" Simon uttered aloud as he sat in the Pontiac and stared at the school. A response rumbled forward from deep within his psyche: You should be dead, not Jake and Dot.

Simon drove to the mansion and had just parked under the sweet gum when he noticed Connie's car had pulled close to the side entrance.

Vivian and Connie sat at the dinette table adjacent to the kitchen as Simon entered through the back door, but not before consoling Cicero, who had been let out and needed to do his business but who became so excited upon seeing Simon that he pranced around him for attention. Connie had just finished sipping coffee, resting her cup on its saucer and taking a paper napkin to wipe a lipstick smudge from the rim before standing up to give Simon a hug.

"Jesus will find a way into your heart," Connie said, pulling away and looking dolefully into his eyes.

"Okay, Connie, I'm stumped. What causes you to bring up Jesus all of a sudden?"

Connie looked at Vivian, who stared back intently. Then she sat down and reached across the table to take Vivian's hand. "It was nice of Thad to bring Simon's things from Hollywood," Connie said, ignoring Simon's question, "but he shouldn't have made your home a den of iniquity." Connie picked up her coffee cup with a gleam in her eye and a curl on her lip.

Confused, wondering what Connie had been saying to Vivian before he entered, Simon decided that Connie would have to hear what he had to say—no more tiptoeing. The news about Jake and Dot was tormenting enough, and he was in no mood for obfuscation. "What exactly does Jesus have to do with anything, Connie?"

Connie went to the window and gazed toward the barn. "I don't think you understand how much Jesus has looked out for you. My prayers have always been that you would leave that group. But then, instead of opening your heart to Jesus, you invited Thad."

Vivian looked at Simon with a plea in her eyes.

A significant lesson Simon had taken from rehab, though difficult to realize in practice, was to let people have their opinions. One could not control the actions of others, only of oneself.

Connie continued, "Jesus found a way to remove Thad; now you have a chance to let him into your heart."

So Jesus sent Thad to provide sound effects for a pornographer? Simon thought. Listening to Connie, he wondered if Thad's desire to leave Sibley had something to do with the times he'd watched soaps with Connie. Thad had never mentioned that Connie had tried to convert him, but now Simon couldn't imagine her not trying. He laughed thinking how miserably frustrated she must have become. Simon had once asked Thad if he believed in God, and Thad had responded that he hadn't thought much about it. If anyone else had said that, Simon would have thought them evasive, but Thad was Dionysus to Simon's Apollo, accepting the obvious if it felt right without the need for the intellectual arguments that Simon demanded.

"Think what you like, Connie. Thad is the best thing that ever happened to me."

The wan smile on Vivian's face told Simon that he was right to temper his response. Vivian dreaded conflict.

Disappointed that her wounding words had not drawn blood, Connie took her coffee cup to the kitchen for a refill and rummaged through the refrigerator, buying time to think of a response. Simon's calm had confused her—she had hoped for an argument.

"Is Thad coming back?" Connie asked.

"He's returning in a few weeks, or I'll join him in California. *We* haven't decided."

"Didn't I just hear from Vivian that you are going back to school in Little Rock?"

"Yes, but my relationship with Thad is more important. If I am forced to choose between school and Thad…well."

"What's Thad doing in Los Angeles?" Connie asked.

Simon considered telling Connie the simple truth but responded obtusely for Vivian's sake.

"Thad's doing sound effects for a video producer."

Connie sipped her coffee. "Is that good money?"

"Enough to get by."

Drama failing to materialize, Connie and Simon continued talking as people do when they have little in common yet want to be connected. Connie and Simon escorted Vivian to a chair in her room, setting a small portable television on a side table to keep her entertained.

Connie and Simon walked to the barn to look at Simon's new work, art providing a neutral ground for discussion. Connie complimented the paintings, even though she didn't know how to carry on an artistic discussion. For Simon, her appreciation was enough.

CHAPTER TEN

"This work is tougher than I thought it would be," Thad complained during a late-night conversation. "I wish Howie would just reuse the stuff I have recorded already, but I've got to make different sounds for each person. There's a few of us in the recording studio at the same time, and sometimes we break out laughing instead of watching the monitor. If Howie's around, he goes nuts and screams, 'Look at the video, not each other.'"

"Too bad you can't work from here."

"It's like you said, though, this takes a lot of equipment, and it works best if all of us doing it are in the sound room together. Howie said he has tried to edit tracks together, but the cost of the engineer was more than having us in the room at the same time. Howie doesn't know how I got to LA, by the way. Once I get a few paychecks, I'll have enough to fly back and forth on my own. Howie doesn't need to know anything; I'm cashing the checks at his bank."

"Howard will get curious and try to weasel information from you."

Thad blew a kiss into the phone with a gentle smack of his lips. "I've got this, Simon."

Eventually, Simon would have to let Wally know he'd moved to Arkansas. Wally was feeling good about himself for giving Simon another chance, and it was easier to honor the terms of their original contract than to pay a lawyer to challenge Simon's rights. A huge concern was Wally's ties to pornographers. Wally several times had mentioned how he'd escaped the business to get away from the nefarious people who controlled the industry—unsavory figures who frightened him. Soft-core videos let Wally work in a familiar format while allowing him to market videos outside the narrow business model of adult bookstore distribution—Wally's videos could be found at discount stores, though relegated to shelves marked "mature audiences."

Even with Thad working for a bona fide pornographer and Simon marketing videos for someone on the outskirts of the industry, however, the specter of David, Irene, and Emilio and the money he owed their Spanish company never left Simon's thoughts. If he had learned anything from the gangster movies he'd enjoyed as a child, it was that criminals never forgave a debt. Simon feared that the trio from Spain would keep looking for him, no matter how long it took.

Simon knew how Wally liked to gossip. Without being aware of the risks, he might mention Simon during a dinner conversation. He might even mention Thad, though Wally and Thad saw each other infrequently, and Wally was unlikely to remember his name. Still, for all its cultural diversity and geographical expanse, Hollywood tended to function like a small town, with people telling stories about each other at every opportunity—the more lurid, the better. Simon hoped his story would be passé. Who in Hollywood had cocaine not driven a rung or two down the social ladder?

Before starting his first semester at university, Simon's agent in Hollywood managed to secure another deal, this one for distribution in the Philippines. The money arrived just in time to cover Vivian's property taxes and for Simon to purchase a new computer with a built-in modem.

"I can't believe I'm doing this," Simon told the admissions officer who examined his reconstituted file, a young man who would have been in elementary school when Simon last attended college. "I'm having serious déjà vu. Eighteen years ago, I sat in this very office, and here I am again."

"We're glad you're back," the man said.

"Do you think I'll be the oldest person in the classes?" Simon worried about standing out.

The young man laughed. "The oldest person I've enrolled was over eighty. I signed her up a year ago. Our policy has always been to keep credits active. You aren't the first to pick up after a long hiatus. Quite a few come back in retirement."

"Well, I'm not quite retirement age yet!"

"We consider age diversity one of our school's assets," the man continued, hoping he had not insulted his new enrollee.

Despite the welcoming attitude of the admissions officer, Simon couldn't shake the feeling that he had lost too much time. If only he had accepted himself for who he was as an eighteen-year-old, Sun Myung Moon's teachings about a heavenly kingdom based on heterosexual marriage might have held less appeal.

"If I may ask," the admissions officer inquired, "what prompted you to return?"

"You mean, what happened during the gap?"

"Everyone has a story."

"Let's just say I fell asleep for many years. I'm Rip Van Winkle getting to know what happened to the world in the meantime."

"Van Winkle slept twenty years, as I recall." The man grinned. "You woke a bit early."

"I'll get my degree this time. I'm resolute. I know what I want."

"Good luck." The admissions officer shook Simon's hand, adding, "I'm sure you'll do great."

Simon might have gone back to university to study art, but perusing the course catalog revived his intellectual curiosity, so diminished by his years as a religious fanatic and drug addict. He examined listings for philosophy, history, and astronomy, and then he noticed a seminar on the origins of religion offered by the anthropology department in conjunction with the department of philosophy and taught by a visiting professor from Paris, Dr. Lucien Dupré.

Simon's failing grade on his anthropology final notwithstanding, he had finished with a strong B, and over the years he had retained much of what he'd learned. Mrs. Hardeman's words, when she'd tried to convince Simon not to join Sun Myung Moon's group, had stayed with him: "If nothing else, look at your experience as field research. Pay attention to the social structures and religious constructs that I've taught you to observe."

Simon had almost left Moon's group as soon as he joined, having moved out of the mansion with the jolting announcement to Vivian and Lenny, simply telling them that he was joining a religious commune. Despite his doubts, he'd been kept from leaving the Unification Church by pride in the arrogance of his decision, fear that the beliefs might be true, and the camaraderie he found among his newfound family. Then, as he rose in the ranks, Simon relished being admired by thousands of members who looked up to him for spiritual guidance. Though recognizing his doubts and failings, he would say to himself, Remember, this is field research. Now Dr. Dupré's seminar might allow Simon to understand a broader context in which to place his experiences.

Before his first painting class, Simon went to the new student union, built on the same spot as the one he had known from before. Near the back wall, at a corner table, he thought he recognized a familiar face. The closer Simon approached, the surer he became—it was Dean Pickett, the former Jesuit who had been a loyal friend during Simon's worst moments before entering rehab. Simon felt bad that he had not visited Dean since retrieving his video and computer equipment.

"Dean, is that you?" Simon called out.

Dean lifted his head from the course catalog, wiping newsprint smudges from his fingers with a paper napkin. "Vivian said you were going back to school, but I didn't realize you were coming here. I thought you might have gone back to Los Angeles."

"I wish I could afford to," Simon responded, thinking what a nice arrangement it would be to attend school in LA—surely that would make Thad happy. "You say you spoke to Vivian?"

"I did, Simon. Don't be upset."

"Never, Dean, why would I be? You helped Vivian during my downhill spiral. When I came by your place to get my things a while back, I don't know, so many emotions overwhelmed me, I guess I felt guilty about not listening to you when I should have."

"It takes more than ignoring my advice to scare me away." Dean smiled. "I was a priest, after all. I'm used to people ignoring what I have to say." Dean paused to look at Simon, nodding as if to say, You look good. "It was a while ago that I spoke to Vivian. How is she? And how's Thad?"

"Vivian's strokes have slowed her down, but she's doing well enough. Thad's in Hollywood."

"Not with Scott, I hope." Dean knew about Thad staying at Scott's and about Thad's infatuation with Jerry the porn star.

"Thad's doing voice-overs for a fellow who produces videos. He's staying at the guy's ranch in Chatsworth."

Dean cast a wary eye, knowing there must be more to the story. "I'm happy you came back to school, Simon. You mean a great deal to me."

"Are you crying?"

"A bit misty eyed, perhaps," Dean admitted. "You came so close to suicide, and now, here you are."

"Even in rehab, I was self-destructive."

"Vivian told me. Thank goodness she got there with Thad and your sister when she did. You could so easily have jumped from that railroad bridge. I wish I could have helped you when you stayed at my house with that adorable Cicero."

"I hate to think about that night on the bridge. I was despondent, and all because some numskull at the rehab center called me a faggot and slapped me on the head."

"Don't ever come that close to ending your life again. Call me first."

"I will, Dean. I promise."

"Well, I better go meet my professors," Dean said, excusing himself. "I can't decide on an elective, but there's still time to choose."

"I've decided on my elective. I signed up for a seminar on the anthropology of religion."

Dean smiled warmly. "That will give us more to talk about."

"I promise I'll drop by soon."

Simon watched Dean disappear down the sidewalk outside and then got a soft drink from the vending machine, sitting for a while to ponder the distance he had traveled to come so completely full circle. As he'd said to himself that first night in rehab after climbing from the railroad bridge, *Only then was I sure I could try living this life one more time.*

CHAPTER ELEVEN

When Simon had last attended the college, the Vietnam War was at its height, and students protested in front of the campus administration offices despite threats from professors that they would flunk those who participated but who backed down when they found their classrooms full of empty seats. A few professors had joined the protests, filing lawsuits against the university when threatened with dismissal. The current student body seemed to lack much interest in politics, oblivious to the pressing issues of the day. The Vietnam protesters had spawned a generation of complacency. The art studio lacked energy as well, populated with students little aware of, and holding little interest in, the art movements of the past, making no effort to discover their uniqueness. Simon wanted art to be a replacement for religion, not the handmaiden of commerce.

Simon's heart raced when he first entered the studio after so many years, his hands trembling as the professor outlined the syllabus with its rigorous course of instruction. His confidence rose only when the class got to work sketching a rather shapeless woman sitting on a stool, draped with a sheet and spotlighted by a focused light. Simon chose an easel and placed a clean sheet of newsprint on the foamboard support, securing the paper with clasps at each corner, gazing back and forth between the model and the blank page, readying himself for an image to emerge, pressing a fat piece of charcoal onto the paper with such force that it nearly tore, then smearing dusty residue from his palms to shade the nude's contours. Standing back to compare his smudges with the reality of the draped model, Simon retrieved a stick of white chalk from the blackboard tray and slashed highlights onto the face and upper arms, producing a work that spoke of the way he viewed the model in the context of his excitement at attending the class—even if the image failed to produce the naturalism requested by the professor.

As a student fresh out of high school, Simon's drawing instructor had criticized the methods he employed, mixing media and making smudges to create the illusion of volume. But this instructor, a well-coiffed woman with intense earnestness in her eyes, spoke with encouragement, sharing many of Simon's views about art, despite her syllabus emphasizing the craft of precise rendering.

"You must have been a troublesome first-year student," the professor noted, "but I welcome this level of expression in a third-year drawing class such as this." She spoke loudly enough for the other students to hear. "The most effective illustrations evoke feeling— everyone responds to passion."

Charcoal smudges on Simon's cheeks and arms gave him the appearance of a chimney sweep, but he had no time to clean up beyond rubbing a dry towel over his skin before rushing off to his next class, a course in college algebra. Contrasting the intuitive realm of the studio and the formulas of math, Simon recognized a narrative that defined his life—seeking a balance between the sacred and the profane: art and math, religion and science.

Home at the mansion, Simon skipped dinner with Vivian, warming leftovers and setting her a plate before heading through the humid night air to start a new painting based on the drawing of the nude that he'd made in art class. Paint covered his hands as he worked frenetically, the figure soon losing its feminine characteristics, the image morphing into a shape that reminded him of Thad, the swirl of somber colors creating echoes of loneliness. Looking at his watch, amazed at how quickly time had passed, Simon realized it was time to telephone Chatsworth.

Vivian's soft snore told Simon that she had fallen asleep. He closed the door to her anteroom, hoping not to disturb her as he walked gingerly up the old stairs, avoiding the creaks in a cadence learned early in childhood. Simon extended the cord on the phone in the upstairs hallway, pulling it under the bedroom door, in the process nearly toppling the lamp off of the mahogany table where it sat on a lace doily. Simon impatiently listened to what felt like fifty rings before Thad answered.

"Simon?"

At the sound of Thad's voice, Simon's heart skipped a beat. "I started to worry we wouldn't get a chance to talk; the phone rang so many times."

"I'm sorry, Simon. I went to dinner with Howard and a few of the guys from the current project. And..." Thad paused for emphasis. "Before you get upset, everyone knows I'm in a committed relationship."

"And you're sure they care?"

"Well, not really," Thad chuckled, "but I know how to fend them off."

"I worry about you."

"I'd leave here and come back to Sibley before anything happened, Simon. I'm with you—forever."

Thad was able to pronounce *Sibley* with the most withering of sneers, a perfect blend of affection and repulsion. "If you're telling people about our relationship, you're not mentioning my name or where I am, right?"

"I haven't…but it turns out Howard already knew something."

"Something? What?"

"When I was hanging around Marvin, when I met Howie, I guess I mentioned you by name, and that you distributed films to foreign countries."

"Sounds like Howard has a good memory."

"It seems I once told him about going to Arkansas with you at Christmas. Howard reminded me what a hick place I thought it was. Anyway, he knows we're together. He assumed that I came out here from Arkansas and that you must be there—and then he saw your number on a phone bill."

"The plan was for me to call you, Thad, exactly because I didn't want this number to show up on a phone bill."

"I know, but I missed you, and I wanted to hear your voice. Vivian's answering machine picked up, but I didn't leave a message. It surprised me what a close eye Howard keeps on expenses. When he saw a charge to Arkansas, he put two and two together and asked if I had called you. What could I say? He wanted to know if you were still in the business and if you might be interested in his videos. I guess foreign deals for gay porn are hard to get. I said that you had gone back to school and left it at that. He didn't ask any more questions."

"Are you sure you don't want to come home?"

"We're wrapping up postproduction. I'll come after that."

"I can never watch one of Howard's videos knowing that might be you I am hearing."

"Did you ever watch one of Howard's videos?"

"There might have been a time."

"Want me to send you copies?"

"No, Thad. I want the real thing."

"Howard says I'm the most convincing of anyone he's heard." Thad went through his stock of slurps and groans until Simon begged him to stop. "When I get paid, I'll fly to Little Rock."

"Best news I've heard in a while, Thad. I can't wait to hold you in my arms."

Simon tried to explain how excited he was about his first day back at school, how much he enjoyed the art class, how Thad's image had worked itself into his newest painting, but Thad kept interrupting, anxious to tell him news about their Hollywood friends.

"Scott is so unhappy," Thad began. "I met him in Hollywood the other day. Jerry left him. Now he's alone."

"Is he still representing that group of gay producers?"

"I don't know. Scott didn't talk business, but he did take me by the law offices, and I met his boss."

"You met Maury Fender?"

"Maury may have thought I was Scott's boyfriend, the way he gave me the once-over."

"Maury knows that Scott is gay, but it isn't something they talk about. Maury lost the Unification Church as a client in large part because of me, once they found out how I was spending my time during Moon's trial on tax evasion. Maury claimed he didn't know anything about my life in Hollywood, but the church said his office had corrupted me."

"Scott told me a little about that. Scott and Sandra can't stand Maury, but you know, they're not going to say anything to cause problems. They like their jobs."

"Was Sandra there?"

"Yeah. She's gorgeous. She said you guys used to call yourselves the three Ss—Simon, Scott, and Sandra. They miss those days."

"So do I, in some ways, but I was confused and didn't have a clue what I wanted out of life."

Thad paused for a moment. "You won't believe who's *living* with Sandra."

"I can't imagine."

"Lyle."

Simon nearly dropped the phone. "Lyle? You're kidding me."

"Scott said he is the guy who was living with you at the Tropicana Hotel when you went to New York to get married to Masako, right?"

"Ancient history."

"Shying away from ancient history?" Thad laughed.

"Some history is just too painful to recall. I'm surprised Scott didn't tell you about Lyle and me—and Masako—when you were staying at his house, back when."

"Scott was either too high or too drunk to tell me anything."

"I'll fill you in sometime, but those final months before I left the church, and then when I was trying to make a go of it in Hollywood, were the worst period of my life. In my own way, I loved Masako, even if we were selected to be married by Sun Myung Moon. If I was going to be married, Masako was a perfect fit—funny, caring, sort of a tomboy cute. I thought after we started living together, I'd just get used to being with a woman. Then I picked up Lyle on the boulevard and fell in love with him. I knew it was stupid, that it wasn't the same for Lyle, but I couldn't hold back. I knew I had to get away from the church after I met him. That's when I went back to Arkansas and severed ties. I left Lyle in Hollywood with some cash. I wanted to take him with me, but I knew that was impossible."

"Scott told me that Lyle never went back to the streets."

"Yeah, he stayed with Sandra after the money I left him ran out—that was around the time Lenny died. I went back to Hollywood, hoping to reconnect—or at least to see that he wasn't in love with Sandra. But it turned out Sandra was simply giving him a place to stay. Lyle moved to Orange County and hooked up with a girl named Sandy, his high school sweetheart. Maybe things didn't work out with Sandy the way Lyle hoped. Maybe he and Sandra really were in love, if he is at her house again."

"Maybe Scott wanted to tell me, but Sandra kept giving him the eye."

"Lyle always said he was into women, that sex with guys was only for the money. I shouldn't say it to you, but he sure was a passionate boyfriend for someone not into men."

"Sandra said to hug you for her the next time we're together. Scott rolled his eyes at her like she was a softy. I can't wait until we finish postproduction so I can be with you."

"How long will you stay at the mansion?"

"A couple of weeks, maybe a month. Howard has another feature lined up, a joint venture with people from Europe. They're coming over to plan the production."

"Do you know who they are?"

"Just a minute, let me run into the other room and ask Howard."

Thad seemed to be away from the phone for a very long time.

"Howie says it's some guy named Emilio, and that he is in partnership with a couple, David and his wife, Irene. Howie is so high on coke, he wouldn't stop talking about them. He thinks the deal will be worth a lot of money."

Simon fell into dead silence.

"Simon? Are you still on the phone?"

When Simon tried to speak, the words barely rose above a murmur as he tried to deflect from his actual fear. "You're around people doing coke?"

"We knew I'd be around it. I won't lie to you. I think about using, especially when someone hands me a straw, but I just pass it on. I found a Cocaine Anonymous meeting in Chatsworth. Turns out a few people on Howie's staff are trying to stay away from coke, so I'm not alone when I go there."

Simon thought the less Thad knew about Emilio, David, Irene, and the deal he had made with them for the money Charlotte stole, the safer Thad might be. Thad knew about Charlotte's taking a large sum of money, but Simon had never discussed the deal or the Spanish clients with him.

"I love you, Thad. Please come home if you can't handle being around the coke. *Please.*"

"I love you too, Simon."

Dreams of pursuit by dark forces caused Simon to toss and turn throughout the night as he clutched a photograph taken with Thad on a trip to Zuma Beach, a reminder of the good times they had shared alongside the turmoil of a cocaine-poisoned love affair.

CHAPTER TWELVE

Howard decided to shoot one more video and enticed Thad to remain awhile longer, offering him double the salary if he would—money that Simon and Thad could hardly afford to refuse. Still, premonitions of danger haunted Simon, and he hoped none of the partners would arrive before Thad returned to Sibley and he could explain the whole story. Until then, Simon felt that the less Thad knew, the better.

A shortened schedule for the video shoot and for postproduction meant that Thad had to stay in the sound room well into the night, sometimes approaching dawn, making it difficult to coordinate a time for Simon to call. One evening, too late for Connie to be calling but too early for Thad, the phone rang. The unexpected call was from Don, the owner of the Spotlight Bar. Simon instantly recognized the familiar drunken slur and the vague Southern drawl diluted by decades living in Los Angeles after leaving a professorship in jurisprudence at Ole Miss. "How's it goin', Simon?" Don greeted.

Simon's first thought was about Don's connections to Hollywood's criminal element. When Simon was using, those connections had made him feel protected when he frequented the Spotlight and bought, and sometimes sold, cocaine—Don bribed the beat cops to ignore improprieties, which they did. And Simon often benefitted from Don's secondary profession: procuring *talent* for the likes of pornographers such as Howard Price and William Higgins. When Don learned of Simon's recovery from cocaine use, he praised Simon, but Simon detected a certain wryness of tone, as if Don would be watching for a relapse. Why is Don calling? Simon wondered now. Is Thad okay? Is there news about Howard Price's Spanish clients—have they figured out that Thad is my boyfriend? Simon's mind spiraled into an abyss, and then Thad came on the line.

"I figured you'd get a shock out of hearing Don's voice," Thad began. "I'm on the phone at the Spotlight. Twiggy says hello." And under his breath, he added, "Don't worry, I dialed the number myself."

"What are you doing at the Spotlight?" Simon asked quietly. Was his number to be on everyone's phone bill in Hollywood?

"Howard brought the crew into Hollywood to have dinner at the Brown Derby after we completed tonight's work. The others are finishing dessert. I said I was going down the street to say hello to friends at a bar. Howard knew right away that I meant the Spotlight. Turns out Don sometimes refers guys to him. Who knew that Don recruited porn stars?"

"It's good to hear your voice, Thad. Tell Twiggy I said hello. Is he still his hefty self?"

"And as graceful as ever," Thad said. "He's at the other end of the bar...I don't know how he moves so quickly and makes the drinks so fast. The other bartender has to squeeze against the bar to make room for Twiggy to pass."

"The Spotlight wouldn't be the same without Twiggy."

Simon heard Don make a comment about the cost of Thad's long-distance call. Don Smite shared the trait of stinginess with other successful businessmen.

"I better join the others back at the Derby," Thad said. "Love you."

The conversation did little to allay Simon's fears.

Studying consumed Simon's every moment by the time Thad returned to Sibley; midterm exams were only a few days away. Reference books in support of an essay required by Dr. Dupré's seminar rested in stacks around the bedroom, each copiously tagged with yellow sticky notes.

"Gawd," Thad inveighed, fresh from taking a shower, picking up a book with orange binding and reading the title, *Death and Rebirth of the Seneca.* He thought for a moment before throwing the volume back on the pile. "Rebirth? Please tell me you aren't getting religious again."

"If I have a religion, Thad, it involves worshipping at a very different altar." To demonstrate, Simon rested his cheek against Thad's thigh. Thad pushed him away and continued to dry off. "That's a book by Professor Wallace. I'm using his ideas to structure my essay on Sun Myung Moon and the way his movement got started as part of the anti-Japanese resistance in Korea before World War II."

Thad regretted putting Simon into professor mode and tried to entice him onto the bed, but Simon kept going.

"Japan was trying to obliterate Korean culture when Moon was growing up. He eventually combined the Pentecostalism of his parents with elements of shamanism and neo-Confucianism and started a new religion. That's what happens in situations where someone seeks to revitalize a culture."

Thad picked out a single word from Simon's lecture. "I'll revitalize you," he said, placing his hands across Simon's shoulders and lowering him to the floor. Thad unzipped his fly, and with a fleshly sword, proclaimed, "I dub thee Sir Simon the Revitalizer."

"I missed you so much, Thad," Simon said, laughing as he played along. "You bring me back to earth when I get lost in my head."

"You're my silly professor, and I love you. Those hunky sex gods I watch all day leave my mind when I go to sleep at night." Thad backed Simon onto the bed. "Sometimes I imagine you are my pillow, and I hump it like a dog."

"Not the image I was looking for," Simon laughed, taking Thad into his embrace.

"No one has your heart."

"You are the best thing that's happened to me, Thad. I wish you would stay here with me in Sibley."

"If temptation gets to be too much, I will, but damn, there's a lot of money to be made—$200 an hour at this point."

Simon almost forgot the reason he wanted Thad to remain in Sibley. "Seriously? How many hours do you work?"

"The clock starts when I get to the sound room. We put in four hours a day for a couple of weeks. Howard isn't asking me for rent or anything, so I can save most of it. I think he just likes having a young guy around after all the stars leave when the shoot is over."

"Does Howard *want* you? I mean, as more than a sound guy?"

Thad lifted his chin as if to say, Who wouldn't want me? "Maybe. Part of the attraction is probably that he can't have me."

"Has Howard asked about me lately?"

"Only that one time, when he asked if you would be interested in his videos. His memory comes and goes. When I was leaving, he told one of the guys I work with that I was going 'somewhere to visit someone' but that I'd be back."

"Your money's going into the bank, right?"

"Yes, Dad," Thad replied, making doe eyes at Simon.

"We may need it at some point, but for now, the deals I'm making with Wally's videos have gotten me into school and covered Vivian's utility bills. I even paid the property taxes."

"Vivian looks weaker than when I left," Thad noted. "I'm glad you're able to help her."

"Connie and Derek are tapped out with their own family to take care of. Vivian needs someone around all the time. She can manage moment by moment, but often I find the mail right where she has set it down. When I am home during the day, I watch soaps with her to keep her company."

"I'm sure you love that," Thad chuckled.

"Not my favorite pastime, but it's for Vivian. She tries to read romance novels, but I'll walk by and see that she's been on the same page for an hour."

"I should borrow Vivian's tapes. I'm so far behind on *Days of Our Lives* I don't think I'll ever catch up.

"Meanwhile," Simon suggested, "I'll bet Ferdinand would like a patch of fresh grass."

"You just want to see me out there acting like a farmhand or something. If you ever take a picture of me doing that, I swear, I'll never forgive you."

"Wouldn't think of it, Thad." Simon tried to remember where he had put his camera.

Thad rose early to prepare a gourmet breakfast, putting a grin on Vivian's wan countenance as he buttered her toast, topping it with fresh honey purchased from a man on the edge of town who managed an apiary of fifty hives, cutting link sausages into slivers to make it easier to chew. The care Thad gave to Vivian touched Simon deeply. He'd rarely seen that side of Thad during their tumultuous days in Hollywood.

While savoring the butter-and-honey-soaked toast, Vivian's eyes rolled as if something on the ceiling had caught her attention. Jerking motions caused her to tip the plate off the table as she tried to regain her balance.

"Are you all right?" Simon implored, knowing something terrible was under way, as did Cicero, who had been sitting patiently beside Vivian's chair waiting for scraps but who now gently pawed her leg to express his concern.

Thad grasped Vivian's arm as she turned toward him, her eyes white as marble, lurching from her chair as if propelled by an unseen force, Thad steadying her before she collapsed onto the floor.

Simon's voice trembled as he said, "Let's get Vivian to her room so she can stretch out on the bed." Then, after taking a deep breath, "She's having a stroke."

Vivian's hands were cold as Simon held his mother close, placing her gently on the bed and pulling the comforter around her neck. Simon had mentally rehearsed such an event many times, but now the preparation seemed for naught. Simon appealed to Thad. "Telephone Connie. Call the ambulance. The numbers are on the refrigerator."

Thad, even less emotionally prepared than Simon, stumbled as he rushed to the kitchen, his voice quavering as he summoned the ambulance, nearly in tears as he spoke to Connie. Simon and Thad held Vivian's hands as they waited for the paramedics.

Sibley's volunteer squad of paramedics tended to Vivian as Thad and Simon watched from the door. Connie had not yet arrived when the assessment was complete. Simon called to see where she was.

"I'll meet you at the hospital," Connie said. "Derek and the girls are sick with a cough and can't come. I sure hope I don't carry anything that Vivian could catch. I've only just got over whatever they've got."

"Maybe you should stay home," Simon offered. "I can telephone when we know something. You're only a few minutes from the hospital."

"That might be best." Connie's voice broadcast her despair, even as she tried to stay brave. "I want to be there, Simon. Vivian's done so much better since you started making sure she takes her medicines and getting her to finish her meals. That's one good thing about you being home."

Simon didn't ask what about his being at home wasn't a good thing.

"This is the first time I have been with Vivian when she's had a stroke," Simon noted. "It's truly frightening."

"Just like Vivian's sisters," Connie sighed. "They reach a certain age, and then it happens. Vivian dodged it longer than the others, though. I used to call every hour to check on her, but she told me if I kept it up, I'd be the one giving her a stroke."

"Vivian's tough. She had to be, the way Lenny treated her."

"Lenny didn't show his mean side when I was at home."

Simon knew that wasn't true, but it was the way Connie chose to remember growing up. Vivian had endured verbal abuse from Lenny as far back as anyone could remember, well before Connie and Derek married. But Lenny wasn't the current issue—Vivian needed everyone's attention.

Thad stood beside Simon in the waiting room as a man and two nurses approached from the intensive care unit. The man scrutinized Simon and Thad as if looking for clues to their relationship. Simon's swarthy looks spoke of genetics different from Thad's Nordic heritage, the olive skin and dark hair of the Powell family casting doubt on the purity of an Anglo-Saxon heritage Lenny had touted as a source of pride.

"Mrs. Powell suffered a stroke, as I am sure you are aware," the man explained. Only when Simon read Dr. Small on the nametag did he realize the man was a physician and not an intern. Dr. Small continued, "Fortunately, we've been able to manage trauma to the brain."

Manage was a frightening term in this context. "Is she conscious? Can we see her?"

Dr. Small looked at Simon, then at Thad, then back to Simon. "Family members only."

"You go, Simon," Thad offered. "I'll telephone Connie from the waiting room."

"Connie must be worried sick." Simon resisted the urge to kiss Thad, worried about distracting the young doctor, or the nurses that accompanied him, from the duty to care for Vivian.

"She's in room 105, down this hall." The older of two nurses pointed down a corridor as the other nurse ferried a cart full of charts to the admissions desk.

Odors from isopropyl alcohol and catheter bags stirred the air in a mix that accosted Simon's sense of smell as he walked through the doors of the ICU. The older nurse—Miss Beckett, according to her nametag—rushed ahead to open the door to room 105.

"Hi, hon." Vivian spoke lucidly, revived by wonder drugs. "I sure did mess up breakfast, didn't I?"

"Vivian, *Mother.*" Simon bent over the bedrail to kiss Vivian on the cheek. "You didn't mess up anything. Whatever you need, Thad and I are here for you."

Vivian struggled to rise up, bracing on her good arm, and gazed past Nurse Beckett. "Where is Thad? Didn't he come with you?" Then a new worry. "Is Cicero all right?"

"They told us visits were limited to family. Thad's in the waiting room getting in touch with Connie. Little Cicero is at the mansion. He's okay, but he sure knew something was wrong. I've never seen such a distraught look on his little mug."

"Go tell Thad to come to this room," Vivian insisted, staring with laser-like precision at Nurse Beckett.

Nurse Beckett started to say something, but Vivian's glare made her think twice.

"That boy is as much family as anyone," Vivian said in a voice as coherent as she had managed in months. "He's with my son, and I won't have him sitting in no waiting room. You tell him to come back here right now."

Vivian turned from Nurse Beckett to look at Simon. "Don't take me for a blind person, son. I know what Thad means to you." Then, addressing Nurse Beckett, who had not yet complied, "You get him back here, I said."

Nurse Beckett left the room, but Simon noticed that she headed in the opposite direction from the waiting room. Simon went to retrieve Thad.

"Connie's on her way," Thad confirmed, just hanging up the pay phone.

"You better get back there to see Vivian."

"But they said no one but family."

"And Vivian set them straight about that."

"Really?"

"She called you family, so get back there."

Thad rushed ahead of Simon as they entered the corridor.

"How's my *Days of Our Lives* buddy?" Vivian asked as Thad entered the room. She tried to smile, but her face refused to conform.

Thad took Vivian's hand as tears formed. Simon placed his arm around Thad's waist. Vivian turned away, but not conspicuously.

"I'm just set in my ways," Vivian said, by way of admission.

During Simon's childhood, he had never seen Vivian and Lenny show affection to one another, so he imagined her reaction might be the same even if he had been there with Masako.

Thad bent over the side rail and kissed Vivian on the forehead. "You're like a mother to me. I'd never do anything to embarrass you."

"I'm glad Connie didn't poison your mind against Thad and me," Simon risked saying.

"Your sister has always had a mean streak," Vivian sighed. "I'm afraid Cheryl and Victoria are going to be trouble. Derek tries too hard to control those girls with his preaching about what's right and wrong."

"I can't believe you said that," Simon laughed. "I always figured you agreed with Connie and Derek, at least Derek's preaching against what I was doing."

"The Bible says there will be false prophets," Vivian pointed out. "That Korean's not the first, and he won't be the last, but I didn't like Connie and Derek going around saying bad things about what you were doing. They should mind their own business and take care of their own family. The Lord God can take care of himself."

As if on cue, Connie appeared at the door. If she had heard what Vivian said, she made no comment.

"Are you feeling better?" Connie asked, marching toward Vivian and taking her hand to examine the swath of tape holding an IV needle in place, then checking the pulse oximeter clipped on her index finger. "Your hands are ice cold."

"Probably the blood thinners," Simon suggested.

"Vivian looks tired," Connie observed. "We should leave her to get some rest."

"I'm fine," Vivian interrupted. "Don't talk like I'm not here."

"You're right." Connie turned to address Simon. "I'm surprised to see Thad here in the room. I thought they only allowed family."

Thad and Simon laughed as Connie shot them a stern look.

Vivian rescued the moment. "I told the nurse to let Thad come to my room. She knew better than to defy me."

"Then I'm glad they obliged you. How are you, Thad?"

Thad nodded as if to say fine, as he took Vivian's hand and cupped her fingers between his palms to warm them. "When you come home, I'm going to fix you eggs and toast soaked in that good honey you like so much. We thought it was gone, but I found a jar in the basement the other day."

Vivian looked at Connie. "Why don't you warm the other hand the way Thad's doing?"

"This is ridiculous," Connie snapped, placing the sheet over Vivian's hand. "Why is Thad here?"

"We're in love, Connie. Why do you think Thad's here?" Simon's statement might have been more direct than Vivian wanted to hear, but he had grown tired of protecting Connie from herself. "It's sin, Connie, worse than the Antichrist. Now you can go tell people your brother is a sodomite."

"That's enough, you two," Vivian said as loudly as she could muster.

Dr. Small and Nurse Beckett rushed into the room. "Mrs. Powell's vital signs triggered an alert. We need to examine her. If you can please return to the waiting room."

Simon and Thad followed Connie down the hall, each finding a seat. Connie sat near a table lamp, retrieving a paperback detective novel from her purse, Thad sat glumly at one end of the sofa, and Simon, unable to control his worries, paced the floor.

Dr. Small came from the ICU. Connie's book dropped to the floor as the group braced for his news.

"We need to keep your mother longer than we hoped," Dr. Small reported. "Despite the medicines, she had another stroke after you left the room."

"Oh God," Simon cried. "Did we upset her? Is that what did it?"

"Mrs. Powell's blood pressure has been elevated since she arrived. The medicines helped to a degree, but it wasn't enough."

"How bad is it?" Connie asked.

"Over the next few days, we'll run tests. If we find blockage in an artery, we can relieve it with a stent."

Thad rose from the sofa and leaned against a wall, wrapping his arms around his shoulders in a self-embrace.

"For now, Mrs. Powell needs to rest," Dr. Small explained. "I suggest you come back tomorrow. The hospital will call if there is any change."

"Could something happen?" Simon asked.

"Mrs. Powell is stable, and we'll be monitoring her closely."

A dark mood followed Connie, Thad, and Simon to the hospital entrance.

"I'd like to stay," Thad said. "I don't mind dozing on the couch. That way I can call if there's any news."

Connie, who had reacted so harshly toward Thad earlier, now looked at him differently. "You really love Vivian, don't you?"

"My parents pretty much kicked me out of the house when I was a teenager. Vivian treats me with respect—and so does Simon. I love your brother."

Connie swallowed hard, her heavily mascaraed eyes beginning to water, her posture becoming less rigid. She hugged Simon, then hugged Thad, and sighed. "It takes some getting used to, but I'll adjust. Thad, if you need me to relieve you, telephone, okay?"

"I will," Thad agreed.

Connie walked toward her car, which she'd parked in an area dotted with islands of redbud and dogwood trees, the pleasant spring air serving as a reminder of nature's indifference to human misery.

When Connie drove away, Simon said to Thad, "I'm not sure the doctor will tell you if there's a change, considering their policy about family members and all."

"I'll say that I am supposed to call you if there is anything to report. I can see room 105 through the window on the ICU doors, and I plan to keep a close eye."

"I hate hospitals, or I would stay with you, Thad. I've felt like escaping ever since we got here. Too many memories."

"I know," Thad said, looking around to make sure no one was looking before giving Simon a quick kiss. "Your father, I know."

"Lenny died a few doors from where they put Vivian."

"I understand, Simon." Thad squeezed Simon's hand. "Take care of Cicero. He must be going crazy."

Simon walked toward the front door of the mansion, illuminated against the darkness by the porch light, the Doric columns fangs to a hellmouth waiting to swallow those who entered. Simon stopped, dreading the emptiness of the house, and headed toward the swing, gently pushing the tire, causing it to twirl in the light wind, swinging just like the body of his ancestor must have swung on the fateful day of his death. Simon stopped the swing and sat, kicking sand

into the air the way Cheryl and Victoria often had when playing on the swing as young children. The limb above, larger than a man's thigh, creaked as the rope pulled taut against his weight. Was it the same branch used by the marauders to hang James Thomas Powell? Simon had once searched newspaper archives for mention of JT's hanging but found nothing. When he commented on the lack of evidence to Lenny, his father had said with a shrug, "Don't matter." The family *knew* it was true.

"A family is defined by its history," Lenny's brother had once told Simon. "You need to listen to what the stories are telling you." Simon wondered if his own tale might one day weave itself into the family saga.

Upon Vivian's death, title to the mansion would transfer to Simon, Connie having long refused to even consider taking responsibility for the place. Simon would not be allowed to sell the mansion, or in any other way dispose of the property, without gaining the signatures of all JT's living descendants. Money for the mansion's upkeep had been put in trust by JT's children, but it could not be accessed without everyone's agreement on what it should be used for. Half the relatives wanted the money to be used for demolition and rebuilding, while the other half wanted the mansion preserved. JT had considered the house as much a part of the family as the people living within its walls. The Powell legacy and the mansion were one. Simon would never be free as long as the mansion stood.

Simon walked across the heavily packed red dirt of the roadway in front of the mansion. Under the brightness of a mercury vapor lamp, installed years earlier to illuminate the family cemetery in hopes of deterring vandals, the granite and marble headstones seemed to glow with their own light. The Powell cemetery had been established during pioneer times, when a wagon train had brought settlers, most related by blood or marriage, on the arduous trip from Alabama. Simon started toward Lenny's grave but stopped. He was not ready to forgive Lenny for making Vivian's life so miserable, for never supporting anything Simon wanted to do. JT had died in 1866, a date scratched below initials on the slate plaque marking his grave. Standing before it, Simon wondered again about the truth of the hanging. Perhaps Lenny's brother had been right: the story we tell ourselves is what matters.

CHAPTER THIRTEEN

D r. Small's prognosis had been correct; tests revealed block-age in Vivian's carotid artery, which a stent could open, likely preventing a significant stroke, but it couldn't reverse damage already suffered. Vivian's most recent stroke had turned out to be considerable, affecting motor skills in her legs and further limiting mobility in her arms. Connie and Simon came to common purpose when contemplating the need to place Vivian in Bobwhite Convalescent Center, the same facility where Mandy had spent the final period of her life, years Simon vividly recalled from his frequent visits to see his grandmother.

Every day, Vivian had dropped off clean clothes for Mandy on her way to work, having washed them the evening before as a way of saving money by not utilizing Bobwhite's expensive laundry service. The smell of ammonia, rubbing alcohol, and cleaning solutions accosted visitors upon entering the nursing home in those days. State regulations had forced improvements, helping to prevent the unpleasant odors, but Bobwhite's cinder-block construction, colorless tile floors, and narrow windows with dirty white blinds continued to make the place unmistakably a warehouse for those approaching life's end.

Connie, Thad, and Simon met at Bobwhite to be with Vivian on her first night. Derek came as well, having recovered from his cough during the two weeks since the night of Vivian's stroke. Derek and Simon had once thought of each other as brothers, not just brothers-in-law, having met when Simon was in second grade. When Simon had dedicated himself to Sun Myung Moon, a man whose mission, Simon believed, was to complete the work of Jesus and build the kingdom of heaven on earth, Derek had become fanatically Christian, crusading against apostasies such as Sun Myung Moon's theology. Simon's current rejection of Christianity deeply concerned Derek, who told Simon on several occasions that he had faith Simon would accept Jesus at some point in his life, arguing that while he was not clever enough to confront the logic of the science in which Simon placed his own faith, "The Lord will work his will." Simon had little to say in response, generally replying, "We'll see."

"I understand you're returning to California," Derek said, addressing Thad as they signed the visitors' log at Bobwhite's reception desk.

"I have to get back for my job," Thad responded. "I'm supposed to be there already, but I couldn't leave until I knew Vivian was okay."

"That's kind of you," Derek said politely but without affection. "But the family has matters under control."

Thad shot Simon a look that stopped him from jumping into the conversation.

"What do you do, exactly?" Connie asked.

"I work for a company that makes videos. I'm one of the sound-effects guys."

"That must be interesting," Derek said.

"Are you still selling films?" Connie asked, turning to Simon.

"It's been tough making sales since I started college, and without anyone in Hollywood to manage the customs brokers and all, but I've made a few contracts."

"What about Thad? Can't he help while he's in California?"

"It's not like that, Connie. The people I deal with expect to work with someone they know."

"Let's go in to see Vivian," Derek suggested, weary of the small talk.

Once winsome and athletic, Derek now hid his weight beneath oversized shirts, and when anyone commented on his baldness, despite a comb-over, he would say he was prematurely bald, "something that comes from the maternal grandfather," as if otherwise baldness reflected on a person's lifestyle.

Derek proceeded into Vivian's room first, followed by Connie and Thad. Simon held back. The short visits with Vivian after the operation made it clear how debilitated she had become. Simon knew that seeing his mother at Bobwhite would bring back memories of the miserable conditions Mandy had endured.

The strong presence that had informed Nurse Beckett that Thad was family had left Vivian's body. She was now a defeated shell whose shoulders drooped, slumped in a wheelchair, knees touching as if bound together, legs shifted to one side.

"Vivian," Simon muttered, kneeling to put himself at eye level. "Mother?"

Vivian lifted her chin from her chest, eyes communicating a vague sense of recognition. Simon rushed toward the door, denying the tears that wet his cheeks. Thad wrapped his arm around Simon's waist and took him to the car.

"Don't think badly of me, Thad."

"Never, Simon. We had a family—I had a family—but now it's lost."

"Being at the mansion without Vivian might be more than I can handle."

"Do you want me to stay another few days? I can change the plane ticket."

"You should go. Howard is expecting you back."

"Yeah, he almost found someone else when I didn't go back when I said I would."

"Can you imagine if Connie and Derek found out what you do actually do?"

"Don't you dare tell Connie or Derek," Thad chortled. "You'd love using me to give Connie a shock. I know how you are."

Images of a closeted Derek secretly buying one of Howard's videos drifted through Simon's thoughts. "Let's hope Derek is as straight as he looks and that he never sees one of those videos."

"Even if he did—God, why did you put that image in my mind?—he'd never know I was involved. None of the postproduction workers are listed in the credits. And no one's real name is used anyway."

"Once, when I was taking out the trash for Connie, I spotted a receipt from Little Rock's only adult bookstore. I think they might experiment beyond the missionary position, despite their traditional values. You never know."

"Not something I want to think about on my way back to LA, thank you," Thad laughed.

"Yeah, you're right. Let's change the subject."

"Let's do some experimenting of our own." Thad smiled. "This will be our last night together for a while. And we will have the mansion to ourselves."

They made the most of it, happily resting in each other's arms, enjoying the simple act of watching television without worrying that Vivian would see them showing affection. Cicero seemed puzzled at Vivian's absence, but he enjoyed snuggling with them, and when Simon and Thad went upstairs, he held a vigil on Vivian's bed.

Over breakfast the next morning, Thad gave Simon a do-you-think-I'm-stupid look when Simon again cautioned about mentioning his name, still withholding the crucial information about Howard's Spanish partners.

"I saw the angry faxes scattered about on the desk when my rehab buddies were helping me load furniture from the Silverlake house into the rental truck. Your clients were livid that you didn't show up at MIFED."

"Even if Charlotte hadn't ripped me off, it was over at that point."

Simon noted the mention of Thad's rehab buddies. He had wondered who had helped Thad load the furniture. Simon knew it couldn't have been Patricia, who never did anything to damage her manicures, and Scott could never be bothered, even when sober enough to consider helping someone.

"You've never mentioned it," Thad began, "but I know how much Charlotte stole from you. One of the faxes listed a company in Spain, Hollywood Pictures something, I forget the whole name. They wanted confirmation that the money had arrived."

Simon considered explaining everything to Thad, to warn him about the identity of Howard's Spanish partners and tell him not to go back. But what if his absence raised questions in Howard's mind and he mentioned to Emilio or the others how he lost his best voice-over artist? What if Simon's name came up? Better that Thad remained ignorant, hiding in plain sight.

"Remember that fellow in Culver City? The one who owned a catalog of movies from the 1960s? I was planning to negotiate the entire library with the money they sent."

"I remember. We watched some of the old westerns. Not awful, but not great, either."

"They were good enough for the Spanish client. Now, that huge debt is just hanging out there. If Charlotte hadn't stolen the money, I would have lost it anyway, literally sending it up in smoke from a crack pipe. That much money in my pocket might have purchased my death."

"Are you saying that in some awful way, Charlotte did you a favor?"

"I don't know, Thad. Those last months I spent in Hollywood are like a dream. I'm not sure I knew what was real and what was paranoia. I knew I missed you and didn't want to live without you. I hated that we weren't together—that I had messed things up so badly."

"Well, however it happened, we're together now. We can figure out the future when I'm done with the work Howard has for me. From now on it is Simon and Thad, together forever."

Simon took Thad in his arms and kissed him as if they would never see each other again. Was he making a terrible decision keeping Thad ignorant of the danger from Emilio, David, and Irene?

CHAPTER FOURTEEN

The next day, Simon drove Thad to the airport and stayed until the plane disappeared into the clouds. Over the next few days, Cicero kept constant vigil, waiting for Vivian to come home, running to the front door if the wind jarred it, and at night hopping onto Vivian's bed to wait for her, then creeping into Simon's room as if to pine over her absence.

Alone with his worries, Simon fretted over the increased difficulty of making sales on Wally's videos, though he scoured the planet for additional markets, looking through a card file of obscure contacts he had collected over the years. Simon considered the possibility of finding other low-budget videos like Wally's; he had contacts for such producers, but if his name entered circulation, he was sure liens on his meager assets would follow. Even if the Spaniards never became alerted to his reappearance, there were plenty of other producers to whom he owed money.

Simon's fantasies about establishing a career as an artist provided sustenance. He believed returning to college had been the right thing to do, but every contemporary artist he researched had found a collector interested in him, made it big gambling with family money, or been able to create a piece of art controversial enough to get noticed by an up-and-coming critic. Simon was simply a fellow from the backwater town of Sibley, Arkansas, a recovering drug addict, and a former cult member—neither failing of much interest to anyone.

In the evenings, listening to LPs of opera recordings, comfortably seated in the plush parlor chair once used by his aunt Opal, Simon became obsessed with ideas. What if he located Charlotte or the complicit Rudy and discovered they still had the money and that they wanted to return it to him, the pressure of a guilty conscience having gotten the better of them—an unlikely scenario, he knew, but one that provided a degree of comfort. At the very least, Simon wanted to know what had become of Charlotte and Rudy. Perhaps Rudy had made an appearance at the Spotlight, and if so, the gossipy bartender, Twiggy, would know about it. Simon jumped from the chair and hurried to the phone before he could change his mind.

"The Spotlight Bar, a delightfully crummy place," Twiggy said cheerfully as he answered the phone.

Simon shouted into the phone so Twiggy would hear him over the din of a rowdy bar crowd. "Twig, it's me, Simon Powell."

"Miss Simon? Where on earth are you? Just a minute, dear." Twiggy screamed at a customer, telling him to pay what he owed or Bouncer Bob would deal with him.

"Lowlifes," Twiggy scolded, returning to the phone. "I hate it when they talk me into running a tab. I'm too nice. I should know better. Oh, fuck me, anyway."

"Some things never change, Twiggy."

"Where the hell are you? Why aren't you here, at the bar?"

"I'm still in the South."

"Oh, *Gawd*. That's right. I forgot. How can you stand it? Is there a gay bar? I hope so. Where's that Thad-pole of yours?"

Before Simon could answer, a brushing sound told him Twiggy had tucked the receiver between his ear and his shoulder to free his hands while serving drinks. "Oh, wait. I forgot," Twiggy continued, "Thad was in here. It wasn't that long ago."

"He called me from the phone at the bar, remember?"

"Oh, that's right. Silly me. I have the worst memory."

"Twiggy, I have a question."

"Fire away, dearest."

"Do you ever see Rudy, or Patricia, or that woman who worked as my secretary, Charlotte?"

"Honey, Patricia's been eighty-sixed out of here for the longest. That girl...do you know she pulled a razor blade out of her purse and swiped it at one of the regulars who tried to reach under her dress? He didn't believe she was a real woman. Well, she's a *real* man, I dare say. Patricia told him he'd be singing soprano if he made another move."

"That sounds like Patricia."

Twiggy yelled at two patrons who were getting intimate with each other. Undercover vice cops frequently patrolled the bar watching for excuses to cite Don for a code violation. The police not on Don's payroll resented the ones who were and looked for reasons to shut him down. Overt sexual contact was the worst offense, next to underage drinking.

"Now about that Rudy," Twiggy continued, "he's another story. Rudy knows not to show his face around here. Don told us all how he ripped you off with that Charlotte."

"Don told you about it?"

"When Thad came in to use the phone. Wait, maybe Thad told us. Oh, honey, I don't know. Anyway, the word is that Rudy owes you money, and Don doesn't like that sort of thing. If anyone is going to rip off a customer of the Spotlight, it's going to be him. Ha!"

"Sounds like you haven't seen Rudy."

"If he dares to come in, should I say anything?"

"No. I just wondered if he had been around. I'll call you another time."

"Okay, sweetcakes. Get on back now, ya hear? We miss y'all."

"Bye, Twiggy. Love y'all."

Sooner or later, Simon was sure that Don would miss his liar's poker buddy and let Rudy back into the bar—Don's banishments were rarely permanent. Charlotte had never liked the Spotlight and was unlikely to show up. She'd first gone there with Rudy after arriving in Los Angeles, and later she'd accompanied Simon to unwind after the day's work. Simon figured she had returned to Miami, perhaps taking Rudy with her.

The call to the Spotlight made Simon long for Hollywood, despite the insanity of the place. Simon remembered the good times at the Spotlight with his bar friends, the regulars who often shared tales of better times—Tinker Bell, the ex-jockey who'd ridden famous horses to victory at the Kentucky Derby; Eddie the Hat, who might have been a hitman—if he were to be believed; Contessa, who claimed to be royalty from an Eastern European country that no one had ever heard of. And then there had been Rudy Gutierrez, a famous chef in his telling, a brag backed up by Polaroids he kept in his pocket showing him beside recognizable if not Oscar-worthy actors and actresses, many of whom had now fallen on hard times, having succumbed to the same fate as Simon.

Simon knew he needed to stop worrying about Thad and focus on school, but school sometimes led Simon into feelings of existential doubt and confusion. Dr. Dupré had complimented Simon for his paper about Sun Myung Moon as the founder of a revitalization movement, advising him to spend the second half of the semester assessing the anticult backlash as a form of moral panic, giving Simon a list of sociology articles and scholarly books to start his research. Connie and Derek and their speeches at Christian churches served as the focal point of his paper, "Moral Panic and the Anticult Movement," which earned him more praise from the visiting professor.

"You should consider a PhD," Dr. Dupré advised Simon during his course evaluation. "Your experience as a leader in Sun Myung Moon's organization and the conflict generated by your sexual orientation is significant material for a dissertation. You'll need to formulate a theory to explain the interplay between sexuality and religious devotion, of course. Catholic priesthood and the doctrine of celibacy might provide background, and then there's the connection between eroticism and visionary experience. Look at the sculpture *The Ecstasy of St. Teresa*, where the love god, Cupid, prepares to pierce Teresa with his arrow."

"The sacred versus the profane," Simon summarized, echoing an idea that informed his art and defined his emotional and intellectual conflicts. "The desire for a sense of order against chaos."

"Apollo against Dionysus," Dr. Dupré offered.

"Against each other or in conjunction—I'm not sure one can be known without the other."

"And there you have it." Dr. Dupré smiled. "The idea for your dissertation."

Thad would have run screaming from the room if he had overheard Simon's conversation with Dr. Dupré. As Thad had once put it when trying to get Simon to stop talking, "Who cares about concepts? Ideas don't put food on the table."

After leaving Dr. Dupré's class, Simon wandered into the lab where he had once pondered a plaster cast of *Homo habilis* soon after his conversion to Divine Principle theology. Simon found the same cast, recalling the fog of beliefs that had clouded his mind for so many years. The cast represented hard evidence of human evolution, a species that had survived despite the odds. Faith had given Simon the idea that behind human evolution stood a divine being. Could Simon now accept a life molded by the vagaries of natural selection and shaped by genetics and the chaos of personal interactions, foregoing the idea that his life had special meaning?

Simon wasn't sure why he still felt conflicted.

CHAPTER FIFTEEN

S imon wanted to get his degree as quickly as possible, so he decided not to take a break but to continue through the summer term, a decision made easier because the university would be offering art classes. Simon especially looked forward to a course on color theory—color serving as a primary feature of his painting. Even so, Simon's mind wandered within minutes of entering the studio as he realized he was being looked at by someone he had seen on campus but with whom he had never spoken, a Ganymede who carried his six-foot frame with swanlike grace and whose hair fell in tufts as if adorning a Greek kouros, someone Simon would have pursued if he weren't in a relationship.

The first project in the theory class, announced by the professor with a handout (the professor being someone who disliked teaching and preferred to keep interactions with students to a minimum), was to create the illusion of depth by painting concentric circles using hues of a single color. The class set to work. Simon struggled to chase Ganymede from his thoughts.

After class, despite realizing that he was placing himself in temptation's way, he followed the student to an open corridor on one side of a courtyard, the morning sun reflecting from a row of windows opposite. Simon introduced himself, calling out, "Hello, I'm Simon."

The student wheeled around, gazing at Simon with an interested look. "My next class is clear across campus. Another time?" The student hurried off.

An acquaintance from Dr. Dupré's seminar walked up behind Simon. "That's Blaine Mathis," the acquaintance whispered. "Gorgeous man, isn't he?"

"Arthur, I didn't know you were gay." Simon also didn't realize that Arthur knew anything about him, having engaged in conversation on a single occasion that Simon could remember.

Arthur, a young man of twenty, with probing eyes that revealed a keen intelligence, wanted to know Simon better. "I knew we were family the moment I saw you," Arthur explained, placing his hand on Simon's arm with a chiffon touch.

"Family?"

"Of course—family, sisters, gay men hiding in plain sight."

"I forget I'm back in Arkansas," Simon confessed. "No one thinks much about the differences between gay and straight where I lived before moving back here."

"Hollywood, right? Oh, I don't mean to sound like the local gossip. People talk, you know. You're something of a mystery."

Simon suspected the admissions officer of sharing information. Simon had supposed the man was gay by the way he looked at him and because of a few questions constructed to find out if Simon was married or had a significant other.

"Thanks for giving me the new vocabulary, Arthur. I haven't met many people in the gay community here in Little Rock. I never thought about the need to be out when I lived in Hollywood. Here, just being oneself is an act of boldness."

"A lot of people fear losing their jobs because they work for a Christian," Arthur explained. "So many of them are intolerant toward employees—and you know the law doesn't protect a gay person from being fired."

"It's a shame. The world has changed, and anyway, the whole point of the American Revolution was to end theocratic rule. There is no Church of America."

"Listen to you!" Arthur smiled. "Well, here's to the Revolution. Meanwhile, you should come to the dance club with me one of these nights. Blaine isn't the only hunk in town—Little Rock has plenty of choice beef on the menu."

"I'm in a relationship, if you weren't aware."

"Aren't we all," Arthur laughed. "Oh, I don't mean to be crass. For goodness sake, that was terrible of me, wasn't it? Where is your boyfriend? I've never seen you with anyone."

"Los Angeles."

"Lost Angels! Well, you know what they say, out of sight..."

"But not out of mind," Simon interrupted. "Thad and I are loyal to each other."

"And what does he do, this *Thad*?"

If Simon told Arthur the truth, it would lead to a conversation Simon didn't want to pursue; on the other hand, Simon wanted to know how Arthur would react.

"Thad provides sound effects for gay porn."

Not skipping a beat, Arthur began, "I had a friend in Hot Springs who did that kind of work. Why doesn't your Thad work for one of the local producers?"

"Seriously, Hot Springs?"

"You'd be surprised what goes on in that little town. As soon as the gambling ended—thanks to mean old Winthrop Rockefeller—delightfully sinful businesses came in to fill the gap."

"You were born long after Governor Rockefeller chased gambling interests out of Hot Springs. How do you even know about it—a class in Arkansas history?"

"Sweetie, I'm *from* Hot Springs. The front door of our house has four bullet holes from a tommy gun, which, by the way, ranks us among the premier Hot Springs families. Happened sometime in the 1930s. No one remembers why they targeted our family, but one of my great-grandfathers managed a speakeasy, so bootleg-ging probably had something to do with it."

Arthur's stories were intriguing, but Simon wanted to know about Blaine.

"Can't tell you much, Simon," Arthur demurred. "Blaine keeps to himself. He will be friendly one moment, aloof the next. I know he's one of us, though. Queer as they come."

Queer as they come. The turn of phrase made Simon recall Lenny and his "queer as a three-dollar bill" comment about Liberace

"Maybe I'll take you up on that offer to go dancing."

"Any time." Arthur risked pecking Simon on the cheek with a light kiss, but not before checking for anyone who might see them.

CHAPTER SIXTEEN

"You remember me telling you about those people coming from Spain?" Thad began during a phone conversation. "The ones partnering with Howard to make a video?"

"Most definitely," Simon replied.

"The heads of the company showed up at Howard's ranch yesterday. Curious thing—a young guy named Felipe came with them."

Simon realized that Thad's opening question had been a setup to see how Simon would react.

"Felipe started telling me about an American film distributor he met in Barcelona. Then he mentioned *Bel Air Babes,* and I realized the American had to be you. Felipe claimed he couldn't remember your name. These are the people who sent the money Charlotte stole, aren't they?"

"Yes."

"I'm going away from the phone for a minute." Thad put down the receiver and shut the door. "I checked to make sure no one was on the extension in the other room. Howard has been putting out rails of cocaine. It's made him paranoid."

"Thad, I hope you haven't…"

"Not even tempted. Seeing the change in Howard as soon as he snorts the first line, I see clearly what it did to me. Howard wasn't doing drugs when I first came here. The drugs started when he found out that one of the new actors used a fake ID to get hired. Turns out the kid is only sixteen. Howard freaked out when the background check came through, since he'd already shot footage with him. Howard destroyed the master tape, but he's worried about blackmail because he thinks the cameraman kept a copy. The other day, Howard installed cameras in the hallways and at each of the entrances; it's like being in a juvenile detention center."

"When you first mentioned Emilio, David, and Irene, I should have explained who there were."

"You let me come back, Simon! Why?" Thad could barely speak through the lump forming in his throat.

"I never imagined you'd meet them, and it never occurred to me that Felipe would enter the picture. I thought it would be worse if you knew the whole story, and worse if you didn't go back. That would have raised suspicion, and I was hoping they'd get their business done with Howard and then go back to Spain. You're just one of the workers, so why would they notice you? I planned to tell you after they left."

"We shouldn't talk much longer, Simon. You were right to be concerned about what would happen if I simply failed to show up when Howie was expecting me. He would have contacted Don at the Spotlight to find out what was up with me—Howard remembers that I went there when the crew was having dinner at the Brown Derby. The way Howard is acting, he'd think I was the one planning to blackmail him, especially if I left now that his Spanish partners have arrived."

"Did Felipe say anything about Emilio looking for 'the American' that he remembers?"

"Not really. But I nearly lost it when Felipe told me about having sex with Emilio and *the American.* I acted as though it didn't interest me, and he didn't say more about it."

"I'm sorry, Thad, we weren't together at the time."

"I know what you were like back then, but Emilio? You and Felipe in bed with Emilio! Oh my God. The problem was keeping myself from laughing."

"Not my proudest moment. Emilio had powerful drugs, and you have to admit, Felipe is hot."

"Yeah, and if we weren't together...well, we better not talk about that."

"Yes, we better not. At least Felipe didn't say anything about the American ripping off his bosses. Maybe it was a big deal to me but chump change in their minds. Maybe they just wrote it off as a business loss."

"No idea," Thad responded, recognizing Simon's statement as wishful thinking. "Felipe's going to star in the video they're doing. I doubt he knows anything about the business dealings. He's a pony in their stable."

"Felipe wanted me to help him come to America."

"I've only seen the company owners from a distance. David wears a dark suit that looks expensive. Emilio wears shorts and one of those cotton shirts with the pleats down the front. Then there's David's wife, Irene. Did I mention her before? That look of hers could shatter glass. Emilio laughs a lot when he tells Howard dirty jokes."

"Don't let Emilio cajole you into talking if he meets you, Thad. He uses charm to get information from people. David is all about the bottom line—making money. He signs the contracts. Irene manages the finances."

"We better cut it short."

"I know, Thad, but now it's better that you know the whole story. The deal I made was to supply American films on a monthly basis. They planned to launder cash from their criminal activities by making it seem as though the money came from video licensing. Charlotte stole an advance they sent so I would have money to negotiate."

"What kind of criminal activities?"

"All I know is what Felipe told me. He knew of drug trafficking and sales of pornography in countries where it's illegal."

"I'd sure like to find out what else Felipe knows."

"Be careful, Thad. This could blow up if Emilio, David, or Irene find out that you're my boyfriend. The money might seem suddenly important if they had a chance to even the score."

"My knees are shaking. I hope I can steer clear of them until they leave."

"Let me hear those sound effects you're famous for." Simon hoped to tease Thad out of his fears. He didn't expect to laugh so much when Thad obliged. "Stop! I can't take it."

"Think of me tonight, Simon."

"Already am."

Thad kissed the receiver. Simon started to cry. Would the crimes of his past destroy everything he hoped to build? Whether through cosmic retribution or acts of human vengeance, was he facing damnation?

To whatever powers that be, he prayed, keep Thad safe.

CHAPTER SEVENTEEN

Thad called from pay phones, sneaking away from Howard Price's ranch on the pretext of grocery shopping, leaving messages because he could only telephone during the day when Simon would be in one of his classes. Simon rushed to Sibley each day to run upstairs and check the answering machine, his heart beating fast when he saw the light flashing. He longed to hear Thad's voice, even through a recording. One message threw him into a panic.

Emilio had stayed behind at Howard's ranch after David and Irene returned to Spain. Thad informed Simon that Howard had stopped using cocaine to focus on the new production, that Howard wasn't asking as many questions as before now that his paranoia had subsided. Simon began to imagine worrisome scenarios, suspicious that Emilio remained in California for a reason other than oversight of the new video production: to look for him!

The mansion creaked throughout the night, a living presence defending itself against, in Simon's mind, hoodlums from Little Rock who were ransacking the place in search of valuables. The act of painting saved Simon from anxiety until he was faced with shadows as he would walk from the barn, across the field, to the mansion's back door. Sometimes he locked himself in his bedroom and read a Steinbeck novel, part of a cache in the same closet where Vivian kept her romances.

Sensing something amiss in Simon's life and assuming the problem to be loneliness, Arthur insisted they meet at Discovery, known for having the best dance floor in the state, an assessment confirmed by the crowds that came from all over central Arkansas, expansive crowds encompassing high-fashion investment bankers along with farm boys in tight-fitting jeans, kickass boots, and wide-brimmed cowboy hats. When Simon scanned the clientele on their first outing, he wondered how many of the young men had sneaked away from their farm on the down low, escaping country homes for queer adventure in the big city of Little Rock. Older men congregated at the bar, their marital status revealed by the light patch of skin on their ring fingers, their intent manifest in the ogling of the farm boys, whose furtive glances signaled the beginning of negotiations.

Arthur stayed close to Simon, keeping a watchful eye, aware of Simon's dedication to Thad but also having witnessed that when Blaine showed interest in Simon, it was hard for him to admit he wasn't tempted. And now some of the farm boys were eyeing Simon with beckoning, half-closed eyes, flexing muscles, and aw-shucks cuteness that made them irresistible, their attentions becoming more of a risk with each beer Simon consumed.

"You know who I saw in here the other day?" Arthur asked conspiratorially. "You'll never guess."

"Who?"

"Kevin Bacon."

"Really? He's gay?"

"I hear he knows people in town, and Discovery *is* the best place to go out dancing. Still, to be *seen* at a gay club—and what a hottie! If he isn't gay, he should be."

"A lot of men have missed their calling," Simon joked. "It's fun to see famous people, whatever the context—that's something I enjoyed about life in Hollywood."

"Tell me who you saw," Arthur implored, hoping for some name-dropping and perhaps a juicy tidbit.

Simon started to tell Arthur about seeing Steve Martin at a video store and Lily Tomlin at a photography studio, but the sound system overwhelmed his voice. Simon and Arthur had grabbed their beers and roamed the perimeter of the dance floor before heading back to the bar when Simon spotted Blaine leaning against the bar in a James Dean pose, sipping a sunset from a tall glass as he studied the dancers as they gyrated beneath the strobe lights and silver disco spheres.

"Didn't you say Blaine tended to be aloof?" Simon shouted into Arthur's ear.

"I've never seen him here before," Arthur tried to respond, but Simon was unable to catch his words over the noise. Arthur led Simon to a quieter area away from the speakers and repeated himself.

"I'm dying to know Blaine's story. He must have a boyfriend—he's too gorgeous."

Arthur shrugged. "No one seems to know."

As they spoke, a man approached Blaine for a dance, an invitation dismissed with a wave of the hand, after which Blaine turned to the bartender and ordered a fresh drink. Simon excused himself from Arthur, who he knew would remain close to overhear the conversation, and set his beer beside Blaine's glass. Blaine eventually glanced his way.

"Hello again. Remember me, from design class?"

Blaine's face lit up in recognition. "Certainly, you introduced yourself. Simon, right?"

"Are you here alone?" Simon pressed.

Blaine offered a diffident smile. "Yes, I'm alone."

"You turned down an offer to dance, so I won't be so bold—but I do like to dance." Simon took Blaine by the hand as if to lead him onto the floor.

Blaine hesitated for a moment, "Okay, I'll dance. But…"

Simon expected Blaine to warn him that he couldn't dance but didn't give him a chance to say anything as he led the way. Blaine released Simon's hand and, with the elegance of a member of the three Graces, glided to a spot under a stationary overhead light. As he began his moves, Blaine's slacks swayed in counterpoint to feet that touched the ground only briefly before setting off on another round of soaring lifts and turns. A circle of onlookers formed as Simon stepped back to admire a performance that challenged the song lyrics blaring through the sound system: "U Can't Touch This."

A different person from the reticent Blaine of moments ago greeted Simon at the end of the spectacle, innocently asking, "Did you like that?"

"Are you kidding? That was amazing. You should have said something."

"I tried to," Blaine reminded.

Arthur held up a mug in salute.

"That was fun," Blaine confessed. "I should come out more often…and I should start earlier in the evening. I'm afraid I have to be going."

"See you in class, then." Simon felt it would be presumptuous to ask why Blaine needed to leave. "I'm just happy to have discovered more about the mysterious Blaine Mathis."

Blaine smiled a sweet smile and took Simon's hand in a grip both firm and gentle before heading through the crush of people toward the exit.

Arthur had shifted his interest to a young man, someone he had dated on and off. Simon bade him adieu and left. As soon as he opened the door to the Pontiac, Simon felt a touch on his shoulder.

"Simon?" came a familiar voice.

"Dean!" Simon exclaimed with a nod of recognition. "We've got to stop meeting like this."

"I saw you leaving the club and rushed out to say hello before you drove away. What a crowd they've got tonight, huh? I've tried calling, but always I get the machine. Vivian doesn't even answer."

"I should have let you know. It's just that with school and Thad being in California and all...Vivian had a stroke. Connie and I had to place her in a convalescent home."

"Oh, Simon," Dean said sympathetically. He'd forged a bond with Vivian during the worrisome time when Simon first arrived from California, and he understood how much Vivian's support had meant to Simon's recovery. "This has to be hard for you. I'd like to visit her."

"I'm sure Vivian would like that."

"Is she able to speak? Did the stroke affect her voice?"

"It's possible to make out her words, but you have to pay attention. The stroke made it harder for her to remember things in the short term. She'll remember while you're talking, but the next day she'll ask why you haven't come by. She's in a semiprivate room at Bobwhite Convalescent Center."

"I know the place. When I was a priest, I visited aging parishioners there."

"Catholics in Sibley? Who knew."

"Ah, who knew there were atheists."

"Touché. But I never use that word to define myself."

"Atheist is as good a term as any to describe..."

"Dean, you're a great guy, but I need to get going."

"I didn't mean anything."

"Don't worry. I'm just tired. I have a lot on my mind."

"It has to be difficult for you. You said that Thad is in California?"

"He went back to LA to work. We need the money."

"You'll have to tell me about it one of these days. Maybe we can have lunch at the student union. Just thinking—Cicero must miss Vivian terribly. Do you take him to see her?"

"I've thought about it, but it might make his pining even worse."

"Sure you don't want to come back inside for a nightcap?"

"I better go. The reason I came here already happened."

Dean smiled. "That doesn't sound rational."

"Yeah, I know. But somehow tonight felt meaningful."

"I can't let you go without hearing what happened for you to talk this way."

"A guy."

"Isn't it always."

"At a different time in my life, I'd pursue him as a boyfriend."

"Anyone I know?"

"He's a student, perhaps a bit younger than me. We're in the same design class."

"Curiosity is killing me. What's his name?"

"Blaine Mathis."

"*The* Blaine Mathis?"

"He definitely is *the* looker. Tall, curly brown hair, slim, elegant, walks with such grace it seems he barely touches the ground."

"You don't seem to know who he is."

"Am I supposed to?"

"Blaine dances ballet."

"Really? That would explain how he took over the dance floor. Everyone stopped to watch him."

"I'm sure they did. Blaine is quite the prima donna. Come to think of it, I've not read about any performances lately. I don't get to the ballet as much as I used to, but I always read reviews."

Simon's curiosity about Blaine grew even stronger.

"You won't you come back inside?" Dean asked again.

"I would, but it's a long drive to Sibley at this time of night, and, well, I had a few beers, which I'm not accustomed to these days."

"I'm glad I ran into you. Call if you need someone to talk to."

"I will, Dean. Thanks."

Dean would leave the club with a date, another in a line of unsatisfying encounters. Dean often told Simon how fortunate he was to have Thad, that finding someone special had been his hope after leaving the priesthood.

Simon knew he must be on guard if he pursued a friendship with Blaine, even as visions of the radiant Blaine pranced across his thoughts during the drive to Sibley. Blaine's beguiling, winsome smile mocked Simon, a smile like those of the pretty boys, self-possessed and unattainable, who frequented the bars in West Hollywood, boys who got Simon to buy them a drink and then flitted away to entice one from someone else. Blaine was the type of person Simon had wanted to find among those West Hollywood men. Then he met Thad, beautiful as well as interested in him, someone who stood out against the backdrop of hard-core hustlers at the Spotlight. If not for cocaine, they would have had an easy relationship—or so Simon fantasized. Simon wished Thad was at the mansion waiting for him. He dreaded spending another night alone.

After letting Cicero run around the fenced-in yard at the back porch while he tended to Ferdinand, Simon settled in the parlor and tried to read a Gore Vidal novel about Lincoln that he'd recently purchased at the university bookstore, believing the great author's captivating prose and vivid imagery would distract him from the gnawing loneliness. Visions of Blaine Mathis on the dance floor stole Vidal's narrative.

Go to Hollywood and be with Thad—now, tonight! So spoke an urgent voice as memories of the better times in Hollywood played like a movie in Simon's mind, interrupted by the scratching of wisteria that brushed against the window. Was that Ernie at the door? How many times Simon had fantasized about his boyhood friend and himself growing up together and becoming partners for life, only to feel the scorch of despair as they learned to hate being gay, Ernie surrendering to heroin for solace, Simon intoxicating himself with the denial afforded by faith, accepting a charismatic figure who demanded sexual abstinence as a condition of discipleship. Not until Simon had learned to forgive himself and sustain his relationship with Thad was he able to forgive Ernie and allow his boyhood friend to rest in peace. Simon grieved that Ernie had never found love.

Simon went across the street to the family cemetery. The tall grass and knotted vines had begun to consume the older stones, and markers bearing etched letters that had once identified those buried beneath were now weathered and unreadable. Simon promised himself that the next day he would stake Ferdinand in the cemetery to deal with nature's unruliness; the goat is a satanic symbol, Simon considered, as he stood before the angel atop Aunt Opal's grave, the distant clanging bell around the goat's neck haunting the cemetery even then.

"Enough!" Simon screamed.

Powell apparitions followed him through the rusted gate as he darted across the barren road and rushed toward the mansion. Under Simon's feet, unstable planks on the porch wobbled, the victims of termite attacks, as he approached the entrance and noticed something stuck in the doorjamb—an envelope, the yellow hue of a telegram. Simon's first thought was that Vivian had died, but the idea made no sense, Bobwhite's staff would have left a message on the answering machine.

"Simon, if you get this, call me right away. Don from the Spotlight."

How did Don have the address of the mansion? Terror gripped Simon as possibilities ran through his mind. Emilio had stayed at Howards...did he learn Thad's identity? Was Thad in trouble? Emotions welled in Simon's heart that made him fear what Don might have to tell him. Hands shaking, he tore the paper to shreds as if doing so would allay his fears. All night, Simon heard footsteps on the stairs, and a car that would typically slow down for a curve within the next block now seemed ready to turn into the driveway, shut off the lights, and release a hitman onto the property.

CHAPTER EIGHTEEN

Following a lecture on standard deviations by the professor of elementary statistics, Simon couldn't wait to get to the painting studio, except that Blaine would be there; Blaine, whom Simon's memory of the performance at Discovery had elevated to cosmic status, as if he were Śrī Naṭarāja, the dancing Shiva of Hindu myth, posing as much threat to Simon as Shiva had to the demon he trounced. The art professor left class as soon as it started—if students wanted advice, they needed to schedule an appointment. Otherwise, as an advanced class, students should work through design problems without help. In fact, with an advanced class, the professor could more easily get away with being absent. Simon began a monochrome painting based on a photograph of the Sibley swamp. Then Blaine wandered in. Without a word, he went to the supply lockers and took out a three-by-four-foot canvas, setting it on his easel and beginning a new work.

"Sleeping until noon?" Simon asked, walking over to Blaine's easel. He intended to sound nonchalant but came across as passing judgment; Blaine's red-veined eyes told the story of a late night.

"Hello, Simon," Blaine responded. Simon could tell that Blaine was happy to see him, but something shadowed his gaze, a sense confirmed as Blaine continued, "No, I'm dealing with some things, that's all. Hey, can you tell me if the instructor took the roll? Probably not, right? She hardly ever does."

Simon reached in his wallet and took out one of the business cards he had ordered from Sibley Stationers. "Here's my phone number," Simon offered, justifying the act by convincing himself that Blaine needed someone to confide in, then added boldly, "What about your number?"

"My hands have paint on them," Blaine demurred. A tube of paint had split at the seam in his locker, and crimson pigment stained his palms.

"It's okay. I have a pen right here," Simon replied.

Blaine gave Simon his number and asked, "When is a good time to call?"

"I'm almost always home by early evening."

"It would be nice to have a friend to talk to. I'm involved with someone, but I can't confide in him."

"I understand," Simon replied. "My boyfriend is in Los Angeles. It's a long story."

"My story is complicated too." Blaine turned to his canvas and added a dash of Mars black to the grisaille—a tyrannosaur chasing a velociraptor, based on a book illustration Blaine had brought into class to tackle a project requiring action to be depicted using shades of gray. It was an assignment that Simon planned to meet with his painting of the swamp, placing emphasis on cranes swooping down to catch catfish in the pond, with a slight violation of the requirement, adding red eyes to an alligator that lurked just beneath the surface.

"I'll call you one night this week," Blaine promised.

"And we can share those long and complicated stories." Simon was happy to make a new friend in Blaine; then Blaine looked into

Simon's eyes, and the rush of attraction that passed between them gave Simon pause. Was he going to be like Thad had been the times they were apart? Simon would never forget the hurt he'd felt when Thad became enraptured by Jerry while staying at Scott's during one of their worst breakups.

Simon cleared his thoughts and returned to his easel, mixing a soupçon of cerulean to a gray sky and in the background adding sunflowers, replanted in Simon's imagination from outside the dinette window to the far bank of the pond, rendered in dark yellow-gray, and, as a final touch, a train of crows in the distance threatening to rob the downcast sunflowers of bloated kernels.

The wall clock signaled the end of class. Simon placed his supplies in the locker and set his canvas in one of the vertical slots. Blaine slipped out of the studio, disappearing before Simon could figure out in which direction he had gone. In the student union, Simon found Arthur sitting in his usual spot—a quiet place for study, but more importantly, a good vantage point for spying the campus goings-on.

"Blaine was late for painting class," Simon reported. "And you should have seen him, the very definition of death warmed over."

"I'm in such a pinch, Simon. I've got an exam in an hour and oh my God, I am so unprepared. What were you saying?"

"Blaine. He looked like a cat dragged him into class. Blaine says he's involved with someone. That's the word he used, 'involved.'"

"Really? That's disappointing. I wonder who it could be? Oh dear, so many questions. I must bury my nose in these books, Simon. Can we chat later?"

Simon left Arthur to his cramming and drove to the mansion, falling into an uneasy sleep stretched out on the couch in the parlor, waking periodically with the memory of Don's telegram. "Call as soon as you get this." Simon didn't consciously realize why a sense of dread overcame him each time he picked up the phone to call. He knew he needed to learn whatever Don had to report.

He rose from the couch and stuck a shaky finger into the rotary dial on the same phone Simon recalled from his first visit to Sibley, when Aunt Opal had pressed a lucky quarter into the palm of his hand and warned him not to lose it. The coin was good luck. Simon wished he had that coin as he waited for an answer.

"The delightfully crummy Spotlight Bar and Thrill," came the familiar voice.

"New greeting, Twiggy?"

"Hmm, some stranger calling? Wait, is that you, Simon?"

"Right on the money."

"Oh my God, Don has bugged me to death about reaching you."

"Is he there?"

"Left for dinner an hour ago but said he's coming back."

"Any idea what he wants to talk about? Any news about Rudy or Charlotte?" Simon specifically excluded Thad from the list, hoping whatever news Don had, it wasn't that Thad was in danger.

"Oh, honey, no, I don't think so. Sweet Peter over at The Pub thought he had a clue on Rudy's whereabouts, but it didn't lead anywhere. Peter wants to kick Rudy's ass for you."

"Sometimes I fantasize about one of you getting my money back."

"There'd be nothing left if Rudy had it—you know what a gambling problem he's got. Not sure about Miss Charlotte. Who knows what a pole dancer does with her money? She hasn't been around… oh my, not since before you disappeared. Listen, Simon, the bar's full. When Don comes back from dinner, I'll let him know you called. Give me your number."

"It's best if I call back, Twiggy."

"Okay, well, give it a try around last call."

Last call in Los Angeles meant waiting another four hours. Speaking with Twiggy, hearing the jukebox blast out a Joan Jett song in background, Simon was there with Thad like old times, drinking the night away, carrying on and having fun with friends,

Simon and Thad swaying on their barstools, arms locked, singing with Liza when she came on the jukebox to sing "Cabaret." Simon needed to hear Thad's voice and risked dialing the number at Howard's ranch they used when the plan was to reach each other at an appointed hour. Simon fantasized that Thad might still wait each night, even though they had agreed to use pay phones, worried that Howard might be recording conversations. Each unanswered ring stung Simon's heart.

Simon tried to work on a new painting, but Ferdinand's braying, an annoyance amplified by an attack by ravenous mosquitos buzzing in one ear and then the other, proved too much. Simon quietened Ferdinand's plaintive calls by filling the water trough, crushed geranium leaves from a pot on the back porch and rubbed the juice on his arms to ward off the mosquitos, and strolled along the creek, following a path barely illuminated by a half-moon.

Not long ago, unsettled with worry or loneliness as he was then, Simon would have gone on the prowl for cocaine, journeying to Little Rock for a rendezvous with the drug dealers BT or Snake, finding them on their patrol of the housing projects on Twelfth Street or along the alleyways of Little Rock's east side, scoring whatever he could afford. How times had changed. Considering the familiar run, tempting as it was, as he threw a pebble into the rapidly flowing creek, he instead went into the house to make a phone call.

"I know it's late," Simon apologized when Dean answered.

"Not so late for me. I'm a night owl. Been sitting here reading. But even if I had been asleep, you know it's fine to call me."

"My imagination is running wild, Dean. I've never told you the whole story about Charlotte ripping me off, and now I'm afraid Thad is in jeopardy."

"That sounds serious."

"The money came from a company in Spain that I made a shady deal with. They planned to use films I would procure to launder illegal money."

Dean didn't respond.

"Did you hear me, Dean?"

"It always seemed like you had a simple business model, licensing old films to foreign companies. I would have thought there wasn't much risk."

"It *was* simple until I went to Barcelona to close out a letter of credit, and the principals of the company offered to front me a couple of hundred dollars to get films for them. I didn't think much about it because the Spanish video market has been hot for old American films. I was aware they produced porn but didn't think much about it until I met one of their young men, a fellow named Felipe. He confided in me that their legitimate film network allowed them to deal with the money they made by selling porn through back channels in countries where it's forbidden."

"Did Charlotte know any of this when she took the money?"

"Nothing about it. When more money showed up than expected, she probably thought I had negotiated another deal. I trusted her too much—I had left behind signed checks for her to pay the bills. I'm sure she thought I was too far gone and seized the opportunity to make a new start."

"Sounds like an old film noir movie. How is Thad involved? Why do you say he's in jeopardy? Was he in league with Charlotte all this time? Gracious, I can see why your imagination is running amok."

"When Charlotte stole the money, I hoped Sibley would be far enough away so that no one could find me. Then Thad went to California to work for a guy that makes porn, and I worried because all over the world, those people know each other."

"You said Thad was in LA to make money, but I never thought he was making porn!"

"He's not performing, just doing voice-overs."

"People do that? I always thought I was hearing the live action."

"Nothing is real in Hollywood. A while back, Thad mentioned that Howard, his boss, had gone into partnership with a Spanish company."

"And it turned out to be the same people?"

"The very same."

"Do you think this Howard fellow is in cahoots with their money laundering?"

"I'm sure it has more to do with the availability of blond California hunks. Adding a few videos with hot California boys to their catalog would increase their profits, sold in a legitimate market or not. Felipe, the young man I mentioned, came with the company's owners when they came to visit Howard. He befriended Thad and told him about having met an American in Barcelona. Thad put it together. I hoped the Spaniards would go back home, but the main guy, a fellow named Emilio, stayed behind."

"Thad needs to get out of there!" Dean said frantically.

"We thought Thad would raise suspicions if he left suddenly and that Howard might mention my name in conversation with Emilio. As long as Thad was seen as just one of the crew, there would be little reason for Emilio to meet him."

"It's too dangerous, Simon. If these people are willing to skirt international laws, who knows what they'd do if they found you, or what they might do to Thad to get to you. When did you last speak to Thad?"

"It's been a while. Thad's boss started using drugs, and Thad became worried he had the phones tapped."

"This gets worse and worse."

"There's more."

"Hold the line, let me close the blinds."

"They won't be looking for you."

"I know," Dean said with a nervous laugh. "I was trying to lighten the mood. This is so worrisome."

"I received a telegram from the owner of the Spotlight Bar. Remember Don?"

"The older gentleman who always played liar's poker with Rudy and the others. I remember him."

"The telegram insisted that I call him right away, but I delayed and didn't try until this evening. He was at dinner, so I'm supposed to call later."

"What do you think Don wants?"

"I don't know. Don procures talent for people like Thad's boss. Maybe Don heard something."

"I know you're tempted to avoid all of this." Dean didn't want to voice his concern by name.

"It's been on my mind, I admit, but cocaine scares me as much as being found by Emilio and the others."

"Maybe you should go to the authorities and explain everything."

"I'd sound like a crank if I called Los Angeles detectives."

"What do you think is going on? Do you think this Emilio has met Thad?"

"I wish I knew."

At last call, Simon again telephoned the Spotlight. An unfamiliar bartender answered and gave the phone to Don. Simon's stomach tightened.

"Mr. Simon," Don began, forgetting Simon's last name. "Have I got news for you."

"How did you get my address, Don? I didn't think anyone knew my whereabouts."

"Resourcefulness. I can find anyone when I put my mind to it, but you were easy. Your friend Scott stopped by with some of the producers he represents. He didn't remember your phone number, but he had your address in his wallet. Arkansas, huh? I can't imagine you in Arkansas of all places."

"Scott is such a blabbermouth," Simon moaned. "What's your news, Don?"

"I know about Rudy and his friend what's-her-name ripping you off. Anyway, Rudy called the bar from Las Vegas about a week ago."

"Charlotte was with him?"

"Right. Charlotte. Rudy had a falling out with her. Sounds like he had been getting money to keep his mouth shut, but you know our Rudy, he does like to gossip."

"Charlotte could have stolen from me before, Don, but she didn't. Rudy probably egged her on while I was in Europe."

Someone interrupted Don, the voice of a hustler pleading for them to leave because it was after last call and the guy wanted more booze at Don's place.

"What's the bottom line, Don? What's so important about Rudy's falling out with Charlotte?"

"Rudy wants you to contact a guy named Wally. He said you'd know who he meant. Putting you two in touch is Rudy's way of getting back at Charlotte. I don't know more than that, just that Rudy insisted, 'Have Simon call Wally.'"

"Thanks, Don."

"Who is this Wally fellow?"

"Just some guy."

The voice urged Don to hurry.

"Is there something else, Don?"

"Only that your Thad is looking good. He was in here tonight."

Simon collapsed into a sitting position on the rug in front of the sofa.

"The guy with him was a knockout," Don continued. "Cutest Spanish accent."

"Don, this is serious. Thad was with a Spanish fellow?"

"I wondered if you two had broken up, but I have to admit, the two didn't seem all that chummy. I asked if they wanted to come to dinner with me, but Little Buddy here wouldn't stand for it, would you?" Don's hustler of the night cooed into his ear. "Thad and the young man sat in a booth and ordered drinks, but they didn't stay long. Some man—who looked pretty tough, by the way—remained close by and then insisted they leave before finishing their drinks."

"I'll ask Thad about it next time I speak to him," Simon told Don, not wanting to raise alarms by telling Don the truth.

"Call if you have anything juicy to report."

"Before you hang up, Don, can I talk to Twiggy?"

"You want to know if he has anything else on that young Spanish guy and your Thad, don't you? Here he is."

Don placed the receiver on the bar and summoned Twiggy. The hustler dragged Don away with an insistent "Let's go, let's go."

"I was at the other end of the bar when you called," Twiggy said apologetically. "I'll bet Don spilled the beans on Thad, didn't he?"

"He said that Thad and a guy with a Spanish accent were there. His name is Felipe."

"I know, sweetcakes. He told Don his name. What a luscious hunk of a man he was too. Not that your Thad isn't...well, I won't salivate over Thad when I'm talking to you, darling."

"Twig, it's okay. I'm just surprised that Thad and Felipe were there. Both of them should be up in Chatsworth. I wonder what they were doing in Hollywood? Don said they didn't look like they were on a date."

"As far as I could tell, Thad was showing Felipe around Hollywood. An older man in a black leather jacket was with them. I figured him for a limo driver, if that makes any sense. He was well dressed, but Thad and Felipe wore simple jeans and tee shirts. The man bought them drinks at the bar and carried them to the table. Don went over to say hello. Thad didn't seem like he was cheating on you. Of course," Twiggy said with a smirk, "that little prince would never do anything in front of me. He knows I'd get the information to you one way or another." Twiggy thought for a moment. "Did Don mention the telegram he asked me to send to you? I felt like a character from a Joan Crawford movie sending out one of those things. Give me your number this time. I don't ever want to send another *telegram*."

"I'll give you my number if you promise not to give it to anyone, not even Don. If you hear anything, or if Thad comes by again, call me. You can leave a message if I don't pick up. I'm worried Thad might be in trouble."

"Well, aren't you full of intrigue? I promise." Twiggy paused. "Now that you mention trouble, the man with them did seem a bit rough for a limo driver. And well, I hadn't thought anything of it before, but a couple of times it seemed like Thad wanted to get my attention, like he wanted me to come to the booth. I figured it was just to make sure I didn't think he was cheating on you. The one time I saw Thad leave the table for the men's room, the older guy followed him. Felipe sat in the booth the whole time. We were so busy, I didn't think much about it, but it did seem strange."

"Thanks for the information, Twiggy. I miss you. And I miss the Spotlight."

"Take care of yourself, sweetcakes. I'll call if there's news."

A thorn stuck in Simon's heart as he raced through the briar patch of possibilities. What was going on?

CHAPTER NINETEEN

During his most recent telephone call with Wally Freeze, Simon had informed Wally that money had been wired to his account following the completion of a deal for *Bel Air Babes*. Simon tried again to convince Wally that he could successfully license new videos, but Wally repeated that new products were under contract with another distributor, and he remained unwilling to reveal the name.

Wally represented Simon's best hope for reestablishing his business. Even producers whose films he had not previously held in his catalog knew he had failed to appear at the all-important MIFED event in Milan and would never consider working with him. With the small number of potential markets remaining for the videos listed on the original contract with Wally, Simon's current business wasn't sustainable. Wally, despite everything, felt sympathy for Simon. Cocaine had overtaken the lives of many people during the 1980s, and Wally had not been untouched.

Since they'd reconnected, Wally expected Simon to contact him on a private phone to avoid contact with his office, which Simon respected, though Wally never gave a reason. Given the message from Don and the fact that Wally wasn't answering his personal number, Simon violated the agreement, which had always seemed unnecessary; after all, Simon had known Wally's office manager, Clarice, when she was Nicolò's secretary. Nicolò had refused to give Clarice a letter of reference when she resigned after bringing attention to the fact that during contract negotiations, Nicolò had included a film to which he didn't own the rights. Simon had recommended Clarice to Wally.

"Hello, Clarice," Simon greeted upon hearing her melodic voice.

"Simon?"

"It is."

"I've meant to contact you since, well, forever. Thank you so much for being my reference. Wally hired me right after I interviewed, then peppered me with questions about our experience working for Nicolò."

"And what times they were, huh? Moe? Remember him?"

"It seems like such a long time ago. Moe didn't last long after you left. Nicolò should have believed it when you explained how he was embezzling, not to mention his problem with alcohol."

"Nicolò knew, he just didn't care, not as long as Moe doctored the books to cut more taxes than he stole. I saw Moe on skid row, down by the Jesus Saves Mission, after I started my own company. It was only a few months after he attacked me in Nicolò's office."

Clarice bellowed a hearty laugh that brought back fond memories of joking around when they'd worked together. Clarice possessed a marvelous sense of humor.

"I wondered what became of Moe. It's sad, what you say, though."

"He was teetering on the edge of sane and dangerous. I mean, when he attacked me with the telephone from my own desk, he could have killed me."

"Oh, don't I know it. What an awful thing. Nicolò and I never spoke about that incident after you quit. I sure can't blame you for leaving."

"You're aware that I still represent Wally's videos, right?"

"Oh sure. Wally mentions it when you call him with news. Wally told me you aren't really in the business anymore. You were such a good salesman, Simon. Nicolò tried to say bad things about you, but it backfired. His clients told him they'd rather deal with you."

"Nicolò was a crook, and everyone knew it."

"Well, Wally is a nice guy, and fair."

"Have you heard what happened?"

"I wasn't going to bring it up."

"It's unfair that I judge Moe, you know. My problems ended up being as bad. Worse, really."

"Wally never mentions it, but I heard some things."

"When I didn't show up at the last MIFED, Wally came to the house and nearly beat the door down looking for me. The truth is, I was too stoned on cocaine to catch the plane to Milan."

"Oh dear."

"Wally didn't believe the cover story that I was too sick to travel."

"He is clever, and he's been around. It's funny hearing Wally talk to people. His voice changes if he's speaking to a female model whom he wants to be in a new video. When talking to the video crew, he's all business. I had to put my feminist views on hold when I started here. Wally isn't sexist on a personal level, but he has no qualms about exploiting tits and ass—God, am I even saying that? The need for a job compromises a person, doesn't it?"

"You know it, my friend. I wish Wally would allow me to market his new products. Then I might not have to leave the business. But I can't hold it against him, not given how badly I screwed up."

"Chanteuse Film Distributors has the contract on his new videos," Clarice said, then abruptly changed the subject. "Where are you these days, Simon? Wally only said that you moved away."

"Let's just say I'm far from Hollywood. I'm back in college and hope to start a career as an artist when I graduate. At least that's the dream. It would be nice to repair some of my business contacts and keep marketing video rights."

"I remember the paintings you hung in Nicolò's office," Clarice said, hoping to avoid more discussion of Wally.

"There just aren't many more contracts to be made on the list on my contract with Wally."

"There's another call coming in," Clarice interrupted. "I have to go."

"Before you hang up, have you heard anything about Charlotte, the woman who used to work for me?"

"It's probably best if you talk to Wally. I need to take the other call."

After Clarice hung up the phone, Simon kept the receiver pressed to his ear, pondering her last statement: "Best you talk to Wally."

Clarice knew something but was afraid to say. Could Wally and Charlotte be in contact—or in cahoots?

More unknowns to disturb Simon's troubled nights.

CHAPTER TWENTY

W as Thad in love with Felipe? Or had he fallen for one of the stars whose erotic sex scenes he watched while creating voice-overs? Simon imagined Thad, guilt ridden, afraid to contact him. Had their relationship always been one of convenience? Simon began to doubt everything he thought to be true about their relationship.

What had happened between the time Thad left the voice mail reporting that Emilio had stayed behind with Felipe when the others returned to Spain, and the appearance at the Spotlight? Who was the rough character, the limo driver? Emilio had once mentioned that his driver doubled as a bodyguard, and Simon had wondered why he needed a bodyguard, not yet aware of the company's shady dealings.

Simon began taking the hallway phone into his room, stretching the cord to its limit and placing it on a chair halfway between the door and the bed, even though, in the mansion, silent as a mausoleum, he would hear the phone from any room. Only once did Simon receive a call during the night, in a moment when the moonlight streaming through the wisteria-burdened trellis provided just enough light for Simon to find the phone.

"It's only me," Dean said, anticipating Simon's disappointment.

"Your friendly voice is always welcome. You know that."

"I do, but it's nice to hear you say it. I've been worrying that the conversation the other night with my friend Allie might have put you off. I can't believe we got so deep into theology—I rarely bring up Kierkegaard, even with fellow theologians."

"Philosophical discussions always intrigue me. Anyway, for a few moments, I wasn't thinking about Thad."

"You held your own, I'll sure say that. Sounds to me as though you have made the leap to pure atheism. I'm still on my existential bent—faith as a passion and all. It's a shame how different ideas tend to separate people. There is so much to learn from disagreement."

"People try to make sense of their lives based on their understanding—whatever it takes to carve out a place in this uncaring cosmos. Dean, my friend. Why are you calling so late? I know it wasn't to continue our discussion."

"I take it that Thad still hasn't called."

"Not a word. I hate leaving the mansion to go to classes. I always think—what if he calls?"

"Thad knows my number," Dean pointed out. "I've wondered if he might try to reach me, especially if he really did fall for one of those porn stars, or even that Felipe character you mentioned, as you have feared. Thad would want to get a message to you somehow."

"It's hard not knowing the truth. If Thad is being held against his will, Emilio and the others must have found out where I am. Why haven't they contacted me? Wouldn't they want their money back? Maybe hold Thad for ransom?"

"Thad went through so much to clean up his act," Dean said. "And no matter what happened, you two always got back together. You are two halves making a whole."

"What a sentimental guy you are!"

"One gets a little syrupy when they pass sixty and still haven't found the right partner."

"What about that fellow that was visiting you from seminary?"

Dean sighed deeply. "Allie and I admitted our feelings during the final year of seminary. We had yet to take our vows, but we understood the church's opposition to homosexual relations. One night, we shared a bottle of scotch and ended up in the same bed. I never mentioned it during confession. I doubt Allie did either. Having gay sex truly was the sin that dared not speak its name. That night remains my most cherished memory."

"I would venture it's Algernon's as well."

"We never refer to it. If we were to continue in our vocation, sex had to be put aside for the greater good."

Simon struggled for words. Anything he might say would sound hypocritical. Denial of his sexual orientation during his decade adhering to Sun Myung Moon's theology was just as severe as the vows taken by any priest.

Dean continued. "I had to respect Allie's decision. He admitted that he loved me, but he believed that allowing our love to grow was the wrong thing to do. He had always wanted to be a priest. Allie was the only man for me, so I became a priest alongside him. Allie embraced his celibacy as the supreme sacrifice. I felt it took me further from God, not closer, so I left the priesthood. Allie and I have remained friends all these years. Like I mentioned, he admits that he's gay but absolves himself by never having sex. I wish he'd leave the priesthood, but he won't even discuss it. No one will ever take Allie's place in my heart."

"Can we talk about something else? This is really depressing. I hate how religious beliefs mangled our lives. I've had it up to here." Simon touched the top of his forehead as if Dean could see the gesture through the phone line. "I am missing Thad more than ever."

"One last comment?" Dean asked sheepishly.

"It's not as though I'm going back to sleep anytime soon."

"Allie and I never understood how we could be so attracted to each other and at the same time be so sure of our calling."

"Biology, Dean, biology versus the force of ideas. Sometimes a person has to decide: follow their heart, or follow the ideas they accept as truth. My thought is that we can change our minds but not our feelings."

"You're a one-person dichotomy," Dean laughed. "Don't be too hard on Allie. He comes from generations of Louisiana clerics. He never envisioned a relationship with another man until we met at seminary—as ironic as that seems." Realizing he should change the subject back to the matter at hand, Dean asked, "Should you go to Los Angeles to look for Thad? The professors are quick to accommodate us nontraditional students. You can tell them you need time off."

"I've thought about it. I keep wondering if Thad is afraid to tell me the truth for fear I would go back to using cocaine. Maybe he's giving me time, thinking I will move on."

"If that's the case, he doesn't know you as well as I thought," Dean responded. "You'll never move on until you know the truth."

"Whatever the story, it's happening because I didn't go to California with Thad. I mean, it's not as though Thad is creating the sound of horse's hooves on a Foley stage with a pair of coconuts. He scrutinizes the intimate scenes of erotic passion and adds a sigh at just the right moment. How could he not be tempted? Thad is handsome enough to have whomever he wants."

"You're taking my breath away just talking about it," Dean quipped.

"Thad is only human—what was I saying about the power of biology?"

"One thing I know for sure: you never expected those Spanish guys to enter the picture the way they did. I wish there was something I could do to help."

"Being my friend is help enough, Dean. How many people can talk about pornography and philosophy in the same conversation? Well, other than the Marquis de Sade, of course."

"First Kierkegaard, now the marquis. You're the first person I've met in a long while who's well versed enough to talk philosophy and sex in the same breath. You obviously learned a lot during your time in Moon's church. For me, leaving the priesthood was the hardest decision of my life. I get why you bottomed out when you left Moon and why cocaine soothed the pain. If I had not held onto my faith in a benevolent God, alcohol would have been my escape. I don't know how you live without faith."

"I don't know either," Simon admitted, "but I just can't reconcile the facts of science with the suppositions of faith, something that always created a barrier between the rest of the family and me. Vivian nearly flipped out recently because she feared I rejected Genesis and believed in evolution. But there's no theory that supports the existence of a deity, so why waste time on God any more than on flying saucers?"

"Conversation for another evening," Dean demurred, realizing again how far they had moved from Simon's immediate concern. "I've been thinking about something. What if your friend Scott spoke to people in that organization of gay producers he represents? Maybe one of them has heard something about Howard, or about the people from Spain. I met Scott when I visited you, and I know you have a complicated history with him, but wouldn't he be willing to help?"

"The thought has occurred to me, but I'm not sure I want to get Scott involved. He can't keep his mouth shut, even if he is a lawyer, and if word gets around that I am looking for Thad, or someone mentions my name to the wrong person, that could make things worse. I should keep a low profile until I know what's going on."

"You're afraid Thad might come to harm, aren't you?"

"I don't know what to think."

"Are they really that fearsome?"

"From what I know, yes. When I was considering their offer to procure films, and Felipe explained that they wanted to launder money, he said that if I didn't go along, they might retaliate. I thought he meant they might badmouth me around the industry, but maybe he meant something much worse."

"I keep thinking that you should contact the authorities. You've done nothing wrong, after all. Not really."

"Except that the original deal wasn't completely on the up-and-up, either. I represented myself as owning exclusive rights to films that resided in the public domain. I'd rather not expose my international business dealings to scrutiny."

"But if Thad is in danger…"

"I know this sounds self-centered, but cocaine had been calling to me every single day since Thad dropped out of sight. I don't want the anxiety of getting the FBI or other law enforcement involved—not yet, anyway."

"It doesn't sound self-centered," Dean consoled. "I feel like getting drunk just thinking about all this."

"One puff from a crack pipe and all my troubles would end. That's the big lie, anyway. Getting high would trade worry about Thad for sheer insanity."

"Thad might be fine, wherever he is," Dean declared unconvincingly. "We don't know, after all."

"Until I know the truth, I won't rest."

"Let's have dinner before long, Simon. Maybe we can come up with a strategy to figure out what's going on."

"Dinner sounds nice, Dean. I'll let you know."

CHAPTER TWENTY-ONE

When Simon finally reached Wally on his private line, they spoke about a sale he could make to an Argentine submarket by dubbing *Bel Air Babes* in Italian. Then Simon asked, "Wally, have you heard from Charlotte since I left Hollywood?"

"She's no longer your secretary, right?"

"We definitely parted ways. I was just wondering."

"I'm willing to keep working with you, Simon, but only on the videos in our contract. I've made that clear. Nothing has changed."

Simon wondered what the contract had to do with having heard from Charlotte or not. Simon didn't get an answer to the question of Rudy's insistence that he contact Wally. He was convinced that Wally knew something, though his evasiveness wasn't unusual. Since they'd reconnected after Simon left rehab, their conversations remained strictly about sales.

Simon considered Dean's suggestion about going to Hollywood, even driving to Howard's ranch and confronting him about Thad. Two considerations stopped him. In the first place, since he'd never received a demand for money, he couldn't believe the Spaniards had abducted Thad. Secondly, having heard nothing directly from Thad increased the likelihood that he indeed was with someone else.

Simon felt helpless. Should he move on? During every class they shared, Blaine stated a conversation. Despite his repeated allusion to being involved with someone, Simon was sure that Blaine wanted to ask him on a date. Simon couldn't help feeling flattered. Someone as alluring as Blaine could have anyone he wanted.

Simon and Blaine often found themselves in the student union at the same time. When Simon took afternoon strolls along the creek that flowed through campus, he would see Blaine walking the same path. Simon knew the encounters weren't coincidental.

One pleasant afternoon, as a breeze rustled the leaves just beginning to fall from the oaks that populated the campus grounds, Simon bought a sack lunch at the student union cafeteria and took it to the creek, laying out his food on the redwood picnic table where he'd once perched with his friend Stanley to talk about the acid trips they had shared the prior weekend. Simon always made extra effort to engage Stanley in conversation because his friend too often secluded himself—a personality trait that had turned a hundred and eighty degrees when Stanley joined Sun Myung Moon's church and enticed Simon to follow his example. Simon had been impressed by the personality change following Stanley's conversion. Overnight, Stanley had transformed into a smiling, joyous person, no longer sullen and morose.

"This is a nice spot, isn't it?" Blaine asked, dispelling Simon's reverie.

"Nearly twenty years ago, I came here for lunch with a friend. It often seems as though my life is a spiral of recurring events. Déjà vu all over again, one might say."

"This is my first time to take college courses," Blaine confessed. "I should have attended in my twenties."

"You look so young, Blaine."

Simon expected Blaine to tell him his age, but Blaine played coy. "Have you been to the ballet?" he asked.

"Not here in Little Rock. I saw *Giselle* at the Palais Garnier once, but I have to admit that I fell asleep as soon as it started. The hypnotic flow of the dances and all. A friend told me that you dance professionally."

The comment seemed to disturb Blaine. Simon added desperately, "We don't have to talk about dancing."

Blaine sat down, his demeanor brightening as he tossed pebbles into the slow-moving stream. Eventually he said, "I'm older than I look."

"I want to know more about you, Blaine. You mentioned once that you'd like to have dinner—as long as it was just between friends."

"Let's set a day soon," Blaine said. "For now, I need to get to the studio. I work best when no one is around."

That night, Simon kept thinking about Blaine while guiltily hugging the picture of Thad and him at the beach.

Thad, my love, he thought. Where are you? What is going on with you?

CHAPTER TWENTY-TWO

S imon's studies in anthropology distracted him from worry
about Thad and deepened his confidence that leaving Sun
Myung Moon's group had been the right thing to do—obvious to
everyone who knew him, but guilt over having betrayed his faith
and abandoning his wife still troubled his conscience. If only he
had paid greater attention to his first anthropology professor and
developed a deeper understanding of the scientific method, he
might have been able to discern supposition and guesswork from
supportable hypotheses; he might have understood the deficien-
cies of the Divine Principle and recognized that ideas based on
assertion cannot be supported. How impressed his young mind
had been with the group's lecture on the parallels of history, which
led—it seemed inevitably—to knowledge of the specific date for
the appearance of the new messiah, and also whom it was. The
magnitude of assumptions about the existence of a God, the reality of a fall from grace, that something called sin affected human
behavior, not to mention acceptance of the supremacy of Christian
beliefs over all others, now overwhelmed Simon when he thought

about it. Though he found the ideas empty, he realized that cold intellect was no balm for a lonely heart.

Simon had joined Sun Myung Moon's fold because he thought he had found an international family to which he could belong—a place to be happy, to thrive. He joined because the group offered an escape from being gay, a way to avoid his fear that he'd never have a happy life if he tried to be himself. Acceptance of a creator god, belief in the primeval taint of sin, adherence to a set of revelatory authorities that pointed to Sun Myung Moon and his wife as the true parents of humankind seemed an equitable trade for his freedom. The irony, he recognized, was that he had been misguided from the start. Life isn't about happiness at any cost; life is about creating the best circumstances one can, given what one has to work with. Simon gave himself permission to love, to pursue his art and his education; he accepted the right to be himself despite what others wanted from him. Science made sense, and that was what Simon needed most—for his life to make sense.

Simon smiled thinking about his conversation with Dean and his friend Allie. For all the intellectual intrigue they'd touched upon when arguing for and against the need for supernatural beliefs, none of it mattered as he tried to sleep at night—he missed Thad! Save for the company of the lively Cicero and the braying Ferdinand, Simon felt more alone than he had at any point in his life. He despaired that his relationship with Thad could be reaching its conclusion. If so, he preferred it to end with a sense of finality, not as it was now, frozen in time, relegated to an aching void.

The highlight of Simon's day was his return to the mansion, the moment when he reached into the mailbox, felt for letters, and, violating his newfound atheism, prayed for a Dear John letter, even a ransom demand from the Spaniards—something!

One afternoon, as Simon exited the library and headed to the student union, he spotted Blaine, who appeared thinner, though little time had passed since they last spoke.

"Blaine, wait up," Simon called out. "You haven't been around lately."

"I hit a rough spot," Blaine replied cryptically as Simon caught up with him.

"Can I help in any way?" Simon couldn't imagine what Blaine meant by a rough spot.

"Just a lot of personal stuff."

"Sorry to pry," Simon pressed, "but you've lost weight. Is your health okay?"

The light in Blaine's eyes, which had flashed so brightly when he'd danced at the club, now seemed devoid of luster. Blaine started to say something but held back.

"You have my phone number," Simon reminded. "I'm at home any evening."

A smile briefly appeared, then faded.

That night, worried about Blaine, Simon called his number but got the answering machine. He left a message saying he looked forward to dinner sometime soon.

Simon stretched the hallway phone into his room before going to bed, an act that now served as ritual, dampening the ache in his heart as he hoped for a call from Thad. The phone rang just before dawn. Simon eagerly jumped to answer, but he heard nothing but the background noises of a crowded bar.

CHAPTER TWENTY-THREE

"You should visit Vivian," Connie chided as she worked in the kitchen while Simon brewed teabags to pour over ice for a fresh pitcher of the Southern necessity. She and Derek had come by the mansion when Simon confessed to living on microwave meals, canned foods, and the occasional pizza.

"It's hard to see Vivian in that place. I think about Mandy and how she spent her final years withering away."

"Bobwhite isn't the same as it was," Connie offered.

"Yes, but even if they cleaned up the facility, it's tragic seeing men and women parked in wheelchairs, waiting to die. Just take me out and shoot me like an old horse."

Connie grimaced as she stirred a pot of boiling potatoes, replaced the lid, and took a seat at the dinette table opposite Simon. Derek, entertaining himself by watching sports on the parlor television, bellowed a whoop as his team scored.

"Please don't be like that," Connie pleaded, recalling how close Simon had come to ending his life when he first arrived in rehab and one of his fellows had ridiculed him for being gay. Simon had threatened to jump from the nearby railroad bridge spanning the Arkansas River as a train approached. Simon never forgot the sound of Connie's voice calling to him, "Brother!"

"Suicide might be preferable to living in one's own filth."

"You have to trust in God." Connie stated the proclamation as much to convince herself as to guide Simon. "If we live to that point in our life, there must be a reason for it. Maybe it's God's will to test a family's love for one another."

"Really, Connie? That makes sense to you?"

"What else should I believe?" Connie asked, perplexed that anyone could see life's events as anything but God's will.

Simon dreaded such a discussion with Connie, sorrowful that he had gone from fanatical believer in Sun Myung Moon's divinity, convinced that Connie's Jesus had failed to create the kingdom of heaven on earth, to eventual atheism. He recalled Connie's and Derek's disappointment when he'd first arrived in Sibley after leaving the group and informed them that he had not come back to be a Christian. Simon had had no answer when Connie asked, "What are you, then?" Only recently had he come to see the question as irrelevant. To be human is to love, he thought now. Without love we are dead. That is what we *are*, creatures capable of love.

Still, God's will?

"Let me put it this way, Connie. How do you discern God's will from random events?"

"You believed in a man who said he was God. How did you know that was true? I have two thousand years of faith to depend upon—the faith of people who sacrificed their lives in order to believe. If the Bible wasn't true—if, as Paul said, Jesus wasn't resurrected—then I am a fool for believing."

Connie's response made Simon wonder if she and Derek had primed themselves for such a question. "Yes, but I admit to being a fool for believing in Sun Myung Moon," he said. "Two thousand years from now, there may be people who still believe in Sun Myung

Moon; his descendants might even rule the planet. But they will be just as wrong then as they are now. If the durability of beliefs is the measure of truth, we should all be Hindu."

Connie held her glass of iced tea close to her lips and gingerly sipped from the rim. "Jesus loves you," Connie sighed. "You try so hard not to believe. It's obvious to me that Jesus lives—I feel joy praising him when times are good and find comfort when I suffer difficulties. When Lenny was on his deathbed, I knew our savior would greet him in heaven, that Lenny would be free of pain in the loving arms of Jesus. How could it not be?"

"That just doesn't work for me, Connie. This life is all we have, and I want to make the most of it."

Connie reached across the table and tenderly placed her hand on Simon's. She had listened to his words but believed they came from his sense of loss, not from his understanding. "Losing Lenny was hard on you, Simon. I'm sorry he never said how much he loved you."

"Believe what you like, Connie. I am fine with it. For me, whether God exists or doesn't exist isn't relevant—other than a topic for debate."

Derek yelled out another whoop from the other room.

"You and Derek are happy," Simon continued. "You have beautiful daughters, you go to church, and you enjoy being part of the community. The words you read in the Bible comfort you. You are satisfied with the story of your faith. You just have to accept that it isn't for me."

"How do you know the right way to live if you don't read the Bible and you don't pray?" Connie asked.

Simon remembered his boyhood—to be an atheist in Sibley was to hail from Zenon.

"Consider this, Connie. People lived for hundreds of thousands of years before anyone ever heard of the Hebrew God or the Christian Jesus. Humans who cooperate survive, and those who sow discord die away. Caring about each other comes naturally. If you weren't a Christian and I wasn't an atheist—if we just sat down to a meal and talked about our relationships—we would find much in common. People are driven apart by ideas—perhaps the biggest risk evolution introduced."

"You should get back to your roots," Connie asserted. "Come to church with us."

Derek entered the room with a curious look on his face. "I'm not sure if the kitchen aromas brought me in or whether it was the conversation I overheard on the way."

"Simon was telling me how he's still searching for Jesus," Connie summarized.

Derek placed rough hands, the hands of a carpenter, squarely on Simon's shoulders. "You'll come around, Simon. I'll bet you find the Lord before your mother passes. Vivian may enter grace first, but you will discover your faith and follow her to glory."

"When Vivian dies, I will grieve because she's gone. I want to acknowledge the finality of that loss, not mask it with the idea that some part of her still exists."

"I find that a sad thing to believe," Connie said. "My prayer is that the Holy Spirit will touch your heart."

"Amen," Derek agreed.

"I'll be on the lookout," Simon offered sarcastically.

"Faith doesn't always make life easier to bear, but the glory that awaits is worth the struggle." Derek's expression shifted from glower to benevolence as he spoke.

Connie ran the mixer to mash the boiled potatoes as Simon and Derek set the table. Simon hoped the meal would encourage the bond their words threatened to destroy.

Simon observed Connie and Derek as they performed the simple act of passing the salt and pepper, giving each other a look that spoke of a deep connection, of abiding love—a relationship supported by family and friends, by their community of believers.

Vivian had averted her eyes when she thought Simon and Thad might be sneaking a kiss. If Simon and Thad as much as held hands at Sibley's grocery store, they might not make it home in one piece. "If God is love, why is some love wrong?" Simon recalled asking long ago. The same beliefs that provided comfort to Connie and Derek had always been a threat to Simon's happiness.

"I hope you go to visit Vivian," Derek said, taking a bite of peach cobbler topped with homemade vanilla ice cream. "Connie and I went to see her yesterday. She misses you."

"I will," Simon promised.

"She really does miss you," Connie added for emphasis. "She fades in and out, but she's still our Vivian."

"When is Thad coming back?" Derek asked. "He's been in California a long time, hasn't he?"

"Too long," Simon responded. Simon wanted to tell Connie and Derek about his worries—that Thad might be in trouble or that he might be ending their relationship for Felipe, but he didn't trust they would understand.

"Call us if you'd like to go to church on Sunday," Connie said as if their discussion hadn't happened.

"Thanks, Connie. I know you mean well by offering."

Derek shook his head almost imperceptibly, signaling for Connie not to keep pressing.

Simon wished he and his family had more in common, that they could speak honestly. For now, sitting down to a meal was family enough.

CHAPTER TWENTY-FOUR

Painting proved to be Simon's one source of comfort, allowing him to explore anxieties he barely considered consciously. A recently begun work consumed much of his time: a vertical canvas depicting a man engulfed in flames and holding the hand of a naked adolescent who stood in the foreground as if waiting for permission to enter our world. Simon stepped back, pondering whether or not to darken the background, but he realized he needed to distract himself in order to free his intuition as to how to proceed. Simon opened a box of photos stacked beside his painting supplies and took out several images from the day with Thad at Zuma Beach. Simon placed the photos side by side on a bench, reminiscing on a happy afternoon, a day that seemed as distant as a past life. Sadness prevented him from returning to work on the painting, so he went back inside the mansion to call Los Angeles, hoping that maybe Twiggy had some news. But Twiggy, drunk from his habit of giving a customer two drinks for a single and swigging the second one himself under the guise of a toast, expressed annoyance at the call and shouted that Don was gone for the evening. Simon knew he wouldn't remember the call, so he didn't concern himself about the reaction. Simon then dialed Scott, thinking that Thad might have been in contact in order to relay a message, but Scott insisted that he knew nothing about Thad. Simon believed him, if for no other reason than that Scott was drunker than Twiggy had been. Scott was unable to refrain from gossip, and if he had heard even a hint about Thad, he would have said.

Cicero, growing impatient with being ignored, clambered into the parlor and leaped into Simon's lap as he went through more pictures from his days in Hollywood, and they slid like playing cards onto the rug. Simon hugged his ever-loyal terrier and scooped up the photos. He and Cicero sat comfortably together until the grave silence of the mansion was broken by the clang of the 1950s telephone on the side table as it disharmonized with the purr of the Princess phone ringing in concert on the kitchen wall. It was Blaine.

"How about Friday night?" Blaine invited. "Let's meet for dinner at the Oyster Bar."

Simon knew that the Oyster Bar restaurant was renowned as a location for a romantic rendezvous, a quaint establishment whose advertisements played into the common belief in oysters as an aphrodisiac, one ad depicting a man and woman, arms intertwined, placing an oyster on the half shell against the lips of the other.

"Sounds nice," Simon responded, making great effort to keep from feeling as if Thad were listening on the other phone, even though Simon was sure, despite the choice of venue, that Blaine simply needed a friend.

Friday after class, Simon changed into tattered Jordache jeans and a baby-blue polo shirt and rehearsed what he might do if Blaine made a pass. Simon arrived early at the Oyster Bar, got seated at a table, and ordered a shoestring-potato appetizer, nibbling slowly as he watched the door, growing more apprehensive as the appointed hour approached—and passed.

Finishing his shoestring potatoes, Simon ordered a plate of hush puppies and drank two gin and tonics over the course of an hour. A meal between friends, Simon had told himself. Then why did he fear Blaine wouldn't show, and with that fear, the dread he always felt when a *date* stood him up? Perhaps Blaine was stuck in traffic, or worse, an accident had sent him to the hospital.

Simon paid his bill to the sympathetic waiter, a handsome man who had tried to engage Simon in conversation as he brought complimentary shots of Schnapps between the glasses of gin and tonic. Staggering to the door, Simon worried about getting pulled over by the county sheriff, sure that his blood alcohol was over the limit. Simon remembered what Arthur had once told him about Blaine, gossip that at the time Simon hadn't taken seriously since he knew that Arthur was attracted to Blaine and wanted to put Simon off of him. Arthur claimed, feigning a conspiratorial tone, that mental illness ran in Blaine's family, that Blaine himself suffered bouts of depression, that rumor had it Blaine's brother lived on the streets of Little Rock, refusing to let anyone provide help. Arthur tended to overdramatize, but on the misty-eyed drive to the mansion, Simon wondered if Arthur had been truthful. Simon desperately needed an alternative explanation for Blaine not showing up at the restaurant, rejection, by friend or lover, being the primary trigger that cast Simon into the abyss. A remedy awaited that Simon both desired and feared.

Along a deserted stretch of road, a few miles from Sibley's decrepit welcome sign, Simon turned onto a dirt trail, one of the many pathways carved into the woods to provide routes for fire trucks trying to navigate their way to blazes begun by a lightning strike or the mischief of local miscreants. Slumping over the steering wheel, anxiety brought forth a familiar voice: the angry god. Not the deity worshipped in temples and churches, but the demon of addicts, a ravenous spirit demanding appeasement through immediate sacrifice. Another voice, weaker, spoke in the cadence of the pastor who'd led him to baptism, a sermon overlaid by the patter of the Korean oratory that had lulled Simon into compliance on so many Sunday mornings at Sun Myung Moon's headquarters in New York: "Have faith, follow your heart."

Simon knew the location of holy places where the strong voice might be appeased, revealed to him upon arrival from Hollywood, sites where priests administered a white-rock sacrament—the holy wafer of Simon's addiction. Commencements would be ongoing at the Twelfth Street chapel, a parking lot of the Delta Express convenience store. The officiators would be waiting to escort those galvanized by sin—those guilty of denying their god—toward salvation, steps away, where for a price, holy men administered relief.

A vortex of darkness opened before Simon as he stared out the window toward a sky devoid of stars, the moon hiding its face behind clouds of shame, the deathly quiet broken when Simon fired the ignition, which throbbed as if humming a chant of blame. Was Simon not to blame for leading so many innocents astray to become disciples of the man claiming to be God? Sacrifice would quell the angry chorus and satisfy the hungry gods. He would offer his conscious mind, served up through the sublime administration of cocaine.

Simon backed out of the dirt fire road, his mind, functioning on autopilot, leading the way toward Little Rock—north on University Avenue, forward to the office building at the corner of Twelfth Street, a right turn bringing him to the Delta Express–adjacent tracts of low-income housing, government projects, dominoes lining dimly lit streets clearly in view—and waited for a guide to take him through to the inner sanctum. A coterie of priestly suppliers each claimed a corner for their particular denomination—here, release through heroin's grant of oblivion; there, dousing of reason through the energetic mania of crystal methamphetamine; and Simon's object of faith, the charity of a living smoke that doused all pain through escape to insanity.

166

No longer could Simon deny the pain he felt that Thad was gone, or entertain the folly that Blaine might replace Thad if he had left him for Felipe. This nonsense would end, and end now!

Simon watched for a hooded acolyte, cautious of the false wafers doled out by the ecclesiastics of trickster gods, those who substituted pebbles for the holy rock. Simon anticipated the aroma of rich white smoke, the sense of an ectoplasmic substance coursing through his sinuses.

Shadows captured his attention, shrouded figures that recognized his car, shadows slinking toward him from the interstices of the complex. Simon slowed his vehicle to a stop, shut off the lights, and waited for a cloaked figure's approach. Other motions caught his eye: men proceeding from the opposite side of the street, the tallest among them reaching beneath a loose-fitting coat to produce a rifle, its barrel aiming through the passenger-side window, and cold metal pressing into Simon's cheek.

Simon hit the accelerator, knocking the rifle askew, nearly sideswiping a parked car as he sped away, an eye on the rearview mirror as one of the ghostly men held a revolver at the end of an upraised arm, pointing the barrel toward the clouded sky. Two shots rang out, shots that echoed through the alleyways as porch lights brightened the dreary housing and curtains parted just enough to check on the action.

Simon had taken a step toward what he believed would be his inevitable death, the final payment of indemnity for abandoning his messiah, the ultimate retribution demanded from the Christian God for Simon's having led so many of his followers to Sun Myung Moon.

"Know thyself," Harris had advised, referring to Socrates, modified for Simon's benefit: "Forgive thyself."

Approaching the gray timbers of the mansion after parking beneath the sweet gum he'd planted as a child with Mandy, Simon entered the empty house as its caretaker, the role once occupied by Aunt Opal, who had gazed from the upstairs window of the room Simon now inhabited, concluding her life in Sibley after seeking the mysteries of spiritualism in exotic lands. Did Simon and his aunt share a common destiny that made them seekers unable to resist the lure of ancient memories? Was the mansion a yoke harnessed to their lives?

When Aunt Opal had pressed the lucky quarter into Simon's palm, she imbued a prescience that set Simon on a course of life he was yet fully to embrace. Aunt Opal now rested under the protection of her tombstone angel, while Simon continued living, trapped in a monument to his family's past.

Ferdinand brayed about his hunger, angry at being ignored. Simon opened the back door for Cicero, who had been frantically scratching at the threshold, and tiptoed across the dew-laden Bermuda grass, unlatching the barn doors and uncovering the painting of the man and adolescent boy consumed by flames. He placed the work under one of the halogen lamps and applied black pigment to the edges of the canvas, as if darkness itself would extinguish the flames and allow the couple to proceed. Ferdinand's incessant plaint grew louder as Simon neared the corral and scooped feed from an aluminum bin. The glow of a mercury vapor light, set high on a pole, reflected in the slit-like aperture of Ferdinand's yellow eyes.

"You're my pet devil, aren't you, boy?" Simon petted Ferdinand between his stubby horns as the goat withdrew to the more important task of eating. Simon filled Ferdinand's water trough from the garden hose, stretching it as far from the back porch as it would reach and adjusting the brass nozzle to stream water the remainder of the distance.

Cicero had been up to mischief before Simon let him out, and his tail—little more than a nub—tried to reach between his hind legs as he preceded Simon back inside. Only Cicero knew what he had done; a quick examination of the room failed to uncover the wet deposits on the rugs or the presence of unseemly odors. Simon lifted Cicero onto Vivian's bed and watched him sniff her pillow before nestling under the comforter, then went upstairs to check the answering machine. The darkness of the indicator light seemed to mock him. No one had called—not Blaine, not Thad, no one from the Spotlight, not even Dean. Simon dialed Blaine's number. No answer, not even a machine. Simon then dialed Howard's Antelope Valley ranch, the number he and Thad had used during their late-night calls.

"We're sorry, the number you have reached is out of order or is no longer in service."

CHAPTER TWENTY-FIVE

Harris spoke from experience when he told Simon not to support his sobriety with intellectual distractions that might inspire the mind's better angels but do little to illuminate the dark corners of the heart. Intellectual distractions were not going to comfort the little boy seeking a place to cry, the little boy unable to get Lenny's attention. Simon might come to understand through reason how Connie and Derek so easily lived a life of faith when a skeptical mind kept Simon questioning, their simple love contrasting with the troubled relationship of young Simon and his friend Ernie, the tumultuous relationship between Simon and Thad. But facing loneliness and despair, reason failed to hold back desire for solace through the absolution of cocaine.

Simon's happiest childhood moments had come through attempting to describe his inner life as he scribbled with crayons on the construction paper Vivian bought for him. Vivian had never understood how much Simon wanted to confide in her, held back by the fear of rejection if he told her what went on during sleepovers with Ernie—forbidden things, things that would make Vivian cry. Simon knew boys weren't supposed to touch each other, but he craved intimacy with Ernie. When Ernie had rejected Simon, puberty arousing in Ernie a desire for girls, the pursuit of art gave Simon access to an inner sanctuary. If only his communion with paint and canvas could hold demons at bay with the same force now as crayons on construction paper once had. Simon needed to know Thad's loving gaze, to feel the softness of Thad's hair touching his cheek, to listen to the sound of Thad's voice, feel his gentle breath, as they lay next to each other in bed.

With palette knives Simon furiously slashed paint onto a fresh canvas, allowing an image to slowly take shape, a semihuman figure holding a caliper as if to measure the enormity of a demon, followed by brushing a patina of dissonant hues over the natty surface—forceful acts that did nothing to quell Simon's desire to escape.

"Find a meeting!" Simon uttered aloud, hoping to summon willpower from his weakness. Simon threw a drop cloth over his painting and went inside the mansion to fill Cicero's water bowl and turn on a few lights so the cavernous structure would seem less foreboding upon his return. Then he got into the Pontiac and sat with the motor running, trying to press the accelerator but succeeding only when he pushed his foot with his hand. Simon drove as if in a trance to Asher Avenue, where he knew of a Cocaine Anonymous group. He nearly turned back as he approached the highway, afraid the car might drive itself to Highland Court, fear of armed drug dealers providing no deterrence. Simon knew the leader of the Cocaine Anonymous group would ask if he had been sober for at least twenty-four hours, and though he had not used drugs for many months, saying yes would feel disingenuous—he had sinned in his heart.

The group's meeting place on Asher Avenue reminded Simon of a Teamsters Union hall from a 1930s socialist propaganda film. As he entered through metal doors wide enough to accommodate a forklift, the leader of the Cocaine Anonymous group, a middle-aged man dressed in faded work shirt and khaki slacks dotted with splotches of white paint, had just begun introductions, making sure everyone referred to themselves by first name and last initial, and reminding them that whatever was said by a member should remain in the room. The eleven men and one woman sat in a circle of folding chairs under a bright overhead light that formed an island in the darkness.

Simon's eyes adjusted to reveal a mottled concrete floor, an abstract painting made by work boots scraping into layers of paint, each revealing an age of use—here some dancehall maroon; there, deeper in, an industrial green pointing to use as a die shop, an era also noted by a rusted sign on the front of the building. Simon took a seat and stared at the floor, discerning further patterns in the worn paint: That looks just like a map of New Jersey, and isn't that the Eiffel Tower?

The moderator, introducing himself as Quincy Z., interrupted Simon's reverie by asking participants to recite a credo. As they chanted, Simon finally looked into the faces of those gathered— Blaine sat opposite!

"My name is Simon P., and I am an addict." In saying the words, Simon felt the depth of their truth, remembering that, only a few blocks away, the priests of cocaine awaited, hands outstretched to offer indulgences as a reward for returning to the fold.

His anonymity defeated, Blaine hesitated, never announcing himself, then abruptly sprang to his feet, pushing back hard on the metal chair so that it collapsed onto the concrete with bouncing clangs.

Simon chased after him, calling out, "Blaine, please stop."

Blaine dashed across the street, ignoring Simon's plea. Simon waited for a break in traffic, arriving too late to prevent Blaine from dashing off in his aging Volkswagen. Simon hurried back across Asher Avenue and accelerated the Pontiac onto the street, in his hurry almost colliding with a pickup truck. Simon anticipated the route Blaine might take to locate the nearest drug dealer. Blaine had never seen the Pontiac, and even if he had, he would never expect Simon to follow him. Even so, Simon stayed two car lengths behind as they maneuvered toward Little Rock's east side, a neighborhood more dangerous even than Highland Court. Simon knew the area well, having faced gunfire while trying to get cash from a drive-through bank, the memory knotting his stomach as they drove past, then along Sixth Street, veering with Blaine toward an unexpected direction, Blaine perhaps worrying that the car matching his every move might be an unmarked police car—they were now the only cars on the road. Simon allowed more distance between their vehicles, sure at that point of Blaine's destination. Simon maneuvered the car into one of the bays of a car wash across from the dance club that dominated eastside social life, the car wash being the spot where Simon had often waited for a dealer going by the nickname BT, so named because people told him it was "'bout time" he showed up, given BT's tendency to arrive pitifully later than promised. If BT was in the vicinity, Simon didn't see him, but he recognized another of his suppliers, a character who went by the street name Snake. BT had explained that Snake earned the nickname because he was a snake in the grass. Simon suspected he'd earned it for a different reason, given the fellow's braggadocio about his physical attributes, which he said men and women both hired him to experience, tales Snake described to Simon in hopes of earning money for more than supplying cocaine.

After hours, the car wash, situated some distance from any streetlights, provided a relatively safe haven. Simon had been able to turn off the headlights and ease into the bay undetected by the people mulling about the club's entrance. If Snake or BT approached—two men who let nothing escape their attention—Simon's resolve might weaken. He didn't want to remain long in the area.

Crack houses dotted the east side, but the dance club was the focal point, with an alley across from the entrance serving as a gathering place for unemployed men to warm themselves during winter against rubbish fires rising from oil barrels and in summer to stand beside air vents from the manufacturing plants that walled the alley, men with connections to dealers higher on the social ladder who were sequestered inside the club. While Simon strained his eyes to see, Blaine's silver Volkswagen passed in front of the club, his arm hanging outside as a signal that he needed service.

Twice Blaine circled, but no one approached; even if his usual dealers recognized the car, they wouldn't want to be seen talking to him, as their peers would assume Blaine was a cop and believe he had become a snitch. Simon's technique had been to drive past the club and wait at the car wash. After his second pass, Blaine parked on a street parallel to the alley. Simon locked the Pontiac and made a stealthy approach to Blaine's window. Thinking Simon was a dealer, Blaine leaned his head out the window.

"Found you, my friend," Simon called out, breathless from the sprint to reach Blaine's car before he could drive away.

"Did you follow me?" Blaine angrily shot back. "Really?"

"Don't shut me out," Simon pleaded.

Blaine fixed his gaze, looking straight ahead as if thinking, This isn't happening.

Simon touched his shoulder. "You can talk to me. I understand." Blaine's pitiable expression tore into Simon's heart. He understood now why Blaine had so determinedly pursued a friendship with him.

Blaine's eyes fixed on a distant point.

"Can I get into your car?"

Blaine nodded.

Simon tapped the hood as he came around, mindful that Blaine might use the opportunity to escape, but Blaine pressed the button to unlock the passenger-side door and allowed Simon to sit beside him.

No words were required—that someone cared enough to make such an effort softened Blaine's resistance. Simon could hear the two voices in Blaine's head, the one insisting he push Simon away, then another, more convincing, urging him to take Simon into his confidence.

"Has this been going on for long?" Simon asked.

"What would you know about it?" Blaine spewed, the first voice dominating.

"You'd be surprised."

Blaine's hazel-green eyes glistened with emotion, his demeanor telling Simon that he had much to share as the second voice claimed victory.

"I was in a religious cult for ten years, and when I left, when I abandoned my faith, I turned to cocaine for comfort and escape."

"What changed, Simon? How have you stayed clean?"

"Can I make a proposition? A voice is telling you to put up with me long enough to make your getaway so you can score some coke. Here's an alternative. Let's go to my home in Sibley. It's about thirteen miles out in the country, very secluded. I have the property all to myself. Let's go there and talk. How about it?"

Simon saw the wheels in Blaine's head turning. If he didn't agree quickly, Simon would have to wait for another chance. Following him farther would be useless—this had to be Blaine's decision.

"All right," Blaine agreed. "Should I follow you?"

"How about this? I'll follow you to the university. You can park your car there; with the student decal, it won't get towed."

Blaine smiled for the first time. "Okay. We'll get on the freeway at the Broadway on-ramp."

"Perfect, and when you're parked, get into my car. It won't be more than a thirty-minute drive to Sibley. Are you expected anywhere tomorrow?"

"Well, kind of..." Blaine stammered.

"I don't know much about your situation, Blaine, just that you dance ballet. I'd love to hear about it."

Blaine brightened at Simon's interest.

"How long has it been since you used last?" Simon asked.

"It had been six weeks until the night of our date."

"Well, not sure how I should take that." Simon smiled. "True confession: I had not thought about using in months before you didn't show up at the Oyster Bar. Like I said, I understand more than you might think."

"Thank you for being kind." Blaine took Simon's hand, a gesture of gratitude and friendship—and yet the simple act sent pangs of loneliness into Simon's heart.

Thad had given Simon such a feeling with the mere brush of his hand. Surely Thad had not left him—but if not, what had happened? Was he being prevented from making contact?

"My car is over there." Simon pointed in the direction of the car wash. "When I pull up, head toward the university. I'll follow."

"Okay," Blaine said, then, noticing the expression on Simon's face, added, "Seriously, I will wait. You're afraid the minute you shut the door, I'll take off. I won't. I'm glad this happened."

Blaine remained true to his word. He parked at the university and climbed into Simon's car. They drove in silence. There would be plenty of time to share stories once they arrived at the mansion.

CHAPTER TWENTY-SIX

S ettled in the parlor with Blaine, Simon initiated conversation with tales of Sibley, introducing the story of JT and his gruesome death at the hand of marauders.

"My ancestor might have been one of them," Blaine sighed. "Our folks lived on the border of Missouri, and whether they said lived there or in Arkansas depended on which state the tax collector came from. My great-grandfather was a moonshiner, and others in the family were bootleggers in the thirties. Dad got out of it when he moved to Little Rock and began work as a truck company dispatcher." After a pause to eat cookies from a crumpled bag Simon had found in the kitchen cupboard, washing down a handful of broken chocolate chips with a sip of milk, and scrutinizing the way Simon was looking at him, Blaine added, "You probably think I'm younger than I am, I'll bet."

"Right now you look like a little boy with a milk mustache."

"How old are *you?*" Blaine asked. "You said you were with that Moon group for ten years, and then you had your own business in Hollywood. You must be somewhere in your thirties."

"Thirty-seven."

In the low light of the converted oil lamp sitting on the mahogany side table, Blaine looked about twenty.

"What if I told you that we're the same age?"

"I would never have guessed it."

"Maybe I froze in time when I left home at sixteen."

"Did your dad make you leave?"

"You mean because I'm gay? No. That wasn't it, though I knew I liked guys from the start. I mean, didn't we all jerk off to underwear ads?"

"Mom often wondered why her J. C. Penney catalog had some pages torn out. She never noticed they were from the men's underwear section."

"Now, that's funny," Blaine chuckled, then looked around the room. "This is such a grand place." Blaine pointed to the quality of the threadbare Persian rug and closely examined the parlor lamps. "I'll bet these bronze pole lamps once had Tiffany shades."

"They were gone by the time my aunt Opal died and we moved to this place from Little Rock. My father found these reproductions at a yard sale. You have a sharp eye to see they aren't originals. I should show you the upstairs gallery of our ancestors."

"I'd like that," Blaine replied, and he followed Simon up the narrow and steep staircase, each step creaking loudly in the mansion's otherwise deathly silence. "It must have been difficult to sneak out at night; these steps are impossible."

"Watch my feet." Simon touched the left edge of a step with his heel, skipped the next, then put his weight on the middle of the one above it, stepping on the middle of the next three and keeping to the right on the final two. Blaine repeated his actions.

"Remarkable choreography," Blaine laughed.

"Years of practice. It's a lot more difficult to navigate across the floor planks from the top of the stairs to my bedroom." Once they arrived on the landing, Simon demonstrated by stepping in several places to compose a creaky rhythm.

"How did you ever sneak out?"

"Held my shoes and slid with socked feet—that is if I didn't climb down the trellis outside my window."

Simon turned on a table lamp, throwing light across the ancestral portraits. "This is supposed to be JT, the guy they hanged." Simon pointed to a portrait awkwardly rendered in charcoal. "I doubt that's true, though; the style of the man's clothes is more like what people wore in the 1880s. And this one, this was my mother's favorite brother, Wesley. He died at eighteen, back in the 1940s."

"He looks like you."

"So I'm told," Simon mused. "Mother liked to compare me with him, which irritated me when I was a boy, but then I understood how much she loved her brother, and that Vivian was trying to tell me that I'd do well to be like him. Wesley was an exceptional young man who probably would have become an artist."

"Vivian, that's your mother?"

"Typical of me, not telling you the names of my *living* relatives. Yes, Vivian is my mother. She recently had to go to a nursing home after having a series of strokes. She was living here in the mansion when I came home from California about a year ago. My boyfriend, Thad, came a bit later."

"Where's Thad now?"

"Back in Los Angeles—to work. It's been a while since I've heard from him. I don't know what's going on."

"That must be difficult, not knowing."

"It is."

"You still love him?"

"Very much."

Blaine studied the portraits, pausing in front of one of the oldest charcoals. "This fellow looks like Chester. His eyes have the same piercing intelligence."

"Chester?"

Blaine ran a finger over the glass covering the ancestor's portrait, outlining the face. "That could be him."

"Is Chester the person you mentioned, the one you're involved with?"

"We're in kind of a similar situation," Blaine began. "I mean, just like you haven't had closure with Thad, it's the same with Chester and me."

"Arthur mentioned the name of the troupe you danced with, the Chester Manley Dance Company, right?"

Blaine grew sullen. "I was going to talk to you at dinner, but feelings overcame me that I don't handle very well."

"And cocaine seemed like a solution."

Blaine nodded.

"Let's go back to the parlor, but first I want to show you something." Simon took Blaine into his bedroom and flipped on the overhead light, which was dimmer than it might have been. Simon had unscrewed a few of the bulbs to make the light softer; the fixture, a conversion from the days of gaslight, was far too bright to create a romantic atmosphere when Thad was there.

"So many paintings!" Blaine exclaimed.

"The larger paintings are in the barn—that's where I have my studio. We can go out there later if you want to see them."

Blaine looked through the canvases, pulling them one by one from stacks propped against the walls. "I can't paint anything unless I am looking at it," Blaine said, noting how Simon worked from imagination.

"Look over here." Simon drew Blaine's attention to the window. "This is what I wanted to show you—my escape route." Simon drew back the full-length curtains and tugged on the stubborn window frame in an attempt to raise it. "It's a small feat to climb down the trunk of this old wisteria—if the darn window would open wide enough."

"I've never seen such a huge wisteria; that trunk must be six inches thick. I bet it would hold our weight, even as adults." Something caught Blaine's attention, and he pointed. "What's that across the street?"

Simon stood behind Blaine to see what he meant.

"Looks almost like a set of uneven teeth sprouting from the ground."

"You have a macabre imagination," Simon chuckled, poking Blaine gently. "That's the family cemetery—the streetlamp makes the marble monuments glow like that. Some of the people in those portraits are buried there. Aunt Opal's grave is the largest; she's the woman who lived here before we moved in. You can see her angel perching on a headstone...just there." Simon pointed until Blaine saw it.

"This mansion, and that cemetery—they're like memories that became solid," Blaine said with amazement. "I can't imagine being so connected to a place."

"I never appreciated any of it growing up," Simon admitted. "The older townspeople blame us Powells for everything bad that happens to them. Aunt Opal let people think she was a witch so they'd leave her alone. The newer residents don't know about our history, but even they cause trouble. There's a petition going around to have the mansion torn down as a fire hazard. The old-timers think that's a great idea—tear it down or let it catch fire."

"Well, I think it's special. It's your heritage, and it's beautiful. Take it from a descendant of scallywags and bootleggers. Let's go downstairs. I'll tell you about Chester."

Simon brewed some fresh tea and poured it into the family's rarely used green Depression glass, placing the antique pitcher on a silver tray with an ice canister. "This is a special occasion," he said, placing the service on a cocktail table in the parlor. "Tonight, we defeat our demons."

Blaine plopped a few ice cubes into his glass using the tongs Simon provided. "I've been drinking instant tea for so long, I'd forgotten how good fresh-brewed can taste."

"It's good to see you smile about something."

"At first, you made me angry, but thanks for following me tonight. I nearly fainted when you walked into the meeting hall. I had no idea about you. You seem so, well...straight."

"You didn't know I'd been through rehab? I figured Arthur would have mentioned it to you. He's such a gossip."

"I don't know Arthur that well. We've had a few classes together, and he's known Chester since he was a boy. Arthur doesn't brag about it, but he comes from a wealthy family; they helped Chester's dance company get started."

"I had no idea."

Blaine set down his glass, glancing wearily at his reflection in the tarnished silver tray. "Chester Manley," Blaine began. "I met Chester a couple of years after leaving home when I was eighteen. I had already started using heroin. A group of us used to hang out in Boyle Park."

"I know the place," Simon recalled. "My first boyfriend in high school took me there."

"The cops left us alone as long as they got a blowjob from time to time. One of them supplied heroin on the sly, drugs from the evidence locker that were supposed to be destroyed."

"That is a terribly early age to start using heavy drugs."

"At least I've stopped with the heroin," Blaine said, remembering close brushes with death. "Chester founded a dance company in St. Louis, modern dance and some classical ballet. He came from Little Rock, and when he got older, he moved the troupe here and focused on the classics. Many of his dancers remained in St. Louis, so he needed to find local talent."

"Did you meet Chester at the park?"

Blaine's chin touched his chest.

"There's no shame in it, Blaine. I know what central Arkansas was like in the seventies. The only way to meet a boyfriend was at someone's party or by cruising in the park."

"Chester Manley made me feel special, loved. He was suave and debonair—a classic. Ha. Sounds like an old Brylcreem commercial, doesn't it?"

"You and Chester became lovers?"

"Chester came to the park one evening. I don't remember what he said, it was so long ago, but I trusted him enough to get into his Cadillac and go to his home on a hill above the river. What I recall most is that we didn't have sex, not exactly. He wanted me to strip and get myself into various poses. All he wanted to do was, you know, please himself."

"Blaine, you are such a gentleman. I get the picture."

"I thought it was hilarious—the first sort of experience like that I ever had—and it was sexy in a way. I'd never thought about having a relationship with someone so much older than me. It wasn't the first time I entertained an older man, mind you, but the other times were part of the games I played to get money for drugs. Nothing serious."

"Chester sounds like a gem."

"We fell in love. Up to that point, I didn't think love was even possible, especially with a man so much older."

"Nothing wrong with that—love finds a way."

"Chester wasn't looking for a lover, and he didn't expect to find a young man he could mold into a dancer. He found both."

"Don't ballet dancers usually start out as kids?"

"Yeah, but in school, I had done well in gymnastics. Chester said that is what made it possible. He taught me in private for five years. When he introduced me to the company, he lied about my age, telling the dancers I had been studying since I was a boy. He said I was eighteen, but I was twenty-three—an old man to start out as a ballet dancer."

"As cute as you are now, what must you have looked like as a twenty-something!"

Blaine blushed as he took out his wallet and produced a laminated picture from his first outing with Chester's dance company—denim-patterned tights, codpiece, shirtless. "This is from Copland's *Rodeo*."

"Cue-tee!" Simon compared the photograph with the present-day Blaine. "Definitely the same person."

"I danced for several years," Blaine continued. "Dancing made me forget about drugs. I never used the entire time I danced with the company. I dreamed about joining a bigger troupe. When I auditioned, I nearly always got an offer."

"What happened?"

"Chester told me I wasn't ready. Each time, he said I wasn't ready. It took me a long time to realize that Chester was holding me back, that he didn't want to let me go."

"You could've struck out on your own."

"It's hard to describe a mentor's hold over someone so inexperienced in the world of dance."

"I'm not liking this guy," Simon fumed.

"By the time I felt confident enough to defy Chester and try one last time, I didn't receive an offer. By then, rumors had circulated about my age. A dancer may as well be dead at thirty."

"Blaine. I'm so sorry."

"Ha. Nothing anyone could have done. When I faced up to Chester's selfishness, I was so angry. I was ready to leave him."

"But you didn't."

"Who else was there in my life? Now Chester's in convalescent care."

"That's why you say you are still 'involved'?"

"Yeah. I spend a lot of time caring for Chester. He doesn't have any family. None of the dancers give a damn."

"You're a good man, Blaine."

"I suppose. And I know it's terrible to say, but honestly, sometimes I wish the heart attack and the stroke had done him in. He's miserable and demanding. He might once have been suave and debonair, but now he's just an ogre."

"You continue to care for him. That's noble, Blaine."

"Maybe, but there's a money factor. Chester's business manager continues to pay my rent, and there's money in trust for me. I started at the university to see if I could begin a new profession in art or theater, and I'm good at graphics. When I'm not in class, I'm mostly with Chester, or recently, going out to score on the weekends to do cocaine. That's the story. You're the first person I've even planned to have dinner with since before I met Chester."

"Not the story I imagined while sitting in the Oyster Bar waiting for you."

"I should have called you."

"We're two peas in a pod, Blaine." Simon excused himself for a moment and dashed upstairs, returning with his favorite picture of Thad from their day at Zuma Beach, a copy of the one Thad had taken to California. "My situation isn't the same, but I can't give up on the man I love, even if I don't know what is going on. This is Thad."

"You look happy."

"Thad is part of me."

"Ha, he's in your heart."

"I love him," Simon confessed.

"What were you doing at the CA meeting?" Blaine asked, sitting beside Simon on the couch.

"As I said, we're a lot alike. When you didn't show up for the date, that was my trigger. I don't handle rejection well, real or imagined. I went into autopilot and drove to the projects to score. A guy had a gun and shot into the air as I sped away. It was the jolt I needed to realize I should find a meeting. And there you were."

"What do I do now?" Blaine questioned.

"Let me take you to the rehab center I went to in North Little Rock."

"If I leave here tonight, it won't be to rehab," Blaine confessed. "I'll drive straight to the east side."

"You're forgetting, you don't have your car, and you're in the middle-of-nowhere Saline County."

"Ha."

"Let me take you to North Little Rock in the morning. Give me your keys and your home address. I'll park your car at your place and pick up some clothes and toiletries for you."

"Okay."

The next morning, Simon drove Blaine to Riverdell.

CHAPTER TWENTY-SEVEN

C hecking the mailbox one afternoon a few days after taking Blaine to Riverdell, Simon found a small package. He examined it and then collapsed onto the porch swing. In his shaking hand rested a parcel bearing a Spanish postmark. They had his address! Any comfort Simon had gained from believing that Sibley might be a remote place to hide now collapsed in a haze of fear. He left the package on the porch and went inside, taking care of Cicero as if nothing in his world had changed. He sat in the parlor, unable to move. Whatever the package contained, he couldn't bring himself to look. He considered throwing it unopened into the pond or tossing it in the corral to allow Ferdinand to make mince of it.

Before his recovery, Simon had rarely sought help from anyone, but he was different now. Just as he had found solace in rehab and was able to help Blaine as a fellow addict, Simon didn't need to face this event alone. He telephoned Dean.

"Can I come over? Something has happened, and I can't deal with it by myself."

Dean heard the trepidation in Simon's voice and knew it must be serious. "Of course you can, Simon."

Upon his arrival, Dean poured glasses of Saint-Émilion, Simon's favorite wine, while eyeing the package resting on his lap as he settled into the wingback chair, a favorite spot whenever he visited, and one denied him when he'd entered into theological debate with Dean's schoolmate and would-be lover, Algernon. Simon had felt he was being displaced, not just in terms of seating priority but in Dean's affections. Simon held an admiration for Dean that bordered on attraction, aware that Dean's amorous feelings toward him were held back by his respect for Simon's relationship with Thad.

"If the Riverdell counselors saw one of their alumni drinking alcohol, they'd go into conniption fits," Simon told Dean, holding the wine glass up to the light to admire the translucent garnet hue.

Dean started a conversation to set Simon at ease. He had already noticed the postmark and knew it must have something to do with Thad. "Do you sometimes visit Riverdell? That place had such a positive influence."

"Visited just the other day, as a matter of fact." Simon took a sip of wine. "I was going to fill you in but haven't had a moment, with school and all. And then you called."

"How's Harris, the counselor who worked with you? I'd like to meet him someday and thank him for helping my good friend find himself. Counselors don't collect many success stories. I know from experience."

"Harris wasn't there."

"You mean not at work?"

"No. I mean he was gone from the rehab center."

"To a better job, I hope. He must be terrific at what he does."

"If not for Harris's approach to recovery, no telling where I'd be. The administrator of Riverdell welcomed me with a big hug and praised the fact I had returned to school. He wanted to chat, but I explained Blaine's situation and that he wanted help. There wasn't an opening, but because it was me asking, the administrator found a bed."

"Blaine? The dancer we talked about?"

"One and the same. Blaine sort of stood me up. You know me well enough—I don't handle any kind of rejection very well, and like an idiot, I went looking for drugs, which didn't work out, thankfully. I decided to attend a Cocaine Anonymous meeting on Asher and found Blaine already there. I persuaded him to follow me to the mansion; we talked all night, and in the end, he agreed to go into rehab."

"Who would have thought…Blaine is so talented." Dean paused. "You're going on dates again?"

"Not really. But I was lonely, and I mistook Blaine's interest in me, and I don't know what I was thinking when we planned to meet for dinner. He didn't show, and that set me off. Blaine's interest came from his knowledge that I had used cocaine and wasn't anymore."

Dean was about to ask about the package, but Simon continued, "Do you know anything about Chester Manley?"

"Of course, the dance company, I'd forgotten the name when we spoke earlier. The newspaper featured him in an article not long ago, saying the dance company has been in financial difficulty since Chester entered a debilitated state of mind."

"Turns out Blaine and Chester have been together since Blaine's teenage years. Chester lives in a convalescent home now, and during most of his free time, Blaine attends to him."

"There's nothing nice about getting old," Dean lamented, reaching for his glass of wine with one hand and rubbing his lower back with the other. "I know of what I speak."

"Blaine and Chester developed a complex relationship over the years; it's hard for Blaine to move on."

"I'm glad you took him to Riverdell, but it's too bad Harris won't be there to counsel him."

"At first, the administrator didn't want to tell me what happened, afraid the news would affect me, but I told him the value of Harris's approach was to put me in touch with myself, not to make me dependent on him personally."

"What happened? It sounds dire."

"During my stay, Harris didn't speak much about his private life, but it turns out he had a glamorous girlfriend. The administrator practically glowed when he talked about the photograph of her Harris had showed him. Seems the girlfriend made demands."

"Demands?"

"She treated Harris as her sugar daddy, threatening to leave whenever Harris failed to provide—reminds me of every guy I fell for in Hollywood before meeting Thad! Harris finally put his foot down, so the woman left, but he followed her to Oregon. The rest is sketchy, but the assumption is that Harris became desperate for money, hoping to win her back. He's in prison for attempting to rob a bank in Portland."

"You're joking!"

"Nope. I wish I were."

"I'm so sorry to hear it."

"I consider it a cautionary tale. A person mustn't depend on others for their sobriety—much less for their happiness."

"On that note, perhaps you should tell me about the mail you received. I see the postmark."

Simon handed the package to Dean. "I can't bring myself to do it. Will you open it?"

Dean took the parcel and gingerly pulled tape from one of the ends, unfolding a flap of brown paper. He suspected what it was before taking out a boxed videocassette. His countenance fell as he turned to the back and studied the film stills used as advertising. Dean slid out the cassette and inserted it into a player on top of the television. He handed the box cover to Simon. "Look at the stills on the back."

The front advertised an X-rated gay film titled *El Amigo Rico*. Simon turned the box over and dropped it to the floor as if it had caught fire.

"I'm glad you came over before seeing this," Dean said.

"My God," Simon said, only half listening to Dean's words. He picked up the box. "That's Thad!"

"I'm sure of it," Dean agreed.

Simon rushed to the hall bathroom and locked the door as he burst into tears and threw up in the toilet.

"Are you going to be okay?" Dean asked when Simon returned, the front of his shirt wet from splashing water on his face and neck.

"What did I expect? The sexiest men on the planet surrounded Thad day and night, and he's had to imagine how they feel having sex so he can add his voice. But for Thad to do this and not tell me!"

"But look at the expression on Thad's face." Dean pointed out one of the images. "Something isn't right."

In the image, Thad and Felipe sat on either side of a heavyset man, the "rich friend," whose face was obscured, but Simon recognized the body—it was Emilio!

Simon took the remote from Dean's hand and pressed eject to release the tape. "I can't do this right now, not the way I feel. I'll call and let you know what I think is going on after I watch it."

"If you need me, I'm here," Dean offered.

"I thought Thad genuinely loved me. But how does anyone know what's truly in another person's heart?"

Simon drove around for hours, passing through parts of the countryside along the Saline River he had not visited since Lenny took the family on Sunday afternoon excursions to see the blooms of redbud and dogwood in early spring and, in autumn, the vivid colors of maple, walnut, black gum, and sassafras trees. Simon recalled the first time he saw hedge apples nestled among the sumac along the roadside and cried for Lenny to stop the car so he could collect some and carry them home, thinking it would be fun to smash the bright green, mace-shaped fruits against the planks of the gray barn.

Arriving at the mansion shortly after dusk, Simon left the dreaded videotape in the Pontiac and walked around the mansion to the corral, giving Ferdinand his evening grain and standing silent to watch as the goat ground the food between his broad teeth, jaw mechanically moving side to side. The beast, gazing up at Simon with yellow slit eyes, seemed to neigh a mocking taunt. Simon felt cursed by cosmic powers beyond his ability to reason away.

"You are Satan, aren't you?" Simon inquired of the innocent goat.

Ferdinand neighed desperately for Simon to pour additional feed into his trough.

"You have your priorities sorted out, don't you, Ferdinand?"

The radioactive cargo remaining secure in the Pontiac, Simon pulled the tarp from a painting he had been working on, an abstract design that allowed him to explore his feelings for Thad through expressive brushwork and slashing palette knife, colors battling for priority, sometimes in harmony, at times dissonant, complicated emotions seizing each moment, fear that he would never see Thad buttressed against refusal to believe it—potentialities now manifest in the toxic video. The painting vaguely depicted sky, land, and sea, with figures trapped in the dark web of a matrix that united the design, and the composition was informed by the photograph of Simon and Thad standing side by side, gazing into the Pacific.

Simon loaded brushes with paint and began to work, avoiding the inevitable viewing of what he expected to put the mystery to rest, the effort unable to dispel the replaying in his mind of conversations with Thad about whether or not he should work for Howard, each memory a path to self-condemnation for not protesting more strongly; then, a disturbing thought: What if, in the recesses of desire, Simon had wanted to be free of his relationship with Thad because he felt undeserving of love such as his? Or worse, what if lurking demons had wanted him to regain his freedom to smoke cocaine? Simon tried but failed to reconstruct the reasons why he had not gone to California with Thad—or why, if Thad deplored living in Sibley, they could not have moved to New York as intended when Simon drove away from Hollywood. Then, moving to New York was a fantasy fueled by cocaine, but now he could manage it. After all, Simon knew the city well from his days as a leader in Sun Myung Moon's apocalyptic army.

Simon retrieved the videotape from the Pontiac, let an anxious Cicero out the back door, and went into the parlor where Vivian and Thad, often joined by Connie, had watched their tapes of daytime dramas. It seemed wrong to insert *El Amigo Rico* into the same machine, remembering how Vivian would chastise a soap opera's character for adulterous behavior. Simon had noted Thad's bemused smile as he nodded in agreement. Simon slid the cassette into the machine and felt it snap into place. A rolling image at the start indicated the poor quality of the technique used in the transfer from a master tape. The US distributor had not bothered to translate the credits into English or to dub the opening voice-over; even so, Simon easily discerned the setup.

In the opening scene, a wealthy man, as evidenced by his Brunello Cucinelli suit, rode in a limousine with two young friends. They were setting out for sexual adventure, the point of view from the front passenger seat allowing the viewer to participate as a voyeur. Emilio—el amigo rico—sat between Thad, who was dressed in jeans and the powder-blue pullover that Vivian had given him, and Felipe, wearing yellow slacks with a blousy white shirt and ascot. Thad's hair was disheveled as if he had just gotten out of bed, while Felipe's hair looked professionally styled. Felipe kept the professional demeanor of a seasoned performer, squeezing against Emilio to fit himself into the camera's narrow field of vision; Thad's awkwardness set him apart.

Someone who didn't know Thad would have seen in his expression the anticipation of debauchery—the effect intended by the editor, whose uneven skills gave the scene a quality little better than a home movie. Awkward close-ups of Thad's downcast eyes shifted jerkily to reaction shots of Felipe, then panned to Emilio, staring directly into the camera as if to convey, with unsavory glee, "This could be you."

Occasionally, the editor inserted establishment shots. Simon recognized the Capitol Records building as seen from the Hollywood Freeway, followed by the exit sign for Cahuenga Boulevard. The car veered south and turned right onto Selma, the establishment footage giving way to a handheld camera positioned outside the passenger window in order to focus on a vertical sign: Spotlight Bar.

This was shot the night Twiggy and Don had seen Thad with Felipe and the limo driver.

The handheld camera followed the trio along the sidewalk until the cameraman rushed ahead to catch Felipe entering through the heavy curtain that separated the mundane world from the Spotlight's inner sanctum. Thad followed, holding the curtain for the limo driver. The cameraman never entered the bar, and neither did Emilio. During the time Thad, Felipe, and the driver were in the Spotlight—when Twiggy and Don saw them—the editor chose to show a montage of hustlers on Santa Monica Boulevard waving at cars or approaching men on the sidewalk, interspersed with shots of hustlers standing on the streets of Gaixample, the cruising section of Barcelona that Emilio had pointed out during a sightseeing tour with David and Irene.

Simon remembered Twiggy saying that Thad wanted to get his attention. If Don had not gone to dinner, he surely would have figured out that something was wrong. Thad would never have consented to a scene being shot in the Spotlight, even if he had agreed to perform in a video, which Simon now doubted.

The video made clear that the limo driver was indeed a bodyguard, positioned to ensure that Thad, and perhaps Felipe as well, were unable able to make a break for it. Simon recalled how Felipe had begged to be taken to America upon his return.

In the scene following the hustler montage, Felipe, Thad, and the swarthy limo driver exited the Spotlight, accompanied by an additional young man that Simon didn't recognize, ostensibly someone picked up at the bar. The voice-over continued in Spanish, but Simon caught the drift: a third boy from the bar had been recruited to provide entertainment for "the rich friend" who waited inside the limousine.

Emilio must have made the fateful associations listening to Felipe talk about the young man providing sound effects and then wormed more information from Thad, who didn't realize that what he was saying would reveal his connection to Simon. Emilio knew how to charm with the tact of a devil's minion. Thad's friendship with the owner of the Spotlight would have been easy to ascertain from Howard. Howard and Emilio had already had plans for a video. Whatever the original story, it would have been easy to incorporate Thad and include a scene at the Spotlight, where people knew Simon, where Emilio could be sure that someone would tell Simon about it, even before completing the video and mailing a copy to the mansion, an address he surely forced from Thad. Simon could only imagine Emilio's plan. Maybe the idea was to make back the stolen money by exploiting Thad, and a fringe benefit would be Simon's suffering upon receipt of the video.

Simon had to find Thad. Would Scott provide some lawyerly sleuthing with his gay producer clients, perhaps weasel a new phone number for Howard Price? What about Sweet Peter, the bartender at The Pub—might he be able to track down Howard for him? What would Howard say if Simon confronted him? Emilio could have absconded with Thad, telling Howard he'd left of his own accord. What reason would Howard have for stopping his new partners from abducting Thad, even if he knew their intent?

Simon paused the video before reaching the scene depicted on the box cover. He telephoned Dean and broke into tears.

"This has to be hard for you," Dean consoled. "Do you want me to drive out to Sibley? I don't mind."

"No. I'll be okay."

"I am here for you. Please call if you need me."

"I'm already convinced that Thad is in trouble and that he didn't want to make this video. One of the first segments was shot at the Spotlight!"

"Then I was right about something being off about the look on Thad's face."

"Howard Price might have sold Thad to the Spaniards. Such things happen."

"I hate to even think about it."

"Thank you for being my friend, Dean."

"Seriously, call me if you want me to drive out there."

"I will—and don't worry, I won't go looking for drugs."

"That possibility had crossed my mind."

Simon returned to the video. More establishment shots put the group on Cahuenga, driving north, before a jump cut to stories of other threesomes, each including Emilio. Simon fast-forwarded and realized that Thad appeared in only one more scene, the one depicted on the box cover. Simon cued it up and braced himself, but nothing could have prepared him for recognizing the same hotel room where he, Felipe, and Sören had engaged in sex with Emilio while they were using cocaine. Thad was in Barcelona!

The camera panned from a close-up of Thad and Felipe servicing Emilio to pause on a framed photograph—the picture of Simon and Thad at Zuma Beach!

The unholy trinity of Emilio, David, and Irene were sending a message with *El Amigo Rico*: they owned Thad.

Simon wished they had sent a hitman instead.

CHAPTER TWENTY-EIGHT

Had an avenging angel been released to cause misery for Simon's abandonment of the faith that had sustained him for so many years, unleashed by a callous deity treating Thad as a pawn in its jealous game? Simon wanted a god to blame but found only himself as he directed his anger at flesh-and-blood Emilio, David, and Irene.

Simon needed information, and the best place to start would be Scott's connections to the world of gay pornography—if only Scott could manage a coherent response.

"Shy-mon? Let me shee," Scott slurred. "I used to know shomeone by that name. I think he died or shomething. Don't tell me you're his ghost. Da-yum."

"Knock it off, Scott. I realize I haven't stayed in touch, but neither have you, neither of you, you or Sandra. And to think we were best friends, the three Ss."

"Aw, c'mon, Simon. When would Sandra call? She passes out when she gets home, and if Maury found a call to Arkansas on his phone bill, he'd blow up."

"Maury's a jerk."

"Tell me something I don't know," Scott sighed, followed by a long pause in the conversation and then a cough.

"You're hitting a joint, aren't you?"

"Yeah, *cough*, and why the fuck not?"

"No reason, I just didn't expect you to answer, considering that it's a workday; I thought the message machine would pick up. I didn't want to risk a call to the office and getting you or Sandra in trouble. Maury lost the Sun Myung Moon account because of me, and I know his resentment runs deep."

"Wouldn't'a reached me if you had called."

"Why is that?"

"Yeah, ol' Maury, he threw me out of the office."

"You mean you got fired?"

"Uh, well, yeah, Maury threw me out. Building security pushed me onto the sidewalk. Guess that *is* how I got fired."

Scott's inability to focus, even when sober, raised the question of how he'd ever managed to pass the bar exam.

"I'm sorry you and Maury fell out."

"Fell right onto the concrete," Scott laughed. "Landed on my feet, though."

"Tell me."

"The Gay Filmmakers Association. Now I have more work than ever."

"That's why I'm calling, Scott. I need information."

"That's me, Miss Information."

"Does Chatsworth Price Productions belong to the group you represent?"

"Howard Price? Why'd you bring up that guy?"

"Why not?"

"Howard's the reason Maury threw me out."

"You mean it wasn't because you showed up drunk?"

"Well, yeah, I *was* drunk...but that's not the reason. A friend of Maury's put him in touch with Howard, said he needed representation on a freedom of speech, uh, pornography case. I don't know...something to do with a state law somewhere in the South."

"I didn't think Maury handled porn cases anymore, not since his partner retired."

"Money, Simon. Come on. You think Maury would turn down a large retainer? Man, oh man, Maury flipped when Howard recognized me. After Howard left the office, Maury made me tell him everything. Was he ever pissed that I'd been moonlighting."

"I'm surprised you hid it from him as long as you did. You're not exactly tight lipped, Scott."

"Not what blondie here said last night. Hey, what are we talking about exactly?"

"Scott, stay focused, something serious is going on. I need to reach Howard Price. Thad's in trouble, and Howard is part of it."

"What do you mean, trouble? Thad told me he was making good money."

"When did you talk to Thad?"

"It's been weeks, maybe, I don't know. What's going on?"

"Thad hasn't contacted me in months. I thought for a while that he might have found someone else and didn't want to talk to me."

"Thad would never do that, not with everything you and he have been through."

"And that includes you and Jerry giving Thad cocaine, but hey, water under the bridge."

"I get it. I'm a pig, and Jerry is long gone. Tell me what happened."

"A video arrived in the mail from Spain. It's made by the Spanish company that sent the money Charlotte stole. Thad's picture is on the box cover, and he's featured in the video. It's horrible, Scott."

"Holy crap! Thad went to work for them?"

"In a way, I wish it were that straightforward. Howard went into partnership with the company, not knowing about my association.

The owners showed up at Howard's ranch from Barcelona. They brought a porn star named Felipe with them, and Felipe struck up a friendship with Thad. Felipe knew me from Barcelona. He told me about the illegal money laundering and warned me not to go into business with them. The Spaniards must have figured out Thad's connection to me and forced him into making the video—payback for the stolen money."

"You sure Thad didn't volunteer?"

"I'm sure. For one thing, the camera lingers on a photo of Thad and me at Zuma Beach—Thad's favorite picture of us. Thad would never have allowed them to use it that way, not if he had a say in it."

"You're thinking he's like a sex slave?"

"Something like that."

"I'm feeling sick."

"If you hear anything about the video—it's called *El Amigo Rico*—let me know."

"Before or after I watch it?"

"Don't joke, Scott. This is serious."

"Not joking. I want to see for myself. This isn't easy to accept."

"If you see it, pay attention to the scene with Thad and Felipe in bed with the much older man—it is staged in the same room, with everyone in the same positions, as a real event with Emilio, Felipe, and me. When I saw the scene, I knew they took Thad to Spain."

"I never mentioned it before, but I heard bad things about those Spanish guys after you told me what happened with the money. I thought you'd figure something out, manage to pay them back somehow. You always seemed to come up with a plan when things went wrong."

"Cocaine took control of my life, Scott. By the time Charlotte stole the money, I was too far gone to think straight. If I'd been even a little sane, I might have found her before she spent the money, or I could have found a way to deliver the films I was supposed to procure with the money, but I was lost. You don't know how bad it got toward the end, Scott. I'd already run away from Hollywood when Charlotte took the money. The terrible thing is I knew Thad was in a dangerous situation at Howard's when he told me about the Spanish clients showing up."

"You should have said something," Scott scolded. "There're no secrets in the porn business. Hell, there aren't secrets in Hollywood; everyone figures out what's up eventually—look at what happened with Maury and me. And now this!"

"I've no idea what they'll do to Thad, especially if he tries to get away from them."

"Now that Howard and Maury are pals, I'll bet Sandra knows how to reach him. Howard didn't come to the last conference I put together for the producers; Maury probably told him to cut ties if he wanted the firm to represent him."

"I'm glad Sandra still has her job."

"Maury will always have a crush on Sandra. She's there until she wants to leave."

"What's Sandra's home number? I'd have to dig around to find it."

Simon heard Scott pop the latches on a briefcase and rummage through papers. "Why don't you just call Maury's office?" Scott said, giving up the search. "Sandra should be the one who answers. Maury doesn't have a receptionist—again. He scares away everyone with that temper of his."

"Be sure to call if you hear anything, Scott. Don't misplace my number."

"I promise. I'll write it down off the phone's caller ID."

Simon braced himself for the call to Maury's office. So much history had passed between the three Ss, the musketeer party animals that had ushered him from a life of faith to a life of choices. Simon didn't blame Scott or Sandra for introducing him to sexual promiscuity and illicit drugs, but that introduction had set him on the path toward the ultimate fork in the road: take responsibility for his actions or surrender to gods, chemical or supernatural. Harris had ushered him into his new life, an existence without mystical guides or cosmic purpose—a simple Simon, free to set his own course in life.

Stepping out the back door and leaning against the porch railing, he watched the sun's rays dip below the horizon and bats begin to stream from the eaves of the barn, a black liquid pouring from the rafters to form a smudge on the twilight sky. The camp soon dispersed into a mist that hung over the swamp to gorge on hatchling mosquitos, with straggler bats swooping low through the cypress limbs to feed on psychedelic garden spiders.

Simon returned to the deafening silence of the mansion, steeling himself as he sat by the phone in the parlor, then slowly dialing, setting down the receiver, then dialing again. Sandra failed to answer as Scott suggested she would. Instead, an unknown receptionist came on the line, carefully articulating the name of the firm as if reading from a business card. Simon hesitated but ended up giving his real name and asking if Sandra was available.

The receptionist introduced herself as Sandy Purchase. "I know a lot about you," she said.

"Good things, I hope," he said, but he knew that any new receptionist would have heard the worst.

"I'm not sure *good* is the word."

"Have you lived in Hollywood a long time?" Simon asked. The name Sandy had a familiar ring to it.

"Not really," Sandy responded, half covering the receiver with her hand, causing a muffled sound that made her difficult to understand. "I knew who you were before I moved to Hollywood."

"Lyle's Sandy?"

"I have to be careful that no one hears me," Sandy whispered. "Maury thinks I'm Sandra's cousin, and he thinks I have experience as a receptionist. I've never answered phones in my life!"

"Where's Lyle?"

"Hasn't Sandra told you?"

"I've been away."

"Lyle and Sandra shacked up months ago." Sandy reported her news in menacing tones. "Lyle's a bum. We were in Orange County. He took my money and split, so I reported him to the cops, and now there's a warrant out for him. Lyle told me all about Maury's firm and about Sandra, Scott, and you partying on some church account—sorry I didn't get a chance to meet that Scott guy, but he got kicked out before I started here. Anyway, I followed Sandra home one night, figuring she'd know where to find Lyle, but there he was, living at her fucking house! Sandra can have the bum for all I care—I just wanted my money. I called the office the next day and told Sandra to help me out or I'd call the cops on Lyle."

"Sandra arranged the receptionist job for you?"

"She did, and it's nice. Sandra's a bum too, but at least she got me this job, and she's forking over cash from her paychecks until the money Lyle took is paid back."

"Fascinating story, but is Sandra there now? I need to talk to her."

"She's entertaining one of Maury's clients. She does that a lot, especially with this new guy—Maury said he's a cash cow. I guess that's like a golden goose or something."

"Must be," Simon agreed. "Can you give me Sandra's home number? I've misplaced it."

"What's it worth to you?" Sandy asked, but when Simon moaned, she continued, "Just joking. Hey, I'm not *that* bad."

Silence.

"Here it is." Sandy read the number from a Rolodex—Simon could hear the squeaky wheel, familiar from the days he'd hung out in the office and watched Sandra scroll for a client's number when Maury asked, rapidly twisting the knob on a Ferris wheel of business cards. "When you talk to her, tell Sandra not to leave me alone at the office so much. Sooner or later, Maury's going to give me something to type, even if I do keep a Band-Aid on two fingers as an excuse—I told Maury I reached into a drawer and got cut on a razor blade that Sandra used to slice letters from cardboard for an office party. Sandra gave me that story, told me to mention workers compensation if Maury challenged me—don't even know what that is, but it sure shut him up."

Relieved to be free of Sandy's unpleasantness, Simon took the first opportunity to end the call and telephone Sandra.

On to call number three of the day. Sandra answered with the sultry voice Simon recalled from the days when he'd first hired Maury's firm to represent the church against ordinances designed to prevent soliciting money from the public, when his offices were still in New Orleans. Sandra's sympathetic conversation had comforted Simon when he'd hired the firm for representation against a Texas sheriff who'd dragged him out of his van and thrown him to the ground, drawing blood as he pressed Simon's head into gravel, angered that Simon had brought Moonie fundraisers to the small town.

"Sandra, it's Simon."

A short silence gave way to a breathy "Simon, my everlasting love. How are you?"

Simon recognized the cocaine-inspired greeting—the drug increasing Sandra's sense of drama.

"I just called Maury's office and spoke to Lyle's girlfriend."

"Oh. Uh. What did she tell you?"

"Enough. I can't believe you got Maury to hire her."

"Hold the line for a minute." Sandra set down the receiver on the nightstand phone and walked soundlessly across the bedroom rug until her heels began to click against the hardwood floor when the rug ended. "I needed some privacy."

"Privacy from Lyle?"

"I guess Sandy told you that. Wee-ell, you knew we were always attracted to each other."

"It's okay, Sandra. I'm not in love with Lyle, but I still care about him. I'd rather he's with you than on the street selling his body—or with that Sandy person. I wasn't even sure she actually existed."

"Lyle never went back to the street after meeting you."

"I'm okay with what's going on between you two, don't worry."

"Sandy's not so bad," Sandra assured. "She came to Hollywood and made threats, but Lyle had taken money from her after all, he admitted it to me, and I told him we'd figure something out. Maury needed a receptionist after the third one left in a month. Sandy's tough. Maury won't scare her away as easily as the others, even if she can't type."

"As long as she's not taking advantage of you."

"She thinks she is, but not really. Trying to manage the typing and having to answer the phone was driving me nuts. At least she can take calls and write down messages."

"Are you and Lyle serious about each other?"

Sandra laughed. "*Serious* is such a grand word."

"Lyle was never serious about me. Maybe he felt some affection, but nothing deeper."

"I can't really say what Lyle feels about you or me," Sandra admitted. "He doesn't talk about his emotions. We're having fun. We'll see where it goes."

"If I ever go straight, Sandra..."

"I'll take that as a compliment, my love. It's great hearing from you, but it's been such a long time. What's up?"

"You remember seeing Thad when you visited Scott's a while back?"

"Yes, I do. He was such a sweetheart toward me."

"Did you hear about his recent job?"

"Scott couldn't keep quiet about it. Listening to Scott imitate Thad's repertoire of sound effects was the funniest thing I'd heard in a long time. Thad was totally embarrassed, but Scott had us rolling on the floor."

"Thad got bored living here in Sibley, especially when I decided to go back to college."

"Is Thad still out here?"

"I'm trying to find him."

"You mean he split up with you? Oh, honey, I'm so sorry."

"It's worse than that, Sandra. I've such a story to tell, I don't know where to begin." Simon described the video and how it had arrived at the mansion in a parcel with no note included. "The people from the Spanish company that produced *El Amigo Rico* are criminals, laundering money with films like I was providing them. I believe they've kidnapped Thad and are exploiting him to make porn because of the money I owe them, the money that Charlotte stole."

"Oh my God, Simon. You must be worried sick."

"You've no idea. The owners of the Spanish company went into partnership with the guy that employed Thad. Did Thad or Scott mention his name?"

"Not that I recall."

"It's Maury's new client, Howard Price."

Silence.

"Sandra?"

"You're joking, right? Howard is in the other room."

"Howard Price is at your house, right now?"

"We went for drinks at lunch after a meeting he had with Maury, and then we decided to come to my place for, well, dessert, if you know what I mean—Howard's very generous."

"This is freaking me out, Sandra."

"Your name hasn't come up, or Thad's. Lyle's in there with Howard right now. He knows Howard's gay, so he's being a prick tease. I don't think Lyle even knows Thad's name or anything about him. This is just too strange."

"Scott told me what happened when Howard showed up at the office. Scott said that Maury took Howard as a client because of trouble in a southern state?"

"Alabama. Police arrested a store owner for selling pornography. Most of the confiscated films were produced by Howard's company."

"Anything international about the case?"

"Howard's company is the only one mentioned in the indictment."

"At least it's not about *El Amigo Rico*. The box cover is in Spanish, and there isn't any mention of Chatsworth Price Productions."

"Howard and Lyle are laughing about something. I better get in there. And, well, I, uh, want to get back to that incredible dessert Howard is serving. Oh my God, I've not snorted coke like that in ages."

"If you hear about anything related to Spain or the video with Thad, let me know. Howard may not realize that the Spaniards have Thad. On the other hand, he may have sold Thad to them. I just don't know, and my imagination is running wild."

"Keep calm, honey. This is a job for sleuth Sandra. Let me put on something more revealing and go back into the other room. Howard might be gay, but I saw him looking down my front."

"You're a wonderful friend, Sandra."

"Aren't I, though? I'll call you later. I'll bet I get at least a tidbit of information."

"Love you, Sandra."

"Love you, dearest."

CHAPTER TWENTY-NINE

S imon knew that if he worked on a painting, he would never hear the phone ring, even if he stretched the cord to its limit out the back door; the deafening natural chorus of the insects, amphibians, and random bobcat howls would overwhelm the pitiful ringer. Simon picked up a book to read, but his eyes fell over the same page without comprehending a single word. He finally set a vinyl recording of Wagner's *Siegfried Idyll* on the parlor's turntable, having failed to locate *Twilight of the Gods*, which seemed a better fit to his mood, sitting alone in the Sibley Valhalla, musing about Brünnhilde on her steed, charging into flames to meet her death.

"The gods are no more," came a soothing voice as Simon dozed, only to be started awake by urgent ringing.

"Hello, darling." A muffled rock-and-roll beat told Simon that Sandra was calling from her bedroom. "I weaseled my best but didn't learn much, dearest." Sandra, thick tongued, could barely articulate her words. "Howard mentioned his next project and then asked Lyle to audition as a voice-over artist. I wanted to get him talking, so I asked, 'Is that a thing?' and Howard said, 'Sure,' and that he had an opening because his last guy 'up and left.' When he heard Lyle trying to make erotic sounds, he said that maybe it wasn't the best use of Lyle's talent, and then he asked if Lyle wanted to perform. Lyle didn't say no, but I don't think he would do gay porn—and then we did lines, and I saw the clock and realized I needed to call you."

"Don't push it any harder, Sandra. It sounds as though Howard doesn't know anything about what happened, only that Thad disappeared."

"Be careful, Simon. Howard looks harmless, but Maury has told me stories, and so has Scott. I hope Thad is okay."

"Me too."

Simon mulled over recent events and could only conclude that sharp-eyed David, wily Emilio, or astute businesswoman Irene had figured out Thad's identify. Had they threatened to hurt Simon if Thad didn't make a movie for them? Confronted, Thad might have divulged what he knew: that Simon was now broke, that their money had been stolen by his assistant, Charlotte, and that no one knew where she had gone. A shudder ran up his spine as he realized that Thad must have been forced to provide the address of the mansion.

The Spotlight would soon announce last call. Simon hesitatingly dialed the number, hoping that Don or Twiggy might have learned more about why Rudy wanted Simon to contact Wally. Twiggy answered, sounding exhausted, granting but a few moments to chat as he closed out bar tabs. "Such handsome men in here tonight," Twiggy giggled. "You should've seen them..."

"Better than usual?" Simon asked. "The Spotlight is a meat market, after all."

"Grade-A prime tonight, honey." Then, "Oh, I just realized, I know what was different about tonight. The Pub got raided the other day when the cops found a fake ID on one of the customers, and they shut it down for a week; all those customers came here tonight."

"How is Sweet Peter?"

"That queen? Gossip is that he's the one who called the police on the customer, pissed off because the owner wouldn't give him a raise. That lovely man isn't the sharpest knife in the drawer. Didn't he know the police would close the bar? A bartender's money comes from tips—salary's nothing. Don doesn't pay me jack shit."

"Sweet Peter has other sources of income," Simon reminded. "Doesn't he supply coke to half the boys on the boulevard?"

"Well, that's true," Twiggy mused. "More than half, really."

"Say, Twig, I'm calling because when I spoke to Don after you sent the telegram, he told me that Rudy wanted me to contact one of my business contacts, and that I should ask the contact about Charlotte."

"Rudy's standing by Don right now if you want to ask him directly."

Simon felt as if someone had stepped on his grave.

"Rudy's been coming in for a while," Twiggy informed him. "He claims he had nothing to do with ripping you off. Anyway, Rudy isn't eighty-sixed anymore."

"Don probably missed his liar's poker buddy," Simon suggested.

"They're playing right now, but I think it's about to end—Don always wins."

Rudy knew everything there was to know about Hollywood's darker byways. If Simon wanted to get information from him, he needed to remain calm.

"Get Rudy to the phone, Twiggy, but don't say who it is."

"Okay, but I *have* to hear to this," Twiggy giggled.

Rudy complained that he and Don were just starting a new game, but Twiggy insisted. A disgruntled Rudy came to the phone.

"You never were very good at liar's poker, Rudy. You're just not a good liar."

Rudy breathed heavily into the phone.

"You know who it is, Rudy, so don't go silent on me."

"I'm just glad you aren't here in the bar," Rudy sighed.

"Why did you do it, Rudy? When we first met, I gave you money so you wouldn't be evicted from your apartment, and then you steal from me in the end? It hurt, Rudy. Your betrayal hurt."

The jukebox blasted out "Life is a cabaret, old chum," inspiring the few remaining customers to sing along.

"I hear that things haven't gone so well," Simon continued. "Did Charlotte toss you aside once she was done with you?"

"Things are more complicated than that," Rudy protested. "What am I supposed to say, Simon, especially on the phone? People are listening."

"By people you mean Twiggy?"

"Well, yeah—hang up the other phone, you fucking queen. This isn't about you."

The phone on the other end of the bar crashed with a loud bang.

"Charlotte can be convincing, Simon. She thought you'd burn through the money, even if she didn't take it."

"That doesn't justify anything. She was wrong, and you had no right to go along."

"Did you get my message? Did you make the call?"

"Remind me," Simon said.

"You were supposed to contact Wally Freeze. Haven't you called him?"

"I tried to reach him, but he wasn't in his office. Anyway, Rudy, I've been in touch with Wally for months. He's allowing me to continue representing his old videos, just none of the new ones."

"Are you in Hollywood?"

"No, I'm far away."

"If you were here, I'd meet up with you."

"You probably wouldn't want to do that, Rudy."

"Come on, Simon. Yeah, I was a jerk, but I couldn't have stopped Charlotte from doing what she did, so I just tagged along."

Simon marveled at the impeccable Hollywood logic.

"I am a queen!" Rudy said, as absolution for his bad behavior.

"I don't know what you've heard, Rudy, but the people whose money Charlotte took have made off with Thad. I think they're coercing him to make porn for them, maybe as a way of recouping their loss. They are dangerous people, and no matter what the motive, Thad's in danger. Tell me if you have information. I promise I won't take off your crown and feed it to you the next time we meet."

"Well, if you're going to threaten me," Rudy pouted, "I'm not sayin' nothin'."

"Rudy, this is about Thad. Please help me."

"That's better. I just can't believe you don't know what happened, what with all the blabbermouths around here."

"Like Twiggy?"

"And Don. Why'd you think he tried to reach you? Anyway, I don't know anything about Thad. What I do know is that after the money arrived, Charlotte sent a message to Spain asking if the people who sent it would work with her. She said that you had disappeared or something—I'm not sure exactly what she said about your absence when she sent off the telex."

Simon's heart stopped at the idea of Charlotte communicating with the Spaniards.

"No telling what my clients thought. And this was after she took the money?"

"Yeah, but they didn't know about that, obviously. She didn't expect there to be as much money as there was. I remember her saying that you must have gotten an advance on a new contract. That's why she contacted them. She wanted to make sure they got whatever new films they were expecting."

"The money wasn't for any films I had in hand. It was capital to look for new ones."

Rudy didn't say anything for a moment. "I don't know if Charlotte heard back from them. I don't think so. Not long after she sent the message, she contacted Wally and some of your other clients. Charlotte was sure you'd never come back—that the drugs would kill you."

"She wasn't far off the mark, Rudy, but still."

"Charlotte told Wally that she was taking over the business. She thought he'd ask questions, but he said he'd rather work with her anyway."

A bolt of déjà vu struck Simon as he thought about Nicolò's clients saying they'd rather do business with him after he started his own company.

"Simon?"

"I'm still here. I'm just flabbergasted. Don said you and Charlotte went to Vegas, that she kicked you out or something, and that's when you wanted to get a message to me about contacting Wally. What changed?"

"I made Charlotte mad because I took money from her suitcase and lost it at a blackjack table. She blew up and said that I'd clung to her long enough. I came back to Hollywood.

"Don hadn't let me into the Spotlight since he found out what Charlotte did and that I was a part of it, but I showed up with a fresh young hunk. As soon as Don saw the kid, he forgave me. I'm not even sure he remembered why he eighty-sixed me."

"That's our Don."

"I wanted to get Charlotte in trouble for tossing me aside, so I gave Don the message that you should ask Wally about her, about where she's living."

"Where is Charlotte?" Simon asked.

"At your Silverlake house."

Simon dropped the phone, catching it by the cord and pulling it back to his ear.

"Charlotte started her own business: Chanteuse Film Distributors."

"You mean this whole time, Wally's been working with her?"

"They agreed not to tell you about it but to honor your old contract with him."

Simon felt bamboozled. Now he understood why Wally would never talk about the company representing his new product, and why Clarice had wanted to avoid the subject.

"Rudy, I'm shocked."

Twiggy announced last call.

"I have to go, Simon."

"You're serious. Charlotte is in Silverlake, at my house."

"She might be in Italy for that film festival or whatever it is. She talked about going when we were in Las Vegas."

"MIFED?"

"Yeah, that's it."

Rudy was no innocent, but it was clear he had little to do with Charlotte's scheme. "I'm glad you told me all of this, Rudy."

"Don't kill me when you come to Hollywood. That's all I ask."

"Don would never let me."

Simon heard "Last call for alcohol!" as he set the receiver back in its cradle.

CHAPTER THIRTY

The evening had begun with bats pouring from their rafter
sanctuary in search of food; the morning started with the
camp of satiated creatures streaming to their home, a black line
drawn against a crimson sunrise. Simon watched as he spread
Vivian's plum jam on a toasted muffin. His course of action was
decided: he would contact his professors and submit his term
papers early, and he'd have his final paintings completed, though
perhaps with less deliberation than he had planned.

Connie, concerned when Simon announced he was leaving for
California, accepted the excuse that Simon needed to meet face to
face with his suppliers if he were to keep his business afloat.

"I know your business isn't what it once was," Connie said, "but
at least you were able to cover tuition. I've never really understood
what you do, but Vivian was impressed with the way you talked on
the phone. She said you knew what you were doing."

"I won't be in Los Angeles longer than I have to," Simon
promised.

"What's going to happen with your schoolwork?"

"I've made arrangements with my professors."

"Going out there is that urgent?"

"Yes."

"And you're taking the Pontiac?"

"I can't afford to fly, and I need a car when I get there. I hope the old rattletrap makes it there and back."

Connie had taken Cicero to her house when Simon mentioned how lonely he had become without Vivian, and with Simon being around so infrequently because of his class schedule. During Connie's visit before Simon's departure, Cicero rushed through the downstairs rooms, toenail castanets clicking on the hardwood floor.

"He's looking for Vivian," Connie sighed.

Simon laughed. "He doesn't even see that I'm here."

Disappointed in his search, Cicero burst across the room and launched into Simon's lap.

"You were saying?" Connie smiled.

"I've missed you too, little fellow." Cicero licked Simon's face, snorting with glee.

"He's been happy with Derek and me. Cheryl wants to take him, but he's become part of the household. Derek spoils him with treats."

"That's where those extra pounds came from." Simon felt his shoulders. "He's still got muscle."

"Running around our backyard keeps him fit—wish I could do that." Connie drew in her stomach, shifting in her seat to assume a more upright posture.

"You're not fat, Connie. If you are, then so am I, and..."

Connie poked Simon in the ribs. "You're fat compared to that skeleton of a person who arrived here from California. Thank God you were able to get help."

"I was skin and bones, wasn't I? Let's not talk about that right now. I hope the mansion will be safe while I'm gone. I'll leave a few lights burning so it doesn't look empty. Someone will need to care for Ferdinand."

"I'll ask Cheryl to drop by. It would be hard for me to do it, what with visiting Vivian every day."

"I know I should go more often."

"It hurts me to see her," Connie admitted. "She's going down fast. We won't have our mother for much longer."

"I hate to think about it."

"Be sure to rest along the way to California. I remember how tired you used to get when you drove home for Christmas."

"I'll be careful. Don't worry."

Connie scooped Cicero from Simon's lap, his ears pricking up at the mention of Vivian's name. Connie promised to take him with her on the next visit. Cicero seemed to understand, opening his wide mouth into a slobbery smile.

Simon's plan included an overnight stay in Gallup, New Mexico, giving him enough time to be rested and alert when he showed up at the Silverlake house to confront Charlotte. He filled a thermos with coffee, placed a bag of Granny Smith apples and five large navel oranges in a box, and made pimento loaf sandwiches, secured in zipper-lock bags that he placed into a Styrofoam cooler with enough ice to keep them until he made it to Gallup. Simon shelled peanuts to eat as a snack to help keep him awake along the dreary plains of west Texas. He stood before an unfinished painting that was propped against a wall on a wooden table that served as an easel, and gestured as if with a paintbrush, an act that helped calm feelings of apprehension—of dread.

Thad, Simon's heart cried out, I will always love you.

Simon stopped at the local Gulf station, the last one in the area still providing a full range of services, and asked the attendant to check the transmission fluid and to add a quart of oil. He hoped, after paying the bill, that he would have enough cash to make it to Los Angeles. He was determined to get there. If the car broke down, he'd hitchhike the rest of the way.

Simon felt a fearful tug as he drove through cities where he had stopped to do drugs during his failed attempt to outrun Hollywood. He kept going, passing through Amarillo and then Albuquerque, finally reaching Gallup as the last hints of twilight disappeared from an alizarin sky and he pulled into a motel parking lot. Simon opened the door and paused to breathe in the fragrant desert air, such a contrast with the swamps of Sibley. He approached the bulletproof window of the manager's office, paid for a night, and fell asleep as soon as he collapsed, fully clothed, on the foamy bed, awakening throughout the night, disturbed by troubling dreams. Expecting it to be near morning, he checked the dim glow of the room's digital clock, shocked that so little time had passed. An hour before dawn, he showered under a lukewarm trickle of water, threw his suitcase in the trunk of the car, forced himself to eat a pimento sandwich, and then went to the motel cafeteria, where the waitress agreed to fill his thermos at half-price. Simon braced for the final leg of his journey, the Pontiac's hood ornament a riflescope targeting Hollywood.

Simon tried to prepare himself for the impending encounter. After Thad had loaded his belongings into the rental truck and left for Sibley, Charlotte must have contacted the landlords, a gay couple who'd bought the house when they first entered into a committed relationship. They would not have thought it strange for Charlotte to assume the lease if she'd told them Simon had moved to Arkansas; they were as familiar with her as they were with Simon, and they'd be grateful that after she began working for him, the rent checks continued to arrive on time. After leaving Hollywood, and after Thad brought his belongings to Sibley, Simon had never thought about the house or his obligations under the lease he had signed. He'd simply disappeared.

For months, Charlotte ran Simon's business, a better negotiator than he, in fact, able to utilize her glamorous looks when necessary.

Charlotte's pixie face and thick red hair, a look reminiscent of the ingenues who posed for 1920s Coca-Cola ads, were irresistible. Charlotte managed flashes of passionate temper, controlled with precision, directing those flairs sometimes at Simon when he missed appointments with clients, other times at lab technicians if they failed to provide quality videotape masters. A heterosexual man stood little chance against Charlotte's wiles if she batted her eyes and thrust forward her ample breasts, highlighted by cleavage-revealing blouses.

The Silverlake house sat perched on a hillside, approachable by a road that wound upward along tight curves from Silverlake Boulevard or, alternatively, by driving more directly from Glendale Boulevard. Simon took the latter route, passing the house several times to study the opaque glass that formed the street-front wall, hoping to see movement inside.

On the fourth pass, the front door opened to allow someone to leave. Simon immediately recognized Wally, Charlotte standing behind him, both aware of the car passing on the narrow street but neither recognizing the driver. Simon nearly lost his nerve, unsure about what to expect from an encounter with Charlotte, much less Wally. Simon drove past the house several more times before curiosity, tempered by rage, became too great.

Simon parked on a wider section of the street toward the downhill curve to Silverlake Boulevard, well beyond the line of vision from the front door. He knocked tentatively, surprised when Charlotte quickly opened the door, anticipating that Wally had forgotten something—and there stood Simon. Charlotte transformed into living stone.

"Hello, Charlotte," Simon greeted.

The two gazed at each other without seeing, an eternity passing within the moment. Simon diverted from Charlotte's blank stare to study the rooms beyond. The ficus tree he had bought from a local nursery, now tall enough for its top branches to reach the loft bedroom, seemed to welcome his arrival.

Charlotte backed away to allow Simon passage. He raced past the kitchen bar, darted through the living room, and threw open the balcony door to take a seat on a wicker chair left behind when Thad had transported his things to Sibley. A recent downpour, washing the air of LA's smog, allowed the Hollywood sign to shine brightly against the backdrop of a brown hillside. Charlotte cautiously sat in the chair beside him.

"No guns a-blazing?" Charlotte asked. "I can't imagine what you must be thinking."

"Best that you don't try."

Charlotte sat with hands folded on her lap, leaning forward from the prickly back of the wicker chair, eyes watching the door, ready to flee upon detection of danger in the tone of Simon's voice. "Do you want me to explain?" she asked, joining Simon at the banister as he stood to gaze at the Hollywood sign.

"Will any of it be true?"

"I deserve that," Charlotte admitted, hesitantly placing her hand on top of Simon's. "I've known where you were, Simon. I was going to fly to Little Rock and drive out to your little town. I even thought of showing up at the college and meeting you in the painting studio as a neutral place to see you after all that's gone down."

"Quite the conspirators, you and Wally," Simon accused.

"Wally found out that you disappeared. I told him that I assumed your lease and started my own company. When you contacted him, we talked about it and decided it was best to keep our relationship from you. He didn't know I had taken money from you. Don't be too hard on Wally."

Simon hoped his expression masked the smoldering anger he feared would erupt at any moment.

"Your clients were glad to hear from me when I promised to pay the money you owed them and explained that I would continue making sales if they would sign new contracts. A few were ready to sue for breach of contract, but I convinced them that no one else would try selling those wretched titles they owned. You really found a niche, Simon."

Simon listened.

"Wally knew all along you had a cocaine problem, but as long as you kept bringing in money, he overlooked it—he said he didn't know many people that weren't into cocaine. But when you didn't show up at MIFED and refused to see him about it, that was the end for him. Anyway, Wally and I figured that if you didn't go back to drugs after rehab, we'd tell you about my new company."

"Then why didn't you?"

Charlotte risked clasping Simon's hand since he had not withdrawn it earlier. "After you started college and seemed stable, we didn't want to mess with it. Wally said he mentioned that he had a distributor for his new material."

"But I never imagined it was you!"

Simon pulled his hand from Charlotte's grasp and leaned over the redwood railing to stare at the century-plant fronds that a drug-crazed boyfriend had once threatened to impale himself upon, prevented only because Simon had grabbed him by the belt and yanked him back to safety in the nick of time.

"What would I say to you?" Charlotte asked. "How could I explain what I had done so you'd understand?"

"I understand perfectly, Charlotte. At the worst moment of my life, you ripped me off! Now I learn that you assumed my life as a film distributor—in my very own house!" Flashes of rage gave way to sorrow and regret. Simon's knees buckled, and he fell backward, catching the arm of the chair just in time to steady himself.

"I didn't mean to kick you when you were down," Charlotte said, straightening her blouse and taking off a hairband to rearrange her ponytail. "I'm no saint, I admit. I did rip you off, and at first, that's all I meant to do—I mean, my God, Simon, you were practically begging for someone to stop you. When the money

225

arrived from Spain, I took what I saw as my last chance to salvage something before you killed yourself. I intended to use the money to start over, but the only sensible thing I did was pay off a loan shark who had come after my daughter in Miami. Rudy and I went on a party binge and burned through a lot of what I had taken. Eventually, I realized I had to get it together. I still had the keys to this place, and when Thad hauled your belongings to Sibley, I contacted the landlords. They said they hadn't heard from you and complained about the overdue rent. I paid it and arranged to transfer the lease—why not? I figured this would be the last place you'd look for me. Then I started thinking."

"You tried to arrange something with the company in Spain, right?" Simon wanted Charlotte to be aware that he knew some of the facts, hoping it might keep her truthful. "Rudy gave me information the other day. That's how I knew you were here."

"Rudy," Charlotte sighed with exasperation. "I don't know what he told you, but I don't ever want to see him again. He's kept needling me for money. I never should have let him know I had the money—but we've known each other for such a long time. Anyway, I was an idiot to get him involved."

"I can't believe you're speaking so freely about ripping me off!"

"If you were going to kill me, Simon, I'd be speared on those fronds down there already. As I said, I'm not a saint, not even a good person, really." Charlotte looked heavenward.

"Damn it, Charlotte. I wish I didn't like you so much."

Charlotte smiled for the first time. "We really were a good team, weren't we? The final few months are what ruined it. If only that damn Axl kid hadn't gotten you to smoke crack. Damn his cute little ass."

"Yeah, cute as a lamb hiding a wolf." Simon scowled, remembering the day on the balcony when Axl had nearly jumped onto the century-plant fronds, trying to escape a paranoid delusion about policemen breaking through the front door.

Just then, a helicopter flew overhead in the direction of Echo Park, a news crew aiming to capture footage of another gang-related crime. When the noise died down, Charlotte remarked, "Don't they know this is an upscale neighborhood?"

"So news copters should only disturb poor neighborhoods?"

"See what living in an upscale place like this does to a person?"

"Let's get back to the story, Charlotte." Simon wanted to explain what a bad idea contacting the Spaniards had been and to lead up to the reason he had come to Los Angeles.

"Thad boxed up your business records and took them when he emptied out the place, but I had made copies before you disappeared," she said. "The contracts with the Spanish company didn't add up to the amount they wired—they sent an extra two hundred thousand. You must have negotiated one hell of a deal! I thought I'd try to honor it, so I sent them a telex saying that you were no longer with the company but that I could take care of the contract you had negotiated if they would give me the terms. They never responded."

Charlotte's communication had alerted David, Emilio, and Irene to Simon's disappearance. They might have thought Charlotte was part of a sting operation, which would explain why they hadn't tracked him down and had instead taken another way to get back at him when the opportunity appeared in the form of Thad—his lover!

"I saw Wally leave here not long before I knocked on the door."

"Yeah, he brought promotional tapes to show at MIFED—and besides, he has a crush on me. He's such a sleaze. I could never date him."

"Keep going, Charlotte."

"I never heard anything from Spain, but I recently sent a follow-up telling them I would be at MIFED, and maybe they could drop by and see me. I figured they might be more willing to work out something if they met me in person."

Simon wanted to explain about Thad at that point, but Charlotte hadn't finished.

"I can't wait to be at MIFED. The booth will have a banner saying Chanteuse Film Distribution—fits my last name of Singer, don't you think?"

"Charlotte, you've no idea what you've done. The Spanish must have thought you were with Interpol or something, that your booth at MIFED was part of a trap."

"Simon, you're scaring me. What were you supposed to do for the money they sent? It wasn't for a new contract?"

"I was supposed to help them launder money by supplying whatever films I could get my hands on. They'd claim sales through their own distribution network and justify the money through phony contracts. When I found out that you had drained the bank account, I didn't know what to do—they're dangerous people. Coming back to Hollywood was out of the question. I hoped that Arkansas would be a good place to hide."

Charlotte's red hair flashed a brighter hue, matching the crimson glow that had risen to her face. "I had no idea you'd agreed to something illegal!" She stood to compose herself, walking from one end of the balcony to the other. "Sounds like I better not go to MIFED."

"What were you doing in Las Vegas so close to MIFED?"

"More of my stupidity. I thought I could win some money before going to Italy. I didn't have much after working out a deal with your former suppliers. I wanted money to have some fun in Italy. I'm a pretty good gambler, and I did win, but then Rudy took half of it out of the hotel room and lost it playing roulette. I was so angry, I told him to get out and forget he ever knew me."

"Rudy was pretty mad at you too."

"Every time I tried to cut him off, he'd threaten to tell you everything. The bastard. I guess he followed through when I cut him off for real."

"There's something I have to show you." Simon rushed to the car, returning to find Charlotte still sitting on the balcony. He handed her the video of *El Amigo Rico.* "This arrived in the mail. Look at the back cover."

Charlotte became white as salt.

"I'm positive that Thad didn't appear in this video by choice," Simon said. "This was made by the Spanish company. Three despicable people are the principles. One of them is Emilio, the 'rich friend' you see in the photo. The other owners are a husband-and-wife team, David and Irene, who handle day-to-day business affairs. They formed a partnership to make this film with a Hollywood pornographer named Howard Price. Thad left Arkansas to work for Howard at his production company in Chatsworth, but not to star in porn, just to provide sound effects—something he used to do when he lived in San Diego. All three of the Spaniards showed up to finalize the deal, and then Emilio must have figured out Thad's connection to me. Either they forced Thad to make the video in an attempt to recoup some of the money they sent me, or Thad decided to leave me and pursue a career in pornography—he might have fallen for Felipe, the other person in the still."

Charlotte's complexion returned to its normal hue. "Don't be ridiculous, Simon. You've already told me that's not what you think. Anyway, I can tell you when I watch it. I know what it's like to fake sex." Charlotte wrapped the thin sweater she had draped over her shoulders more tightly around her arms. "It makes me sick to think I'm responsible for this. Damn."

"The scene on the back cover was shot in Spain. That's where they've taken him."

Charlotte listened to the details about Thad's appearance at the Spotlight, and about the scene of the threesome featured prominently in the early part of the video. Simon explained that it reenacted Simon's night with Emilio and Felipe.

"Stay here at the house," Charlotte insisted. "I'll watch the video after you go to sleep."

"Strange being a guest in my own house. I've definitely stepped through the looking glass."

"Sitting here with you now, all sober and everything, I don't know how to feel," Charlotte sighed. "After you left, I expected the police to call and tell me that you were dead. I'm sorry for what I did, Simon, and for not contacting you sooner."

"I want to hate you, Charlotte, but I can't. This is like having the memories of someone else, and then I realize it is me, and I can't deny it. What a nightmare I lived! It still isn't easy. Some days I struggle more than others." He thought about Blaine and his near brush with relapse.

Simon bid Charlotte good night and went to the guest room, falling asleep within minutes of crawling into bed. Sometime later the smell of coffee and the rattle of dishes woke him up.

"Here's fresh-squeezed orange juice," Charlotte said, handing Simon a glass as he came into the kitchen. "Welcome back to California."

Simon felt strange greeting the personable, self-confident Charlotte that he remembered from better days.

"Do you realize that you slept for two days?" Charlotte asked. "I've poked my head in the door a few times to make sure you were still breathing."

"I had no idea. That explains why my head feels bloated to twice its size." Simon drank two cups of coffee in rapid succession, filling his stomach with eggs and sausage.

"I've been busy while you slept," Charlotte said. "I've made some discoveries, and I have a plan."

Simon steadied himself for whatever Charlotte had in mind.

CHAPTER THIRTY-ONE

Simon and Charlotte changed planes at London's Heathrow Airport on the last leg of a flight to Milan. Charlotte complained about the cramped seats in the coach section, the best she could afford after trading in the single ticket she had purchased earlier.

Simon, now having someone to talk to who knew his history with Thad, kept trying to reason through the possibility that Thad made the video of his own free will.

"Good grief, Simon, enough already!" Charlotte scolded. "I was there through your arguments—Thad stealing Cicero to spite you, you running after him with a carving knife—oh my God, thinking back on all that! You wanted to destroy each other. It has to be true love!"

"Always the cynic!" Simon shot back. "Our life has been different since we both went through rehab. The fact that we kept coming back to each other is what speaks to me of love."

Charlotte flashed a huge smile, the reading light overhead causing her eyes to glisten.

"Damn it, Charlotte. I keep looking over at you and feeling like I'm the one who should apologize, when you are the one who stole from me."

"Do you want to spank me?"

"Don't make me laugh!"

"You should never trust someone as completely as you trusted me. I mean, you simply accepted Rudy vouching for me. And oh my God, Rudy. You definitely shouldn't trust him."

"Guess that's why I take betrayal so poorly. I keep expecting the best of people."

"You make yourself suffer when people don't live up to your expectations. That's your nature, and it's not healthy, Simon."

"I've never been good at forgiving myself."

"I didn't mean to do that."

"What?"

"Make you sad."

"You haven't. I've made so many bad choices over the last few years. I thought giving you so much responsibility for my business was one of them, but I see that's not the case."

Charlotte reached over to stroke Simon's cheek with backs of her fingers. "This cute face was so full of sorrow. Every time a hustler ripped you off, or won your heart and then hurt you, I saw a part of your soul disappear. When Axl left, I worried what you might do. I've got to admit, though, heading off to New York thinking you'd be a famous artist wasn't on my list."

"Axl! Another gift from Rudy. I wish he'd never seen Axl at the Spotlight and called me to take him in. I saved the little Adonis from the street—I even kept him from throwing himself off the balcony. What thanks was there? An introduction to smoking crack."

"You can't give hope to a hustler," Charlotte challenged. "It causes them to despair over what's become of their life, and then they want to end it. That's what happened to Axl. It's not your fault. You were trying to be a good person. When you left Hollywood, I was sure I'd never see you again. Communicating with you when you were on the road, I was sure you'd lost your mind."

"Not sure I had a mind to lose."

"But look at you now." She again brushed her fingers across Simon's cheek. "All peachy and clear-eyed," she said as she clasped his hand.

"You understand me better than most people, Charlotte."

"I understand one of the Simons. Not the religious nut or the Simon in love with that Japanese woman. What was her name?"

"Masako. I did love her, but I should never have gone through with the marriage." Simon took back his hand and called the steward to serve drinks.

"I didn't mean to upset you again."

"No, it's just, so many different paths might have unfolded. What if Masako and I had had children? I would have tried harder to stay married but almost surely would have started living on the down low—trying to love my wife but having sex with men. I've always dreaded such an existence. Practically all the gay men I met growing up in Arkansas lived that way."

Charlotte set the bloody mary mix aside and drank her vodka straight from the little bottle. "This conversation is depressing. Let's talking about rescuing Thad."

"Any more psychoanalysis and I'm going to be in tears."

"I noticed that the company owned by the Spanish trio you described purchased a full-page MIFED advertisement in the *Hollywood Reporter*." Charlotte took a folded copy from her purse. "See here? These are titles you licensed to them. The titles have been translated into Spanish, but growing up in Miami, I learned to read Spanish a little." She kept a finger on the page as she lifted it closer to Simon's eyes. "Look at the small box here in the corner. They list *El Amigo Rico* along with ten other films with porn-like titles. There's no description, so I'll bet the clients who want them know that the small box on the page refers to the hardcore stuff."

"It makes me sick that men will be getting off watching Thad."

A passenger across the aisle held a cassette player in his lap with a set of headphones loosely covering his ears. Simon noticed that the play button wasn't pushed and motioned to Charlotte.

"Take off the headphones," Charlotte called to the man with a laugh. "You'll be able to hear better."

The embarrassed man hit the play button and made a display of more firmly positioning the headphones. Charlotte grinned and turned to Simon. "Nosy people."

Just then the plane went through turbulence, and the fasten seatbelt lights came on.

"I've never liked flying," Charlotte admitted. "And this is my longest flight. It's lucky I had my passport. I've not needed it since flying to the Bahamas from Miami, and that was at least five years ago."

"Brought mine to LA because I figured Spain might be on the itinerary, but I had no idea how I'd manage a flight. I barely had enough to cover the gasoline."

"You were right about the shot in the video panning to the headboard, then pausing on the photograph; that was deliberate. It served no purpose but to send you a message. They may be trying to recoup their losses, but those monsters want you to know they have control of the man you love." Charlotte drank another bottle of vodka, saying it was to steady her nerves.

"It should have been obvious to me that they'd find out Thad was my lover. I should have told Thad about Emilio, David, and Irene when they showed up at Howard's ranch—and explained about Felipe! The first time that Thad asked me about going to LA, I should have gone with him. I can be so self-centered sometimes! All I could think about was going back to college—and I didn't see any way to do that unless I lived at the mansion. I knew Thad was unhappy."

"Hindsight being twenty-twenty and all that," Charlotte pointed out, her words beginning to slur with her fourth bottle of vodka. "Let me go over the full plan with you before we land."

"Good idea. I need to convince myself it's going to work." Simon took a long sip of the drink he had been holding, now watered down from melted ice.

"We have surprise on our side, Simon. I spoke to Wally when you were sleeping, by the way. We have to visit him when this is over. He's more of a friend than you realize."

"I know about his past with drugs. I'm sure he understands what I was going through, but I threatened his livelihood. I can't blame him for being so pissed off at me."

"While I was on the phone with Wally, he looked at his copy of the MIFED catalog and realized that one of the titles listed in the company's ad belonged to him."

"They probably got a stolen master tape. The night staff at the labs sometimes sells tapes out the back door. Nicolò acquired many of his best titles that way, but at least he made sure the films were in the public domain, even if he didn't point that out to his clients."

"Them having *Sorority Lettuce Fights* gave me an idea. Wally agreed to put his notarized signature on a statement confirming that he owns the copyright and that Chanteuse Film Distributors has exclusive international representation. Wally said when this is over, I can keep the rights; I know I can make money on it. What straight guy wouldn't want to watch dorm girls drenched in salad dressing, rolling around in a gigantic bowl of lettuce? As soon as we get to the MIFED exposition center, we need to see if Thad is their office. I'm betting they have Felipe and Thad there to promote *El Amigo Rico*. Don't porn stars usually hang out at the office to attract buyers?"

Simon nodded. "Having the boys around is the safest way to do the promotion, especially for gay videos. They're still illegal in a lot of countries—actually, straight porn is too. Even in Italy, a company can't be open about what they have in their catalog. The authorities overlook little ads that don't call too much attention to themselves, like the one they put in the *Hollywood Reporter*."

"Once we confirm that Thad is in the office, we'll make our move. We'll get the Italian authorities to confront them on a copyright violation, and we'll follow right behind. That Emilio guy and the other two will freak out when they see the authorities heading toward their office." Charlotte's eyes gleamed mischievously. "And you know Thad will find a way to bolt when he sees us."

"The first year I was at MIFED with Nicolò, something similar happened—Vestron Video came with a letter of ownership for one of the films he had in the MIFED catalog. Nicolò bribed his way out of the situation, but the ordeal took an entire afternoon. We had to shut the office down and follow the police to their station in the exhibition hall."

"While the police are around, we'll have a chance grab Thad and get the hell out of Milan."

"I'm nervous about seeing Thad."

"Stop worrying about that, Simon. For Pete's sake."

"That's not it, Charlotte. I'm afraid I'll melt into a bundle of emotions at the very moment we need to act."

"I'll kick your butt if it comes to that—and I'll kick Thad's if he dawdles."

"We'll be landing soon," Simon noted, looking out the window and recognizing the Italian Alps.

"It won't take long to rent a car and check into the hotel. I've arranged everything," Charlotte said. "Tomorrow, we put the plan into action."

CHAPTER THIRTY-TWO

S imon knew his way around from past visits, easily navigating the rental car from the airport to the old quarter of Milan, directly to the hotel that Nicolò had chosen when the two of them had first traveled to Italy, and which Charlotte selected because Simon had mentioned it while bragging to hustlers at the Spotlight about his world travels: the Hotel Windsor. Charlotte checked in, conversing with the desk clerk, who spoke English—a requirement for staff, since the hotel catered to British buyers who came to Milan for fashion shows.

Despite the urgency of the situation, Charlotte wanted to sight-see, perhaps go to a club, but in the end she admitted that they needed a good night's rest before setting the plan into motion. The hotel's proximity, however, allowed a brief excursion to the Piazza del Duomo, which at night took on particular allure for curio shoppers roaming the Galleria Vittorio Emanuele II. Simon pointed out the pasta bar located inside, which specialized in gourmet spaghetti dishes, one with popcorn shrimp being Simon's favorite. The pair quenched their hunger before exhaustion hit hard—the meal proved to be an enervating feast—and then collapsed on the single bed. They were sure no time had passed when Simon awoke to the street noise below their window and roused Charlotte, laughter overtaking weariness as Simon pointed out that they could now tell people they had slept together!

The October air, crisp and biting, arrested their sluggishness as Simon and Charlotte started the day with a plate of assorted cheeses and ciabatta—advertised by the hotel restaurant as nouvelle cuisine. The two-cylinder rental car seemed to take an eternity to warm up as Simon studied the map of Milan provided by the concierge. In the past, he had taken taxis from the hotel to the exposition center, and now, even with the map to follow, he took several wrong turns before recognizing any landmarks that seemed familiar.

Simon flashed Charlotte's MIFED credentials to the guard manning the heavy pole that served as a barrier preventing people from entering the crowded exposition center, the film market overlapping with an event that showcased industrial machinery. The small car became sandwiched between tractor trailers loaded with earth-moving machinery, a mouse among dinosaurs. Simon maneuvered to a parking lot by a rear exit to MIFED's main building. The same hall had been assigned to the event each year, allowing Simon to know where the exit could be found from inside. Simon led the way, trekking between cars, to the main entrance, where Charlotte signed a form, received a guest pass for Simon, and hung her exhibitor card from the lanyard provided in the welcome package. Simon kept a sharp eye for anyone who might recognize him, people to whom he owed money, or worse, a premature encounter with Emilio, David, or Irene. Charlotte located her booth among a carnival of kiosks, each decked with displays in various stages of completion, with half-unloaded boxes of advertising posters, video machines, and other wares needed to get buyers' attention. Charlotte's space was delineated by poles, white

canvas flaps, and a small sign with blue lettering: Chanteuse Film Distributors. Charlotte admired the booth for a moment before taking out her camera and snapping pictures that would form the basis of future advertising, allowing her to legitimately claim a presence at MIFED.

"So much potential at this market," Simon noted, remembering his successful days in the not-so-distant past. "I see lots of buyers that never made a contract with me—not every bridge was burned."

"I'm with you—so much potential," Charlotte pined. "Let's forget about Thad and start distributing the brochures I had sent to the business center over there."

"Evil, evil woman," Simon growled.

"This was supposed to be my coming out a businesswoman. If the plan succeeds, we'll both have to go into hiding, at least for a while."

"I can't consider it possibly failing," Simon responded. "Thad is being held captive, and we have to save him—we have to."

Setting a map of the exhibitor halls on a table at the coffee bar, Charlotte found the location of Hollywood Pictures, SA, marking the proximity of the building exit.

"It's down there." Simon pointed toward a sign above an archway that read Exhibits D–H, a corridor with ceilings high enough to allow twenty-foot actors to gaze upon the crowd from movie posters, Greek gods watching the affairs of humankind, ready on a whim to assert their will.

Simon grabbed Charlotte's arm and froze—a few yards away stood a man akimbo in the archway! Simon ducked behind a line of customers waiting for their cappuccinos, but Charlotte stared, studying the details of the man's manner and dress as he extended his hand toward a fellow in a tailored suit, a buyer who had arranged an early appointment.

"That's Emilio."

"Of course." Charlotte grimaced. "My God, he's uglier than he looks in the video."

"His suits are always shabby like that. It's a thing with him, puts people off guard. He isn't like David, who's younger and somewhat handsome, always in a black suit and dark tie. Irene is the brains behind their evildoings; she'll be dressed in the height of fashion."

Simon heard a familiar voice approaching from one of the corridors and motioned for Charlotte to stand with him behind a wall of movie ads. David and another man—the chauffeur in *El Amigo Rico*—flanked Thad and Felipe. They were so close that if any one of them turned around, the plan would be foiled. David and the chauffeur were engaged in some manner of argument, paying little attention to their surroundings, unlike Thad, who spotted Simon and Charlotte immediately.

"That was a close one." Simon could barely get out the words in his agitated state.

"Poor Thad! I can't stand this." Charlotte's face contorted into a mask of anger. "Did you see Thad's expression? I thought he was going to call out to us."

"He's smarter than that. Thad drew Felipe's attention in the opposite direction as soon as he saw us."

"Thad knows we're acting on a plan," Charlotte surmised.

The brief glance was all Simon needed to forget his worries that Thad was in Spain by choice. Charlotte was right that his first impulse had been to run into Simon's arms.

"Let's have an espresso and wait until more of the offices open for business and the crowds arrive," Charlotte suggested.

Slowly sipping espressos, the pair nervously watched the corridors fill up with buyers, many accompanied by translators whom they'd hired at the central office, until they finally summoned the courage to act. The map had shown them the location of the *posto di polizia*, which was close to the registration desks. The chief of police spoke English.

"Sir," Simon began, "here's a document proving that the catalog of a distributor at this year's event includes a film that their company does not own. My colleague here, who is exhibiting as Chanteuse Film Distributors, has a contract for exclusive rights worldwide."

The chief closely examined the letter; notarized papers held significant legal weight in Europe, a discovery Simon had made when negotiating the original agreement with the distribution company owned by David, Emilio, and Irene. It had been an agreement for films that had passed into the public domain but nonetheless could be treated as licensed films because of the notarized documents he provided, allowing a defense if challenged by competitors. The trick was to be first on the market.

After a few questions, which Simon responded to as if he were an attorney, the chief marched the group toward the office of Hollywood Pictures, SA. From his experience with Nicolò, Simon knew how threatening it was to have Italian authorities come to an office. Simon's heart pounded as loudly as the poor soul's in "The Tell-Tale Heart," and he was sure someone would hear it, especially as they neared the office and he began to fear the randomness of fate. Nicolò had bribed the authorities when they confronted him; the fearsome trio in the office they now approached might have the chief of police on their payroll. Perhaps Simon and Charlotte were being delivered not to a confrontation on a copyright issue, but to whatever dispensation Emilio, David, and Irene commanded.

Simon clasped Charlotte's hand as they approached the entrance to Corridor D–H, Simon's knees buckling as he struggled to regain his composure. Their success depended on quick reflexes, alertness the key to seizing the advantage once the chief brought out the notarized letter. Simon hoped a subtle hand gesture would be enough to alert Thad so they might slip away to the exit and dash off in the two-cylinder Citroën. So much could go wrong.

Businesslike David, stern Irene, and jovial Emilio stood in their office greeting potential buyers, handing out one sheets, and depending on Thad and Felipe to draw attention to a table by the door with stacks of postcard-sized ads for the pornography. The police chief, accompanied by two deputies, blocked the doorway, with Simon and Charlotte a few paces behind them. Attentive to a plan being put into motion, Thad, followed by Felipe, casually moved past the officers as if they had just completed browsing advertisements that, if the officers had looked closely, would have revealed the identity of the two men leaving the office as the stars of an illicit video. The officers didn't notice; they remained dedicated to the task at hand, focused on the owners of the company who had rented the office, the confrontation catching Simon's nemeses off guard—they didn't notice Simon and paid no attention as Thad and Felipe escaped.

Simon took the lead, briskly walking toward the end of the corridor near the espresso kiosk, the machines spewing steam and grinding coffee beans, providing a noisy soundtrack to the group's flight. The chauffeur, a ruffian in the guise of bodyguard, driver, and gofer, balanced a tray of six espresso cups as he determinedly retraced his route to the office, lost in his effort to keep the drinks from spilling, and though he approached within a few steps, he failed to spot Thad or Felipe. The group entered the main hall and headed toward the exit, their pace increasing to a brisk trot when the illuminated red letters of USCITA came into view above doors that beckoned with the allure of pearly gates. When Simon pushed hard against the metal bar and threw wide the double doors—alarms sounding because it was an exit meant for emergency use only—the group filed into the parking lot. Simon pressed against the resistance of air compressors designed to keep the doors from slamming shut, maddening work as they refused to comply; he stayed until they latched into position and the alarms stopped blaring. Charlotte was leading the way toward the rented Citroën as Simon caught up. Fear glowed from their ashen faces;

only Felipe held his composure, his feelings of gratitude overcoming trepidation.

"No time to delay, jump in," Simon insisted, pulling forward the bucket seat to allow Thad and Felipe to squeeze into the back. He caught Thad's glance and softly touched his arm, that brief moment charging him with such affection he almost lost the sense of urgency—but they had to move, and move with haste. Thad folded his long legs against the front seat and motioned for Felipe to squeeze in next to him. With Charlotte beside him in the passenger seat, Simon drove as fast as the labored engine could manage, but not before glancing in the rearview mirror to see that the exit doors remained shut.

The next obstacle was the front gate—what to expect? Hopefully, the police remained with Emilio, David, and Irene; they would never have indicated that the two men leaving the office were associated with their company. But what about the coffee-carrying bodyguard? He would have hesitated within sight of the office when he saw the police and would have noticed the absence of Thad and Felipe. Would he race off to find them, knowing that whatever the police wanted with his bosses, his job was to keep Thad and Felipe from escaping?

Simon's throat tightened as the gate attendant approached the driver's side window. Think rationally! Simon told himself, to little avail, fully expecting the attendant to draw a weapon and order everyone from the car. But the attendant waved in a friendly manner and pulled a lever that caused the red-striped pole to rise—and the group's spirits with it. Simon drove toward the main road, closely watching the speed limit until he made it through the city center and onto a highway heading south out of Milan. Charlotte and Simon had only thought about the rescue, giving no thought to what would come next.

Felipe, his face dead center in the rearview mirror, remained expressionless, his eyes refusing to meet Simon's as he periodically turned to peer out the back window, unable to believe the success of their escape.

A large billboard with a hand waving at its edge directed traffic off the highway toward a gas station, an advertising suggestion that Simon followed, pulling to the back of a major truck stop to find a secluded place to park behind an eighteen-wheeler, where he collapsed, resting his forehead against the steering wheel, emotions drained, courage spent.

Thad reached around the seat to touch Simon's shoulder and said, "Let's get out of the car."

The group unfolded from the tiny vehicle. Thad rushed around the car to take Simon in his arms. The feel of Thad's skin, the familiar brush of his Thad's soft hair, the warmth of Thad's tight embrace electrified every cell of Simon's body. "I love you so much!" Simon cried out.

Thad pressed his face against Simon and wept.

Charlotte found a bench near the restrooms and sat with her knees pressed against her chest, her arms wrapped tightly around them. Felipe steadied himself, propped against the hood of the car.

"I was so confused," Simon whispered into Thad's ear. "For the longest time, I didn't know what was going on."

"I wanted to get a message to you. I tried."

"Don and Twiggy thought something was wrong when they saw you at the Spotlight, but they didn't figure out what was going on. Anyway, nothing matters but this moment—we're together! I can take you into my arms!"

"I never wanted to be in that video," Thad cried. "That's how you knew, right? They made such a deal about planting that photo of us. It was a safe way of sending you a message. As soon as production was complete, they mailed a videotape to Sibley."

"I was so scared when it arrived that I took it to Dean and let him open the package." Simon shuddered, realizing they had known his whereabouts. "Dean was sure from your picture on the back cover that you were scared."

"Forgive me, Simon."

"There's nothing to forgive, Thad. This is my fault. I should have gone with you to California."

Thad held Simon's face between his hands and gazed into his eyes. "I was afraid you'd think I left you. I couldn't stand you thinking that."

Felipe overhead the conversation. "Señor Simon," he said sotto voce, approaching them. "Señor Simon, Thad was made to do. Never he betray you, señor."

"I believe that, Felipe."

Though Felipe had starred in numerous adult films, he had never lost a sense of shame, and because of that, his humanity remained intact.

"Señor, please, never watch film of Thad. Please, señor. That is not Thad."

Simon reached out to bring Felipe into the embrace with Thad. Felipe, vulnerable to feelings of forgiveness and redemption, burst into tears.

"This is a touching scene," Charlotte interrupted sarcastically, and with reliable pragmatism she insisted, "but let's get the hell out of here."

Felipe straightened his back to stand proud and with a renewed sense of dignity. "You are Carlotta. Is true?"

"Yes," Charlotte confirmed, surprised that Felipe knew her name.

"Sí. Irene—eh, wife of David—she mention company you made—eh, Chanteuse?"

Charlotte tightened her scarf against the autumn breeze, an act signaling discomfort more than a reaction to the chill wind. "I want to hear what they know about my company, but for now let's get moving. I don't think anyone followed us, but I'll feel better when we are farther away."

The foursome crammed back into the car. Simon drove to the front of the truck stop's central building, past a group of shops, parked in front of a Howard Johnson's restaurant, and dashed inside for a coffee to go. Afterward he filled up the efficient car's minuscule gas tank and proceeded toward the highway with no plan except to drop off the car wherever they ended up, despite the extra charges they would incur for not returning it to the original location. He hoped Charlotte had enough money to cover it.

"Felipe," Simon called out as they entered the on-ramp, "what should we do? Do you need to stay in Italia? Do you have your passport?"

Felipe laughed. "You make many questions. I have passport because MIFED police, they look for people illegal. I keep in pocket."

"You took a big chance leaving with us. You've made yourself part of this."

"Eh, sí. Emilio, David, they become very angry. Irene most bad, she make trouble for people."

"Then why are you laughing?"

"Emilio y David, they fear la polizia when no in España. Italia is católico, home for Vatican. No like the people with sex film. You take risk, señor, go to polizia to make trouble. Is thing they most fear, the polizia."

Simon felt so weakened by apprehension, he could barely command his foot to press the accelerator.

"Is no problemo, Señor Simon. David y Emilio, they will make argue, maybe give polizia money, eh, bribe. MIFED muy importante. They must sell film. No lose time. Now, they no follow us."

"And later?"

Felipe's face darkened. "Do not know, Señor Simon. Maybe they make much money. Maybe no more care."

Charlotte kept her attention fixed on the outside mirror. No matter how improbable it was, she worried that someone could have followed them.

"They'll want to get back at us, one way or another," Thad sighed. "They are connected to the Mafia and know people all over the world. One call and a person drops dead."

"Charlotte, you might be right," Simon hollered over the traffic noise.

"What?" Charlotte asked incredulously. "Oh, you mean about hiding out? Damn, Simon, I don't know what we should do."

Thad leaned forward to be heard more easily. "I need to explain a couple of things. When Emilio was at the ranch after David and Irene left, he kept flirting with me, saying that I could be a star—that he'd make a movie with me. One evening, in front of Emilio, Howard asked me how you were doing. Emilio had been pushing him for information about me, hoping to find the reason I didn't want to be in a movie—that maybe I had a boyfriend or something. I tried not to react when Howard said your name, and Emilio didn't flinch—but I saw his eyes burning. I wanted to get away that night, but Howard's ranch is in the middle of nowhere. I was hoping I'd get the chance to drive his car to the store the next morning, ditch it, and catch a bus into LA."

"When you stopped calling, I tried to reach you. Howard disconnected the phone."

"Yeah, he did that the next day. Howard turned out to be a real dick. I wasn't supposed to see it happen, but Emilio gave Howard a pile of cash."

"I worried that Howard might have *sold* you, and it sounds like he did."

"The cash also paid for a cameraman. Emilio asked Howard if there was a place in Hollywood where people might see me, people who would let you know about it."

"That scene at the Spotlight!"

"Exactly. Howard remembered that I went to the Spotlight the night he took the crew to the Brown Derby for dinner. The cameraman Emilio hired is a real jerk. He wouldn't have cared if they'd paid him to shoot a snuff film—with me as the victim. Before we got to Hollywood, Emilio said that if I tried anything funny, the next stop would be the desert, that I'd become food for coyotes."

"Sí, he would do." Felipe nodded.

"Do they know it was me who actually took their money?" Charlotte interrupted.

Felipe listened intently to Charlotte's question. "They know something wrong soon after send money. They get message and think you and Simon work together with police to catch them. Emilio try reach you, Señor Simon, but never get answer. Then no office telephone, no fax, no telex. Many months go by and they get very angry, but they give up—how you say, cut losses. They come to Howard only to make porno in Hollywood, not to find you."

"I should never have sent them a message," Charlotte lamented. "But I had no idea Simon had worked out a shady deal, that they were criminals. I just thought they were clients with a lot of money, and I didn't want to lose them."

"When I was in the Barcelona office," Thad remembered, "they were talking about the MIFED catalog and said that it listed some of Simon's titles under your name and the company Chanteuse—Irene mentioned the telex you had sent. Felipe is right that they wondered if the note and the booth at MIFED were part of a setup to entrap them. They thought it was possible Simon had landed in jail and made a deal with the police. That's the way their minds work. I wouldn't know any of this if they had realized I understood their Spanish."

"I forgot about hearing you speak Spanish to our drag friend Patricia," Simon recalled.

"Just high school classes."

"Please, no speak Español to me," Felipe laughed. "You understand, but, eh, speak no good."

Thad tapped Felipe on the head in a congenial way.

"God, this is horrible," Charlotte shouted. "Fuck, I started this."

"Yes, you did," Simon accused.

"At least the truth is out," Charlotte sighed. "That's something."

"Not much of something," Simon chided.

"Maybe all good," Felipe offered. "David and Emilio have video and make much money."

"You mean the one with Thad and you?"

"Sí, señor. They have video, you have Thad."

Felipe's facial expression, as Simon glimpsed it in the rearview mirror, and Thad's furtive response told Simon that making the video had not been entirely unpleasant.

"How did they manage to get you to Spain?" Simon asked, still talking loudly to overcome the road noise.

"After we got back from shooting those scenes in Hollywood, they locked me in a bedroom for two days. Then we all crammed into a private jet. We landed in Mexico without going through customs and from there took a commercial flight to Barcelona. They had found my passport going through my things at Howard's. They gave it to me so I could get into MIFED and hadn't had time to get it back from me."

"At least you and Felipe are free now," Simon sighed.

"You got paid for *El Amigo Rico*, didn't you, Felipe?" Thad asked.

"Sí. And much money in banco, eh, bank. I no more need make porno." Felipe paused for a moment, then addressed Simon, leaning forward to put his mouth closer to his ear. "Can you take me to España? Yes? To Madrid? There is mi familia. Señors Emilio y David, they no think I have familia."

"As far as I'm concerned, the farther we get from Italy, the better. We can drop off the car in Madrid and fly back to the States from there. We'll have enough money, right, Charlotte?"

Simon saw Charlotte's tentative nod in the rearview window. "Yeah, I guess," she said.

Thad waved something over the seat. "Thank God we needed our passports to get badges at the MIFED registration desk."

"Charlotte and I never even talked about how we'd get you home, Thad. We'd make terrible secret agents! Felipe, are you okay to cross the border?"

"Sí, señor." Felipe reached into his jacket pocket and held up his passport.

The little band fleeing the world of kidnappers and pornographers drove across the border from southern France into Spain. Thad and Felipe felt the joy of released prisoners on their first day out. Charlotte felt more anxious than ever, and mad that she was losing her big chance at MIFED. And Simon, finally free of doubt, was more confident than ever of Thad's love for him.

CHAPTER THIRTY-THREE

S imon wanted to explore Madrid, to visit the Prado, and, if nothing else, to see *The Garden of Earthly Delights* and the corresponding hell-scape panel of Hieronymus Bosch's famous triptych. But anxiety pressed the group onward, despite Felipe's assurance that no one could possibly know that they had gone to Spain. Simon argued that Felipe's dialect gave him away as someone raised near Madrid and that Emilio, David, and Irene would expect him to have friends there, even if they didn't know about his family.

"Eh, they think I go America," Felipe assured. "They know I save money; now I have chance to go. Never think Madrid."

Simon hoped Felipe was right as he guided them to a small town about fifty kilometers southwest of Madrid.

"Oropesa, it is muy small," Felipe said as they approached the city.

Oropesa was small, but the sight of its medieval castle made Simon wonder about visiting under better circumstances if he ever returned with Thad to see the Prado.

"Mi familia, work at el Parador."

Simon paid little attention to what Felipe said until they neared the city and Simon realized that the restored castle was a luxury hotel.

"Maybe best leave me with cars, eh, parking lot. I find family."

The tone of Felipe's voice made Simon doubt his earlier assurances about them being followed. Watching for any strange vehicles following them, Simon found a parking space in the area designated for staff. Thad spoke to Felipe in awkward Spanish as he struggled from the back seat. Simon refused to allow jealousy to demean their moment of parting, though he knew a bond had formed between them.

As Simon, Thad, and Charlotte drove away from the castle, Felipe stood at a service entrance waving vigorously until the car turned a corner and disappeared from sight. On the open road, flanked by sparsely populated farmland, Simon pondered his journey in life, starting when he'd first met Nicolò and embarked on a career in business after leaving Sun Myung Moon's group, instead of following his true desire to pursue a career in the arts. Though Simon had no faith in providence, he firmly believed that people should pursue the life they were inclined toward, having no doubt where his heart resided.

At the Madrid airport, Charlotte paid a hefty fee for crossing borders and traveling so many miles in the rental car. The flight they booked should have been direct to Los Angeles, but a strike by baggage handlers detoured the plane through Paris's Charles de Gaulle Airport. Simon never felt such relief as the moment when a dour customs official completed his scrutiny of their passports, and they set foot on home turf. Even the taxi from the Los Angeles airport, bouncing on questionable shock absorbers, felt luxurious.

Thad led Simon upstairs as soon as they entered the cliffside house through the tall front door, undressed, and watched as Simon shed his clothes. They held each other tight on the narrow guestroom bed, two bodies melded into one, love warding off worry and doubt—whether lingering from the past or gathering strength for the future. Nothing mattered but this moment in time.

"Never doubt it, Simon, I love you," Thad said consolingly.

Simon had never felt as safe as that moment provided, but as he tried to sleep, held closely by Thad, his mind raced through recent events, worried he had allowed himself to be lulled into a false sense of freedom. He carefully unwound himself from Thad's arms and ventured downstairs in his robe, discovering Charlotte in the office beneath the garage, poring over recent faxes and downloading telexes through a dial-up modem. Simon remembered the space beneath the garage as cloistered and gloomy but private, a space to engage hustlers in sex while smoking cocaine. Entering now was to transverse a parallel universe.

The message machine's red indicator light flashed to alert of a new message—people had been calling. Charlotte held up a pile of faxes and pointed to the number of telexes still downloading. "I don't know what I am going to say to people," she sighed. "So many questions about why the booth at MIFED is vacant."

"I hope I never hear the term MIFED again," Simon said wearily. "The film business did nothing but expedite my ruin."

Charlotte put down the faxes and placed her hands on either side of Simon's face. "Stop it. You're just going through a phase, some recovery step or something. You'll get over it. The film business made you almost rich. Your problem has to do with that religion that screwed with your head. Give it time—you'll get back into the swing of things. You're a natural-born businessman, Simon."

Inwardly, if not to Charlotte, Simon admitted that the capitalist game could be alluring: negotiating, logistics, challenges...profit! For all the personal and public turmoil Simon had endured as a member of Sun Myung Moon's organization, he had been good at raising money, never letting himself consider the Moon family's opulent lifestyle, a lifestyle he'd enabled by sending hundreds of

members to parking lots and stoplights to sell cheap wares, sending millions of dollars to church bank accounts, accounts used to
pay for mansions, private schools, and expensive wardrobes for the
True Family.

Charlotte replied to some of the telexes, using vague statements about medical issues coming up that made it difficult to
travel. Disheartened, she led Simon upstairs, where they sat at the
counter separating the kitchen from the dining area, balancing
on barstools. Charlotte poured fresh brew from beans ground in a
recently purchased coffeemaker.

"I don't know where my energy is coming from," Charlotte said.
"Coffee is the last thing I need, but I just can't go to sleep. There's
so much work to do."

"We need to talk, you know."

"I know, Simon. But not now."

The coffee gave Simon a few moments of alertness, but soon
exhaustion caught up with him. As Charlotte returned to the
downstairs office, Simon retreated to the bedroom, crawling under
the covers and embracing Thad. Images from *El Amigo Rico* played
through Simon's mind, images he tried to deny—that isn't Thad,
that's a shadow of Thad; remember the love we shared—but it was
Thad in the mental panorama, Thad making love to Felipe, both
servicing Emilio. In a half-waking dream, David and Irene watched
the threesome, jotting down notes; Irene, wearing an emerald robe,
set down her pad and keyed numbers into an old-fashioned adding machine, pulling a level to print the results, the gray machine
emitting the same sound that Vivian's made when Simon had sat
with her as a child and admired the speed with which she tallied
the grocery store's daily receipts. More dreams pursued Simon,
spawned by anxieties from childhood: Simon's abuse during baptism, his questioning mind succumbing to errant beliefs about the
kingdom of God, and later, his drug-addled paranoia fueling fits
of hysteria—Thad running off with Cicero—Simon rampaging

through Hollywood with a butcher knife to kill anyone who might interfere with his vengeance—the tenderness of his lovemaking with Thad—theft—betrayal—the soft murmuring of Thad and Charlotte speaking downstairs—Simon forced himself awake.

"Irene's an ice queen," Thad was saying as Simon listened at the top of the stairs. "I don't think she once looked me in the eyes. I was nothing but a pony in her stable. Anyway, one of the times they didn't think I understood their Spanish, Irene laughed in a shrill voice and asked David if he had sent the video to *Seeblee*. Her pronunciation was so bad, I wasn't sure I understood correctly, not until David laughed in a voice as creepy as his wife's and confirmed that *El Amigo Rico* was on its way."

"Holy shit!" Charlotte shouted. "You're saying that they had Simon's address in Arkansas?"

"I didn't have a choice," Thad said.

Charlotte glanced at the glass forming the wall beside the front door if expecting to see figures beyond the opaque murkiness.

"Since the authorities confronted them, they'll lie low," Thad mused. "I just hope they got their revenge with the video and they'll leave us alone after this."

Simon didn't want to enter into the conversation between Thad and Charlotte, so he returned to the bedroom, followed shortly by Thad, who kissed Simon on the back of his neck and sighed as he pulled up the covers, placing his arm around Simon in a tight embrace.

"What might have happened if we hadn't rescued you?" Simon asked.

"They figured they owned me, paid for me with the money they sent without getting the films they expected. I'm not sure how many movies they wanted to put me in, but more than just the one, I'm sure of that. I wish I could have found a way to get a message to you. Twiggy was catching on that I wanted to tell him something, but then he got busy, and the bodyguard wasn't about to let me get

255

his attention again after he realized what I was up to. The bar was busy that night. We stayed just long enough for you to hear about me being there with Felipe."

"You must have been scared when they took you to Spain."

"Felipe kept me from going nuts. He's a funny guy. He made me believe that everything would work out. He said he prayed that everything would work out, which seemed crazy—pray? And then get fucked for money?—but his faith put him a positive frame of mind. It was like he separated who he was in his mind from what he did with his body."

"Do you really think they'll be satisfied with the one video? That it evens the score?"

"I don't know, Simon. I'm more worried about the way we embarrassed them at MIFED."

"I have to ask you something."

"You thought I'd been seduced into making porn, didn't you?"

"When I saw *El Amigo Rico*, I wasn't sure what to think. I saw fear in your eyes, and then there was the photo of us, but you and Felipe didn't seem to be acting."

Thad couldn't address Simon's suspicion, so he merely said, "I was acting in the scene with Emilio, trust me."

"I can't get the image out of my head."

"Emilio found the picture of us in my room at Howard's," Thad continued. "He's the one who placed it on the headboard so it would be in the video."

"But it could have been your way of telling me our relationship was over."

"I'm not in love with Felipe, Simon. I know that's what you're worried about. But if Felipe hadn't been kind to me, I would have tried to run, and that bodyguard—Alfonso the Merciless, I called him—would have shot me in the back or something."

"I have a confession to make, Thad. The scene with you and Felipe in the room with Emilio was staged as a reenactment of

what happened when I was in Barcelona and made the deal with them."

"I know. Felipe thought I didn't, but I heard him talking to Emilio when the scene was being planned. Do you honestly think I would have let them do that—what, as a way of telling you we were breaking up or something? You know that's not me. I would just have told you. I'm not a tricky person like that. You know I'm not."

"Dean tried to assure me; he saw the fear in your eyes."

"Emilio sometimes laughed off the fact that you stole their money—nickels and dimes, he would say—but David always shot back with remarks about honor and revenge. Irene would nod, spewing words in Catalan that I couldn't understand."

"We can only hope they forget about us."

"What about Charlotte?" Thad asked. "What's up with the two of you? Did she return the money or something? I can't believe she's living in our place!"

"Long story. She contacted my clients, telling them she'd bought the business. She started with Wally, whom I called after leaving rehab. He would only allow me to represent the films in the original contract, saying he had made arrangements for the new ones, but he never gave me a hint the arrangement was with Charlotte. Charlotte has been keeping tabs on me through Wally. I had no idea."

"And you're okay with all this? What about Rudy? Don't tell me he's your friend again."

"He's back at the Spotlight, in like Flynn with Don. Rudy and Charlotte had a falling out, so Rudy spilled the beans about Wally to Don. That's what set things in motion that led to working with Charlotte to rescue you."

"She ought to give back the money."

"Maybe, over time. Charlotte and I agreed that after I finish college, if I want to come back to Los Angeles, we can stay here in Silverlake. Quite a reversal of fortune, isn't it?"

"Well, maybe a transfer of fortune. She still stole from you. I've never seen you so forgiving. Anyway, I miss Vivian. I even miss watching soaps with your sister."

"And Cicero misses you."

Thad puckered his face and snorted, imitating an excited Cicero.

"Cicero's with Connie. Cheryl is dropping by to feed Ferdinand. Vivian had another stroke, and we had to put her in a nursing home. We'll go visit when we get back to Sibley—you will go with me, right?"

Thad held Simon close. "The mansion, the goat, Cicero, even that haunted graveyard across the street—can you believe that I really do miss it?"

Simon thought for a moment about how he felt toward the Sibley mansion, about its legends, his mysterious aunt Opal, the childhood adventures of Simon and Ernie. The mansion and the lands surrounding it were as much a part of him as his arms and legs.

"That mansion is my Valhalla, Thad, a fortress against the darkness. It's my bond with the past as much as Vivian is my tether to the present."

"Let's hope the devil got his due, and we can live happily ever after," Thad whispered.

"Listen to you." Simon took Thad's hand. "The devil his due. You've been around me too long."

"I hope it is forever, Simon. Get that video out of your mind. Forget Felipe. You're the only person I want."

There was a gentle knock at the door. "Simon, if you're awake, can you answer?" Charlotte spoke in a subdued but urgent voice. "I need to tell you something."

Simon and Thad both got up, dressed, and joined Charlotte downstairs.

"This is so weird," Charlotte began. "I just got off the phone with Wally. By the way, he said to tell you that he's relieved he doesn't have to pretend any longer."

"I'm surprised he was able to keep your secret as long as he did."

"I can be persuasive," Charlotte said, flashing a sexy smile. She seemed refreshed after doing her hair and putting on makeup.

"What is that lipstick you're wearing? I love the color."

"What do you mean?" Charlotte demurred. "I'm au naturel today."

"Okay, but there's a tube of lipstick beside your purse there on the end table."

Charlotte scooped up the cosmetics and closed her handbag.

"What were you going to say, Charlotte? What's so weird?"

"It's that Howard fellow."

"What's up with Howard?"

"He's dead. Two days ago."

Simon backed toward a chair and sat down. "Oh my God. Foul play?"

Thad's complexion grew ashen as he steadied himself against the bar and sat on a stool.

"I asked Wally the same thing. Wally said the police raided the Chatsworth studio. Someone tipped them off about an underaged actor."

"Howard knew he'd screwed up when he accepted that fake ID," Thad interjected.

"Did Wally know anything more about what happened?" Simon asked.

"Evidently, Howard was drunk when the cops served the warrant. He pulled a gun from his desk drawer, and a rookie cop shot him in the head."

"Holy shit," Thad blurted out.

"Maybe this will send a message to Emilio, David, and Irene that they better not fool around with American police," Simon said hopefully.

"Can we hit the road to Sibley? Like, today?" Thad asked.

"Don't you want to visit Scott or Sandra or drop by to let Twiggy and Don know we're okay?"

"No. I just want to get the fuck out of town."

"I have to agree. I'm getting nervous."

"You're going to abandon me, just like that?" Charlotte complained. "With all that's going on?"

"Maybe we've met the end of our trouble, Charlotte, and I've barely got enough money for the drive back to Arkansas. Emilio, David, and Irene will return to Barcelona after MIFED, and they'll have new contracts to manage. Can what happened with Thad and Felipe matter so much? It should be obvious we're more trouble than we're worth."

"You think I'm safe, really safe?" Charlotte implored. "I'm not sure I can forget the last few days."

"Maybe one of your hunky boyfriends can stay with you."

"I guess you're right. But I keep seeing Emilio's eyes when the police showed up—so much anger. And the other fellow, David, he looked like a rattlesnake coiled and ready to strike. And that woman, Irene. Good God, she's Medusa with that stare of hers."

"They're not here now," Simon said consolingly, as much for himself as Charlotte. "Forget them."

"I hate this," Charlotte moaned. "We interfered with their business at MIFED and made off with Felipe and Thad. They know who I am and that I'm involved."

"What would you have us do, Charlotte? You can move to a different place. I am joined to Sibley and the mansion until death do us part."

"It's just a building," Thad said. "You're not married to the place."

"I feel like I am."

"Damn it, Simon. It's just a house."

"Someday I want my portrait to hang in the gallery." Simon surprised himself with the statements; most of his life he had professed disgust with Sibley. "I want to be one of the ghosts that haunt the place. A hundred years from now, someone will look at my picture and wonder about my story."

Thad laughed. "My God, Simon. You said the right word, ghost. Let's make a life together, whether it's at the mansion, Los Angeles, New York, or wherever you want to live. I don't care, as long as we're together."

"Being kidnapped seems to have matured you," Simon noted with a gleam in his eye.

"Being forced to have sex to keep from ending up on a Spanish garbage heap or buried at sea makes a person think about what matters."

"Been a trip, guys," Charlotte interrupted. "But my moment of fear has passed. I'm not letting those assholes get the better of me." She did a mock pole dance against the bar. "I'll be damned if those nasty people from Spain are going to take anything from me. I'm not moving out of here, and I'm not giving up Chanteuse Film Distributors."

"You've got spunk. You'll be fine," Simon reassured.

"Okay, you guys, get more rest, hit the road, whatever. I'm going into Hollywood. I'll drop by the Spotlight and let Don and Twiggy know you're safe and that you're back together. I'm going to confront Rudy. And now I have juicy gossip about Howard being shot to spread around."

When Charlotte left, Simon suggested they start on their journey, knowing they'd be unable to sleep. Thad agreed.

"Good-bye, Silverlake house!" Simon said as he closed the tall front door.

"It was strange to see Charlotte living there."

"Treat Charlotte well," Simon told the house.

"You are so weird."

Thad fell asleep in the passenger seat before they made it to the Hollywood Freeway. Simon, uncannily alert, set their sights eastward—to Sibley.

CHAPTER THIRTY-FOUR

T had checked every room in the mansion, frantic to assure
himself that no one lay in wait, no hitmen lay ready to attack,
not in the upstairs rooms, the basement, or the attic. Simon was
less concerned about bad guys than about making sure his paintings were safe and Ferdinand was fed. Cheryl had done an excel-
lent job; Ferdinand's trough was full of alfalfa pellets, and the
washtub overflowed with fresh water. The paintings had survived
a wooden door being blown open in the hayloft, caused by winds
during recent heavy rainfall, Simon surmised, judging by the level
to which the pond water had risen, high enough to cover the flat
rock where the green turtles sunned themselves. The roof made it
through the storm unscathed, a fact Simon appreciated not only
because his paintings were dry, but because he dreaded climbing
into the rafters where the resident bats would soon return from
their nightly foraging, dawn just breaking through the spindly top
limbs of the nearby cypress trees.

Simon made iced tea, a welcome change from the bitter roadside coffee that had sustained them during the long drive from

Hollywood, and joined Thad at the dinette table. Sunflowers as large as dinner plates, now gone to seed, bowed under their weight in a familiar sight, one that reminded Simon of his grandmother Mandy, who would sit for hours staring at this crop's forebears.

"You should telephone Connie," Thad suggested. "If she brings Cicero when she comes over, I'm afraid the little guy might have an asthma attack. He gets so excited when he sees someone after a long absence."

"I should call Cheryl too, let her know that I appreciate the care she gave Ferdinand. Cheryl dislikes coming to the mansion, especially when she's alone. She's convinced a resentful ancestor will slam the doors and windows to keep her inside. Cheryl has a vivid imagination. I wish I had been around while she was growing up…and I missed Victoria's childhood."

Thad set down his glass of tea and looked around. "Yeah, but it doesn't take too much imagination to agree with Cheryl. I know you regret not being close to your nieces, but they both seem to love you."

"I represent a kind of freedom for them. I don't know what Connie and Derek have said about me over the years, but the few times I visited, they jumped into my arms as if they missed me more than anyone." Simon stood at the window, surveilling what he could see spotlighted under the mercury vapor lamp beside the corral. "Looks like the grass around the pond is close cropped. Cheryl must have staked Ferdinand there longer than other places. One more cold snap and his diet will be limited to oats until spring comes."

"I never thought I'd be happy tending a goat," Thad laughed, "or living in the middle of nowhere. But you know…I couldn't be happier right now."

"Being with you makes everything seem new, as if I've never before gazed on the sunflowers or watched the bats flow into the rafters."

Thad plopped ice cubes in his glass from a freezer tray and brought the Princess phone to the table. "Connie will be up by now. Let me say hello before you hang up."

Simon prepared himself for Connie's inevitable questioning about his trip to California. He was not prepared for her news.

"I'm glad you're back," Connie said, her voice faltering. "Vivian had another stroke last night. I went to see her this morning. The doctor said she didn't have much longer…"

Thad understood Connie's message through Simon's expression, mouthing the words, "It's Vivian, isn't it?"

Simon nodded.

"Vivian is completely out of it," Connie explained. "I tried to lift her chin this morning to see if she would recognize me, but she couldn't keep her eyes open."

"Did the doctor say anything specific—I mean, about how long…"

"It could be hours, it could be weeks. The nurse has been giving her vitamin milkshakes, but when they put the straw to her mouth, she doesn't respond. If she doesn't eat, they can't force her. That's what Vivian wanted."

"Seems that Thad and I returned just in time." The drama of recent events played through Simon's thoughts as he considered how lucky they had been with the rescue. He was unwilling to consider what might have happened had they failed.

"You should be thankful to the Lord, Simon. Vivian was saved. She'll go to heaven."

Simon stopped himself from commenting, knowing how Connie depended on her beliefs to see her through the loss they were about to share. Simon braced himself for the unfiltered agony of losing his mother, holding no idea other than death as the gateway to oblivion.

"Do you want to visit Vivian with me?" Connie asked. "I can drop by and pick up the two of you."

"Actually, Connie, I'd like to be alone with her. Please don't be upset."

"I'm not upset, Simon. I understand. Let me know how she looks after you see her."

"I will."

Ending the conversation, Simon knew that Connie would say a prayer, while a quiet but persistent desire would hum in the recesses of his mind: to stem the emotional tide through the numbing grace of cocaine. Simon recalled the trust he had once placed in Sun Myung Moon's vision of building the kingdom of heaven on earth. Sacrifices, deaths, hardship—all of it fit into the plan for a new world, the idea of a glorious future making life worthwhile. Connie's faith in an afterlife and Simon's conviction of the possibility of an earthly paradise mitigated loss and gave hope that pain could be endured for the sake of the future. Those who followed Jesus must have faced an indescribable sense of sadness and loss at his death; consumed with such grief, they must have denied he had died all. Their grief had transmuted loss into visions of a resurrected Christ, loss transforming their denial into grief so profound it spread through humanity and survived two millennia, recreating the visionary Jesus with each new convert. Simon could see Vivian at that very moment sitting in the parlor reading one of her romance novels, as real as if she were flesh made manifest.

"This place needs a lot of work," Simon noted, distracting himself with consideration of the mundane world. "I should get estimates on the cost of restoring this place."

Thad stood at the window as a murder of crows swooped at a desperate Ferdinand, who stomped and jabbed his horns, trying to keep the pellet-robbing thieves away from his food trough. "The mansion is in worse shape than you realize," Thad pointed out, running his finger near the cracked edge of a glass pane.

"If only it were possible to tap into the fortune that's been put in trust to maintain the place. But no one has wanted to try to gather all the signatures it would require for the bank to release the money. The money has been earning interest for generations, all the way back to JT Powell, the man hanged from the oak tree. I'd have to track down every descendant and get them to agree that the mansion should be restored."

"You never told me about a trust fund!"

"Lenny's brother tried to piece together the legalities when he was young—at least that's what Lenny once told me. But he gave up, saying it would take a lifetime to track everyone down, sort of like the ending of *Bleak House*—nothing would be left after all the squabbling. Lenny wasn't interested in the money because he thought he could do the work himself, but then his heart gave out."

Simon wondered if he and Thad remained in Sibley whether he could find the dispersed relatives by searching message boards and newsgroups, technology coming into greater use with each passing day.

"I'd hate for all these pictures to get damaged by a leak or something," Thad said as they went upstairs.

"There's an attic above those planks." Simon pointed at the hallway ceiling. "I haven't looked up there since I was thirteen. I remember seeing stacked crates and barrels filled with packing straw. Ernie and I found such a barrel in the basement and discovered items that had once belonged to Aunt Opal. Maybe the effigy of JT that used to swing from the oak tree on Halloween is up there. I looked high and low in the basement, but the only things we found were Aunt Opal's books, a box of scents, and a corn-husk doll like the ones slave children made."

"I remember," Thad said, rolling his eyes as he recalled Simon talking about the discoveries made with Ernie.

Thad stood in front of Wesley's portrait. "This is such a spooky image. You should get a good thirty-five-millimeter camera and take pictures of them all."

"Too expensive to do it right."

"Maybe so."

"On the other hand, a photography student at the university might take on documenting them as a semester project."

"I really caused trouble going to work for Howard, didn't I?" Thad said. "I hope your professors let you catch up on what you missed."

"I'm as much to blame for not just moving to LA with you. Anyway, right now I need to rest before going to see Vivian."

"Our bed!" Thad swooned as he entered the bedroom and got under the covers.

"What was it like, Thad? Really like," Simon asked, snuggling close as he got in bed.

Thad's heart pounded at the question. "Scary as hell. I was terrified that Irene would put me in one of the bondage videos she directed. Felipe told me that young guys from Serbia came to Barcelona to appear in them, and if the films didn't sell, no one heard from the Serbians again."

"You mean…"

"Taken out to sea and pushed overboard from Emilio's yacht, according to Felipe."

"Why not just send them home?"

Thad shivered. "Less trouble just to dispose of them, I suppose. That's what Felipe thought, anyway, and he was the closest to Emilio, sleeping in his bed and all. He worried that when he got older, that's what would happen to him."

"I love you so much, Thad. Whatever we have to do, wherever we have to go to be together, that's what I want."

"Please don't ask me any more questions about what happened. I did what I had to do. I didn't want to end up like those Serbian boys."

"This moment is all that matters."

Thad wept as Simon held him close.

The next morning, Thad having gone downstairs to make breakfast, Simon listened to the wind as it brushed the wisteria branches against the window, tapping as if crows were pecking on the glass. From downstairs, the aroma of sizzling bacon nearly levitated Simon out of bed toward the kitchen.

"How soon until breakfast, Thad?" Simon called from the top of the stairs.

Thad stood at the bottom of the stairs, holding a spatula and wearing one of Vivian's frilly aprons. "Give me twenty minutes. I have a soufflé in the oven."

"Using those eggs from the farm down the road?"

"The small brown ones. Connie must have stocked the refrigerator before we arrived. She even left bacon wrapped in butcher paper from Sibley Grocery."

Simon telephoned Connie from the hallway phone to thank her and to let her know he hadn't yet visited Vivian, that he and Thad had slept all the previous day and night.

"That wasn't me," Connie said about the groceries. "Cheryl mentioned restocking when I told her you'd be returning with Thad."

Simon again felt pangs of regret that he had not been at home to see Cheryl and his younger niece, Victoria, grow up, remembering how joyously they'd greeted him on his infrequent visits over the years.

"Brace yourself before you see Vivian," Connie cautioned. "She probably won't recognize you. She's likely to be unresponsive."

"Thanks for preparing me, Connie."

After the call, Simon lit the gas-powered wall stove in the upstairs bathroom, waiting until the air was heated before taking a shower. Though the efficient stove quickly warmed the air, the black and white floor tiles felt like ice against Simon's feet. He laid out a towel to serve as a rug before stepping into the footed tub and pulling the white plastic curtain along the aluminum rod.

Refreshed from his long, luxurious shower, Simon joined Thad in the kitchen for the soufflé, crisp bacon, and coffee. "Do you want to go with me to see Vivian?" Simon asked.

"I'll stay and clean the house. There's so much dust everywhere!"

Thad's expression told Simon the housework wasn't the issue, that seeing Vivian would be hard for him as well—better to stay busy.

CHAPTER THIRTY-FIVE

E ach time Simon visited Bobwhite Convalescent Center, he remembered trips from home on his bicycle to visit Mandy, memories ripe with the odor of unlaundered bedsheets, unemptied bedpans, soiled diapers thrown into hampers, and the pitiful pleas of residents unsure of their surroundings or their very identities. He recalled the nickname given to the place by Sibley residents: death's waiting room. Stricter laws and better enforcement had improved Bobwhite's reputation; it now claimed, euphemistically avoiding the word death, that the facility offered end-of-life care.

Visitors gained entry by pushing a red button beside a sliding glass door. Exiting was made more difficult by requiring a numeric code long enough that most residents would have trouble remembering it. One of the many volunteers, recruited by the Baptist charity that operated the facility, escorted Simon along a narrow hallway, past nurses on their rounds and others whose job it was to lift men and women from their beds onto mobile contraptions so they could be taken to a shower stall and held aloft in a swing-like harness. One of the nurses, a woman who looked familiar but whose name Simon could not recall, took him to see Vivian in a semiprivate room located in a wing for those needing extra care and attention. Simon knew what to expect, having experienced Mandy's last days as well as Lenny's final hours, but prior experience failed to buffer the impact. Whatever had constituted the mother Simon knew, only an emaciated shell remained, barely resembling the vibrant woman who'd defended Simon at the family reunion in Magnolia, who'd told him about Lenny's sad childhood, who'd helped him understand that Lenny's bitterness arose from the sacrifices made for family, and who'd made Simon feel loved, made him know that he deserved love. If only Simon had told Vivian about the man who had corrupted his sense of self-worth instead of ushering him unmolested to the absolution of baptism.

The nurse addressed Simon as he stood at the door of Vivian's room. "We've met before," she said.

"Jennifer Calumet, right?" The woman's voice had shaken loose old memories that caused her name to pop into Simon's mind.

"I didn't think you'd remember me. It's Mrs. Hinkson now."

"We went to Sibley High School together. I remember. You were a year behind me."

"Seems like such a long time ago, doesn't it?"

"It was a long time ago." Simon smiled. "Over twenty years." He didn't want to press the issue of memories. His former classmate's brother, Benjamin Calumet, had gone into a coma after receiving a concussion during the season's championship football game, and her aunt had succumbed to flames during a fire at the store where she'd worked as a bookkeeper.

"I've never held that article against you, you know," Mrs. Hinkson said, referring to an essay Simon had written for the school paper, arguing that the administration should care as much about academic achievement as it did about success in sports, pointing out that the school had won three consecutive championships and that therefore it was time, as the headline suggested, to start "Letting Others Win," to move away from sports and begin paying to attention to the humanities and sciences.

"I was young and idealistic," Simon said, averting his eyes from Mrs. Hinkson's.

Lenny and Vivian had endured weeks of phone calls after the school allowed publication of Simon's column, parents and classmates accusing them of Communist sympathies for raising a son to think it was acceptable to just give up—their interpretation of the headline, having never bothered to read the actual article. Simon remembered Lenny railing at one caller, "That boy don't listen to nothing I tell him."

Simon had stopped himself from saying to Lenny, "Like the time you told me that if a boy or girl wasn't white, I wasn't to play with them?"

"The school newspaper published your column before Ben's injury," Mrs. Hinkson pointed out. "If the coach had understood what you were trying to say...Ben is the reason I went into convalescent care. I was lucky to get this job so I can be near him. I read to Ben every night when I get off work. People wake up from these things all the time, you know."

Simon placed his hand on Mrs. Hinkson's shoulder in a gesture of sympathy before walking toward Vivian's bed and putting his arm through the railing to take her hand, almost recoiling at the touch of her skeletal fingers and the feel of her skin, as dry as waxed paper. "There's no chance she'll improve, is there?"

Mrs. Hinkson fluffed Vivian's pillow, set her head at a more comfortable angle, and pressed another pillow between the railing and the mattress for added security, noting that Vivian sometimes slipped to the floor. She checked the oxygen tubes helping Vivian breathe and jotted down readings from a blood pressure and pulse monitor. "Poor dear hasn't taken a drop of fluid in three days."

Mrs. Hinkson looked at Simon with penetrating eyes. "Are you sure you want us to continue this way? Not even an IV?"

"I understand the consequences of the do-not-resuscitate order," Simon responded. "I hate seeing her this way, but my sister and I talked to Vivian many times about her wishes. She never wanted to be kept alive artificially." He put his hand on Vivian's forehead.

"We try to make her comfortable," Mrs. Hinkson said. "She's had a fever today, but the antibiotic suppository we administered is bringing it down a bit."

"Connie told me she doesn't have long. Do we know?"

"Her diaper has been dry, which tells us that her kidneys are shutting down. I'd be surprised if she lasted more than two or three days."

"Thanks for being honest about it. I'll be here as much as I can. Vivian shouldn't die alone."

"Mrs. Powell was so nice to everyone down at Sibley Grocery. Everyone liked her."

"Vivian enjoyed people."

"I know this isn't easy. I am on call if you need me, and the rest of the staff is ready to help. Oh, and I'm sure you know, but Lordy, Mrs. Powell told us every chance she got that if she has a funeral, the casket must be closed. Poor dear, she had the worst fear of people looking at her body. I hope you don't mind me saying so. It's just that it mattered so much to her. I'm sure she told you the same thing."

"She made it very clear to Connie and me."

Mrs. Hinkson went about her duties. Simon pulled up a chair and sat close to Vivian's bed. He spoke aloud, sure that she heard his words, even if she couldn't respond.

"Your son is here," Simon began. "I love you."

Vivian's temples felt hot from her fever. Simon caressed her forehead and stroked her hair. Against his palm, he rubbed the

cranial bumps that had made Vivian self-conscious when she went to the beauty parlor, always worried that the beautician would embarrass her by commenting on them.

"These are wisdom bumps," Simon said. "Remember how I told you? Just like Moses. Remember the picture I showed you, the one of Michelangelo's sculpture? Remember the bumps?" Vivian had recoiled the time he'd opened the book to show her the sculpture, Simon not yet having realized how much they embarrassed her. "It wasn't fair of me to join that religious group the way I did," he continued. "I didn't mean to hurt you. I never wanted to embarrass you."

Simon clasped Vivian's hand. In seeming response, her eyes partially opened. "You were the best mother a son could want." Her eyes closed again. "Wherever you are," Simon whispered, his lips close to Vivian's ear, "I hope you find comfort."

It was the closest thing to a prayer Simon could offer for the woman who had raised him, a woman who believed in a god and an afterlife. Simon felt grateful for the moment of intimacy, soon interrupted.

Connie and Derek, with Cheryl holding Victoria by the hand, filed noisily into the room, accompanied by Thad, whom they had picked up at the mansion on the way.

"Uncle Simon, you're looking good," Cheryl remarked as Victoria hugged him.

"Between international flights and cross-country driving, I hardly know what day it is. I must have bags under my eyes."

Connie, never one to be left out of a conversation, asked, "When were you flying internationally? I thought you went to Los Angeles for business."

"The dealings led to a quick trip to Italy. I didn't have a chance to mention it before."

"Well," Connie harrumphed, registering displeasure that she had not been told the whole story, "it's good you completed your affairs so you can be here for Vivian."

Derek went to Vivian's bedside and lifted her hand, holding it as Simon had done, praying in a manner foreign to Simon. "Lord, grant your daughter peace. In Jesus's name." Derek shut his eyes and continued his prayer in silence.

"Connie, don't think badly of me, but I'm going back to the mansion." Simon didn't explain that he wanted to hold onto the feeling of closeness he had shared with Vivian.

Thad took Simon's hand in a gesture of understanding.

"You all better come over here," Derek whispered as he placed Vivian's hand by her side.

Simon rushed toward the bed. Vivian's eyes were half-open, glazed in the same way Lenny's had been when he collapsed from heart failure before paramedics arrived at the mansion and revived him. Simon couldn't help thinking that Vivian had chosen that moment while everyone was in the room. Simon's tether to the earth was broken.

Cheryl broke into tears, seeking comfort in Thad's friendly embrace. Simon placed his arm around Connie's waist to provide support. Victoria wept. Derek touched Vivian on the forehead, praying as Connie came to stand beside him. She clasped Simon's hand, and he took Thad's. Cheryl and Victoria completed the circle. Personal beliefs about God and the afterlife made no difference at that moment. Love for Vivian bound them as a family.

CHAPTER THIRTY-SIX

Shortly after Lenny died, Vivian had had a local attorney draw up a will making clear her wishes for the disposition of property and stating unequivocally that she wanted to be buried in the family plot at Holy Oak Cemetery in Magnolia. (When Vivian had had Simon read the will at the time, he'd suspected that Vivian wanted to spend eternity far away from Lenny.) The will underscored Vivian's demand that she be in a closed casket during her funeral.

"I want to be with you," Thad said when Simon told him where the service would be held, "but do you think I should go to Magnolia? I remember what you told me about the last time you went there."

"I'm more worried about Derek than you. He can't resist an argument if he hears someone make a religious comment that isn't precisely what he believes. Vivian once made a remark about the way her Southern Baptist church viewed the will of God, and Derek went into a tirade about free will. Vivian was taught a strict idea of predestination when she was growing up. Lenny didn't have time for any of it, satisfied with his notion of once saved, always saved."

"My head hurts already," Thad said, holding his palms against both temples. "As a boy in Idaho, my parents railed about the Campbellites. If you asked one of them, they'd tell you they belonged to the only true Christian faith and that my atheist parents were blaspheming apostates."

"Listen to you." Simon smiled. "Blaspheming apostates. Who knew you were such a theologian?"

"Theologian! Never in a million years. It's just that I heard that kind of stuff when I was a kid. Apostate means believing in the wrong things, doesn't it?"

"I didn't mean to make fun of you, Thad. You said it perfectly—believing the wrong things. Christians talk about grace and a lot of noble ideas, but in the end, they fall back on the exactitude of one's beliefs. What a person believes matters more to them than the way someone behaves—it divides Catholics from Orthodox, Baptists from Methodists, and subdivides people within those churches. Everyone tells everyone else they're going to hell. It is going to be a crowded place, that hell of theirs!"

Thad sat on the edge of the bed, paying more attention than usual to Simon's philosophizing. "I hate this," he said solemnly. "Vivian would be so sad if she thought her family couldn't stand each other long enough to mourn her death. When I was alone with her at the mansion, while you were in classes or out in the barn painting, she never once asked what I believed or if I went to church or anything like that. She worried whether she could ask me to stake the goat around the yard, knowing I didn't like to do it. The Bible wasn't the reason she cared about people; she cared about people because she understood how they felt."

"You make Vivian sound like a saint. Trust me, she had her failings."

"The way she treated me is what I'll remember, though. Your sister and brother-in-law use their beliefs to justify their bad feelings toward people. Vivian wasn't like that. She tried to be kind, even if she wasn't perfect."

"Lenny mistreated her from the moment they were married," Simon said. "Sometimes I wished she had fought back, but I guess putting up with Lenny made her an even more compassionate person."

"It's strange, but going through that ordeal with Emilio, David, and Irene changed my viewpoint on a lot of things, and before working for Howard, I never realized how porn stars separate their emotions from their sex lives—and how sad that makes them. You and I don't just have sex, we make love. Oh my God, I sound so old fashioned!"

Simon and Thad lay on the bed beside each other. The chandelier threw rainbows across the ceiling and walls as dangling crystals caught the broken rays of sun streaming through the wisteria and the opaque glass of the aging window.

"Sometimes, when I look at that gaudy thing," Simon commented, pointing at the ceiling, "I wonder what it's seen over the years."

Thad rose from the bed and opened a dresser drawer, lifting a pile of underwear under which he had seen Simon place the copy of *El Amigo Rico*. He brought it to the bed and showed Simon an image on the back, a young man on the receiving end of anal sex. "That guy shot heroin right after the director took this picture."

"What are trying to tell me, Thad?"

"That these videos murder people's souls." He pointed again to the young man. "This is Esteban. He kept telling me he wanted to be in adult films because it made him feel in control. Then I'd watch him shoot drugs after the filming stopped. Doing porn didn't make him strong; it killed his emotions, just like heroin.

Emilio's chauffeur started out making porn, then became a body-guard and a hitman if they asked him to knock off someone."

"Hitman?"

"He's the guy that took the Serbian boys out to sea. He'd come back; they wouldn't."

Simon held Thad's hand as he came back to bed.

"That video will be around a long time," Thad cried. "Men will jerk off looking at it—looking at me! They won't know I was forced to do it. They won't know about my love for you!"

"Can this be the same Thad who left when I was sick with hepatitis?" Simon immediately regretted his statement. "That was cruel, Thad. I'm sorry."

"Yeah, but you're right, I was a dick. I didn't realize how I felt about you until after we split up, and then I didn't think you'd take me back. When I brought your things to the mansion from the Silverlake house, I never thought we'd stay together."

"I wish I could burn every copy of *El Amigo Rico*. But I guess only gay guys will see it—and they're not going to judge you."

"You'd be surprised who watches those videos," Thad sighed.

"Look at it this way—it adds to your mystique. And if my friends see the video, they'll be jealous."

"I *am* a stud," Thad said, laughing mischievously.

"My blond hunk of burning love!"

"Kiss me, Simon."

"All night, my love."

The next day, before leaving for Magnolia, Simon called Arthur to catch up on the classes he had missed. Arthur, always current on gossip, reported that Blaine had gone from the rehab center to a halfway house. After returning from Vivian's funeral, Simon planned to visit—taking Thad along with him.

Connie suggested that Simon and Thad join Derek, Cheryl, and Victoria on the ride, but Simon chose to be alone with Thad in the Pontiac.

"Your uncle Jared sounds like a jerk," Thad said after Simon recounted the events of the family reunion he had attended with Vivian.

"Uncle Jared wasn't so bad when I knew him as a boy. His sons and I used to play together whenever we visited my grandmother. I even stayed in Magnolia during the summer a few times. I can still smell the pine needles that kept the underbrush from growing in the woods but made them seem like a carpeted wonderland—so different from the swamps around Sibley. My cousins and I fished with bamboo poles and caught box turtles that crossed the roads early in the morning. I'm sure Uncle Jared was just as narrow minded back then, but I never crossed him, so he had no reason to show his cruel side. I didn't start challenging people's beliefs until high school. By then, we rarely visited Magnolia, and the family there didn't come to Sibley, not even when Mandy died. I'm sure there's history that I don't know about. Maybe they objected to Aunt Opal—the word *heathen* comes to mind when I recall family conversations, but as a little boy, it didn't mean anything to me."

"Will Vivian's service be in a church?"

"That's why we had to dress up in suits. I wouldn't have had us bother for a graveside ceremony." Simon stuck a finger in the neck of his shirt to free his Adam's apple, then checked his watch. "We're cutting it close timewise. I've only been to their Baptist church once, when an aunt of Vivian's died. Funny, I don't remember Lenny ever going to Magnolia."

"We just did graveside services in Idaho—family and friends standing around the grave, each paying their respects. Nothing religious or anything."

"Arkansans are big on church funerals. Vivian would have preferred a graveside service, but after we die, it's all about what the living want, isn't it?"

Derek led the way to the church once the two cars arrived in Magnolia. They parked at the end of a row of cars on a patch of gravel where the asphalt-paved lot ended. Simon pulled along-side, noting the change from the smooth surface to the crunching sound of rocks beneath the tires.

As Derek, Connie, Cheryl, and Victoria entered the church, Simon and Thad got out of the car, straightened each other's ties, and shook their legs to straighten out their slacks—delay tactics, since neither wanted to go inside. Simon looked in the rearview mirror on the driver's side door. "I wish I had brought a camera. Who knows when we'll dress in suits again? We make such a hand-some couple."

"I'm glad you *didn't* bring a camera! I don't ever want to see a picture of me in a suit."

They walked toward the church and fell under the shadow of its tall steeple as they climbed the steps toward massive bronze doors.

"Do vampires feel this sick about entering a church?" Simon joked.

Thad brashly planted a last-minute kiss on Simon's cheek. "Let's just get it done, for Vivian."

Simon pushed open the heavy door. Slowly his eyes acclimated to the mustiness of the dim sanctuary. The auditorium was not large, making it easy to see past the pews. Between volumes of white chrysanthemums crowding the casket, made bright by a track light, heavy cosmetics made Vivian's face glow with the waxy sheen of a mannequin.

"Close that fucking casket!" Simon screamed before he could stop himself.

"Let's go, Simon," Thad urged. "You paid your respects at the nursing home. Vivian knows that."

Derek glared at Simon over his shoulder. Connie trembled. Victoria looked confused. Cheryl knew of Vivian's wish not to have an open casket but had not protested when she realized what the family had done. Derek raced toward Simon and Thad, but not before Uncle Jared, the tails of his suitcoat flaying to the side as he rushed forward, came face to face with Simon.

"How dare you blaspheme in the house of God," Uncle Jared yelled. He stood in the frame of the church door with Simon just beyond the threshold.

"And how dare you disrespect Vivian's wishes," Simon shot back. "She never wanted to be seen like that."

The arteries on Uncle Jared's neck throbbed as he clenched his fists, clearly itching to pound Simon into the ground, and his bloodshot eyes fixed on Thad in a deadly stare. "Remove your ungodly selves from this property. I curse you in the name of Jesus Christ. Get thee behind me, Satan!" Uncle Jared took a small Bible from his inside coat pocket and held it to the sky as if summoning God's wrath before thrusting the book at Simon.

Simon slapped away Uncle Jared's hand with such force that the Bible flew into one of the evergreen trees lining the steps, slipped through the limbs, and landed on the ground.

Half a dozen relatives, many of whom Simon knew only by sight, filed from the church. Simon felt a tug and realized it was Thad, urging him toward the Pontiac.

"Let's go, Simon. Vivian would not want this."

"But Thad!" Simon cried. "Vivian's body is in there, exposed to the world, and damn it, Derek and Connie just sat there like it didn't matter."

"I know," Thad consoled, placing his hand on Simon's forearm. "*I know.* But more than the open casket, Vivian would never want her funeral to be a source of conflict."

Derek and Connie, followed by Cheryl, with Victoria close behind, rushed down the steps between the crowd of relatives and approached Simon and Thad.

"Let's go home, Simon," Derek said in a controlled voice. "I heard what Thad said to you, and he's exactly right." Derek turned to Uncle Jared. "Forgive Simon, but he's right. You knew Vivian's wishes."

Uncle Jared pointed an accusing finger at Simon and then at Thad. "Don't you think I know what my sister really wanted? Viewing the deceased is our church's tradition."

"This is a day to respect Vivian," Derek said firmly. "She told us many times she didn't want people to see her in death."

"Vivian was foolish. This is a day to acknowledge the corruption of flesh and praise the inheritance of God's kingdom."

Uncle Jared's elder sons, whom Simon had played with as a boy, echoed their father, one adding venomously, "The Powells are devil people! You put ideas in her mind."

Simon and Thad managed to slip away, secure within the protection of the Pontiac. The youngest among his cousins pummeled the cars with gravel, and the adults watched without scolding them.

Simon couldn't shake the image of Vivian's body, her face so white and pasty under the garish spotlight. He wanted to turn around, rush into the church, and slam the casket lid shut, but, outnumbered by the rabid clan, he knew he'd never get that far.

"If only I could drive this old car through the front doors of that damned church," Simon fantasized aloud.

"Please don't," Thad pleaded.

"It's as though we were in a Frankenstein movie, pursued by villagers."

"Pretty much," Thad agreed. "Let's get out of here."

Simon did his best to spray gravel on the crowd, who continued to stone them as he floored the accelerator and sped away.

Derek had driven from the parking lot first and was idling the car at the street, waiting for Simon to proceed around him after he motioned through the driver's side window. The two vehicles escaped the city limits and reached a heavily wooded stretch of highway after crossing the county bridge at Franklin Creek. Derek flashed his headlights so Simon would pull over.

"Let's drive to the mansion," Derek suggested as Simon approached. "We should be together and share memories. We'll have our own memorial."

"That sounds nice, Derek. I know we've had differences over the years, but thank you for standing up for Thad and me."

"We all have much to learn about the will of God. I knew what Vivian wanted, but I didn't have your boldness to speak up."

"Okay, Derek." Simon nodded. The language of religion made Simon uncomfortable, but after the events of the day, he tried to find more acceptance of Derek than he'd been willing to consider in the past.

For the remainder of the drive, Simon stayed a car length behind. As darkness fell, the headlights of both cars cast cones of brightness onto the stands of oak along the roadside, which transitioned as they neared Sibley, first to long-needle pine and then to a mix of sweet gum, elm, and catalpa.

Turning off the main highway onto the narrow road leading to the mansion, the Mercury and the Pontiac struggled to find enough shoulder to pull over as fire trucks came roaring from behind. Narrow streets had always posed a problem in the area, making navigation difficult for emergency vehicles trying to reach the fire lanes carved into forests prone to catching fire from a lightning strike or, more often, a cigarette butt casually thrown out a car window. The road became exceptionally narrow in the vicinity of the mansion as it wound along the top of a levee built to prevent flooding from the Saline River.

About a half mile from the mansion, Thad spoke up. "Oh my God, Simon, do you see that glow above the trees? The clouds are lit up pink."

Simon leaned forward and stared at the sky. Derek slowed so quickly that Simon almost rear-ended his car. In the distance, crimson lights from what must have been a dozen fire trucks flashed like a psychedelic aurora. That many trucks would include some from Little Rock, adding to squadrons from Benton.

Derek pulled off the road behind the truck farthest from the blaze and leaped from the car. Connie raced forward to join him. Simon found a place to pull over. Thad jumped out before the car had stopped. Simon slumped over the steering wheel.

Connie and Thad spoke to a man who, according to the identifying label on his coat, was the fire chief. Thad stood transfixed beside Connie as Simon made his way toward them. Connie held out her arms to take Simon into an embrace. Cheryl and Victoria had not left the Mercury, transfixed by disbelief, only leaving the car when Derek motioned for them to join the family.

Everyone faced the smoldering ruins of what had been the mansion, now a collection of blackened beams falling crossways in a desolate heap. Embers drifted upward with crackling noises into the night sky, fretting the earth's majestical roof with golden fire. Some volunteers tended a generator pumping water from the pond, while others worked in pairs to hold aloft hoses soaking the trees near the mansion's remains as well as the lawn where Ferdinand strained on a rope to get closer to the woods.

Simon ran through thick smoke that drove through a persistent wind, hoping beyond hope as he came within view, but nothing remained of the barn. Firefighters had arrived soon enough to move Ferdinand from the corral, staking him by the creek where a fallen tree had once formed the bridge that allowed Ernie a way to visit. Ferdinand's neighing provided a soundtrack to the horrific scene, as if the devil himself were commenting on the tragedy.

Simon had once set fire to his art as a sacrifice to God—a choice made of his own volition. Who had decided to destroy generations of remembrances? Simon wished there were a God, some being upon which he could heap cosmic blame.

A fire had consumed the mansion like a ravenous, uncaring beast. The gallery of ancestors, the esoteric books once owned by Aunt Opal, the wisteria that Ernie had climbed to join Simon in forbidden rendezvous—ashes. The empty look in Simon's eyes drove Thad to hold him firmly around the waist, frightened that Simon, in a panic of despair, might throw himself on the red-hot, glowing remains.

Connie fell to her knees, defeated, sobbing. Cheryl was a statue, eyes transfixed by the dying embers. Victoria held her hand, two sisters facing an unknown future, watching traditions they had wanted to believe meant nothing disappear before them, the family legacy, the repository of memory, vanishing in an orgy of flames. Derek broke free of his stupor and crouched beside Connie, even as he kept a watchful eye on his daughters.

The fire had not touched the hangman's oak where the pious JT Powell had died, nor had it reached the sweet gum that Simon as a young boy had planted with his grandmother Mandy. The fire had not crossed the road to where Aunt Opal's granite angel seemed to bear a message of grief as it stood sentinel in the cemetery.

Simon and Thad walked toward the street, barely aware that the others followed. The family stood hand in hand in the same order as when they'd surrounded Vivian's bed, gazing now on tombstones engraved with the names of ancestors, some long forgotten and some who remained in vivid memory.

"It's gone, Aunt Opal," Simon said, a four-year-old boy addressing the funny old woman with the frizzy hair, the aunt who'd given him a lucky quarter.

Simon knew the others felt as he did, that they had witnessed the end of a history handed down to them—the nobility of the hanged JT, the endurance of the ridiculed Aunt Opal, the sacrificial legacy of Bartholomew, who'd proclaimed the family motto that it is better for one family to sacrifice than for many to do without. Bart's motto had been a source of pride when Simon had left home to build the kingdom of God on earth. Had Simon brought this devastation upon the family through denial of the new messiah? Was this merely an accident? Arson? Could it be payback from the unholy trinity for absconding with Thad and Felipe? Was it the will of God?

Simon knew what he believed, but would he ever know the truth?

ABOUT THE AUTHOR

Author and artist William Poe draws inspiration for his novels from his own upbringing. He grew up in the American heartland and joined the Unification Church of Reverend Sun Myung Moon at eighteen. He stayed there for nearly ten years, all the while struggling to reconcile his identity as a gay man with Moon's teachings. Poe eventually left the group and pushed back against the ideology he'd first embraced and then rejected.

After recovering from drug addiction, Poe began to find peace and understanding in his art. He received his bachelor's degree in art from the University of Arkansas at Little Rock and his master's degree in anthropology from the University of Nebraska. He worked at the National Museum of the American Indian (part of the Smithsonian Institution) as well as for several government agencies. Poe retired in 2018 and now focuses on writing, painting, and researching his family history.